The Ones closest to You

a novel

STEPHANIE VERNI

The Ones Closest To You is a work of fiction. All of the characters, organizations, and events portrayed in this novel are either products of the author's imagination or are used fictitiously.

Book cover designed by Stephanie Verni

ISBN 9798332594458

MIMOSA
PUBLISHING

For Anthony...for your loving support of my "passion projects." I love you.

For those who believe that there is a LIGHT that guides us, and for my family, who always tells me to enjoy the whole process of storytelling. I love you all.

Books by Stephanie Verni

The Ones Closest to You
The Letters in the Books
From Humbug to Humble: The Transformation of Ebenezer Scrooge
Anna in Tuscany
Little Milestones
The Postcard and Other Short Stories & Poetry
Inn Significant
Baseball Girl
Beneath the Mimosa Tree

Textbook, with Leeanne Bell McManus & Chip Rouse
Event Planning & Management: Communicating Theory and Practice

The Ones closest to You

a novel

STEPHANIE VERNI

"Incarcerated mafia dame Rosa Manetti is unlike anyone I have ever met. She is shrewd and smart. Savvy and secretive. She answers questions, sometimes sharing bits of a broken life that can be both disturbing and understandable. Her icy stare makes your bones quiver. And yet, if you look deeply enough into the recesses of her hazel eyes, you might be able to decipher that it was family betrayal that led her here."

Excerpt by writer Veronica DeMarco, from a series of articles entitled "Rosa's Revenge" from NYC's The News, 1956

Chapter 1

Essie positions her cane at the edge of the table. Preparing my sister's breakfast every morning is part of our daily routine. She glances at the plate, then eases herself into the maple chair across from me. Her mouth appears to be incapable of forming the words "thank you." Rarely are there words of appreciation.

"How are you feeling today?" I ask her. It's a question I pose daily because of her condition and the way it's affected her. The bitterness comes and goes.

"Same as always—uncomfortable."

"I'm so sorry. Is there anything I can do for you before I leave?" I have a nine-thirty meeting, and I can't be late for it. Essie is still in her nightgown and robe, her feet tucked into fuzzy pink slippers. She's always been fond of the color pink.

"Not really," she murmurs.

I pour myself a second cup of coffee and return to the table, fully dressed and ready to go. I take another bite of toast and organize my briefcase. My father bought it for me the day I got the job as a journalist at the newspaper, a grandiose gesture for him, and one of the only gifts I remember him giving me in my adulthood.

When I finish eating, I wash the plate and cup and place it on the drying rack. "Gertie should pop by around eleven-thirty.

She's bringing you lunch, and I believe some new yarn for your knitting. I should be home at my normal time, if not earlier. I'll pick up food from the market on my way home for supper."

Sisters and roommates, this is typical morning conversation for us. I work and Essie stays at home, her condition precluding her from holding a full-time job at present.

"Today's the signing, right?" she asks.

"It is," I say.

"Well, I hope it goes well for you." She repositions herself at the kitchen table.

"I appreciate that," I say, and I kiss her on the top of her head and move toward the door. "Let's hope it goes the way we want."

"I'm sure it will," Essie says, and I see her pick up the fork and take her first bite.

*

Early is on time. I can hear the words my mother preached to Essie and me echo inside my head. Despite my punctuality, Alice has beaten me to the office, and motions for me to take a seat.

Documents are strewn across the desk. Alice leans across the table, pushing my copy of the contract in front of me. I'm moments away from signing on the dotted line.

"I'm happy to offer you this book deal, Ms. DeMarco," the publisher says. He's a tall and lanky man with a receding hairline, who smells of Yardley soap. Everyone calls him by his last name only: Henderson.

"Yes, Mr. Henderson," I say. I'm not one to shorten anyone's name or refer to them in a disrespectful manner. Then, I straighten my gray tweed pencil skirt and readjust myself in the seat of the chair. Admittedly awestruck, I find it difficult to offer anything more than a one-word answer.

"Just so we have an understanding, Ms. Hawthorne and

Miss DeMarco—this is a one-book deal." We both nod. "And the edits are almost done?" His voice is low, its cadence melodic.

"Yes." I rest my hands across my lap so that he can't see them shaking.

My agent looks at me from across the desk and smiles, knowing that I'm nearly finished polishing the draft. *Never tell them more than they need to know*, she had said. *Surprise them with an early manuscript.* I am no dummy. I listen to every bit of advice Alice Hawthorne offers me. I respect her too much not to do so.

"Excellent, then here you are."

We have already perused the text of the document privately, making sure every detail has been included, and have no further questions. Alice hands me the paperwork, and I begin to sign on the lines marked with a check. Seeing my name on the contract makes it binding, and I am giddy with delight, though I keep that excitement to myself. I've worked hard to get to this point.

There are days when I write so much, my fingers grow weary from pecking the keys, the result of dual jobs as journalist and author. I thank my lucky stars for typing class; knowing the keys by heart definitely helps me to be efficient with my writing. From an early age, storytelling has been in my blood. My mother always said, "If you leave your gift unrealized, it is a snub to God." I don't forget her words; I don't want that on my conscience.

The truth is, I never could have come this far in either of my careers without Robert, who taught me to be a writer. He took a chance on me and hired me to work at The News, the place where I smoked my first cigarette and learned how to interview people and listen to their stories. When I saw my first by-line, I squealed with delight. Editor-in-chief, Robert Barone, has been the mentor who groomed me as a journalist, taking me under his wing. An old family friend, I suppose he felt obligated to both my mother and father for their years of friendship with him. Willing to take me on board, most of what I've learned about writing well has been instilled in me by Robert, a man with an infinite amount of patience. My writing career blossomed under his tutelage. I owe Robert a debt of gratitude. And as he seems intent on assigning me longer, in-depth features, I've become passionate about them over the years.

While we wait for the carbon copies of the paperwork to be assembled, Alice and I shake hands with Mr. Henderson. When the copies are placed in Alice's hands and we've said our goodbyes, Alice invites me back to her office three blocks off Madison Avenue for a quick celebration. She and her associate are keen on raising a glass of champagne for each new book signing. I can hardly decline such an invitation. Plus, I believe a payment is coming my way.

"I can't tell you how wonderful this is for you," she says to me, in her expressive Barbara Stanwyck way of speaking. "You are still so young. Think how many books you have ahead of you!"

"That's a lot of pressure, Alice," I say, wringing my hands.

"Nothing you can't handle." Alice opens the champagne, pours the content of the bottle into flutes, and places them on a tray.

"Still, it's all a bit daunting, don't you think?" I feel slightly overwhelmed, though grateful to have someone I trust implicitly, like Alice, in my corner.

"You have a good imagination. I'm sure you'll surprise us with loads of interesting tales and epic romances." Alice flashes her knowing smile.

"I'm surprised I can write these stories at all, having minimal romantic relationships to refer back to in order to get them right." I'm half joking and half serious.

"Well, my dear, maybe your imagined stories are better than the real thing. At least they can have the ending you want, instead of the ending that may never happen. Look at me. I never wanted the divorce. It was thrust upon me. Not at all the happy ending I would have liked," Alice laments.

"But perhaps it's the ending you were meant to have and it's leading you to a new beginning with Edward."

"Right, honey. I like Eddie. He's sweet and helps pass the time. But I'm not so sure I'm in love with him the way I was with Adam."

Alice says those words in a matter-of-fact way, and it causes me to pause. I never want to feel like that, as if I am settling for someone because the man I love doesn't want me. It's a melancholy statement, and although I'm not presently in a romantic relationship, one day I hope to fall in love with someone decent and kind and to have a good life with him.

Just then, Mel Jenkins walks through the door. He's been Alice's associate since they started the literary agency, and I'm convinced he's in love with her. Unrequited love. They began the business by working from Mel's second bedroom in his East Side apartment, until they could afford this office space, which is beautiful and boasts expansive views of the city. With pastel couches and sleek end tables, the agency office is modern. I accept the champagne flute from Alice.

"Here's to you, darling," Mel says, in his tailored plaid suit with straight legs, his shiny new loafers catching the light from the large window. "One book down. We can't wait to see what's in store for your next one. May every book forward tantalize your readers!"

"I'll drink to that, and I'll do my best to keep you in business." I take a sip; the champagne tickles my nose.

"Cheers, darling," Alice says. "And don't forget to take a short vacation to recharge your battery and get that creativity moving again for your next project."

"I can't. I've got Essie."

"Doesn't Essie deserve a vacation, too? Take her to the shore so she can see the ocean."

Of course, Essie deserves a vacation. She probably needs it more than I do. I think about the notion, and wonder if I can make it work. "I will, but not just yet," I say. "Robert's scheduled me for a new feature."

"Another one? I thought you were going to slow down on that front now that you're an author, Veronica."

"I'm not an author yet," I say, laughing. "But I look forward to seeing my book in its published form and getting it moving."

"Oh, we're going to get it moving, darling," Mel says. "You're going to help us retire early!"

"Not that you're heaping loads of pressure on me," I say, teasing them.

After our short celebration, I leave their office and hop into a taxi that takes me home to our two-bedroom apartment in Greenwich Village. Inserting the key into the lock, I remove a small pebble from my shoe, banging the heel of it on the brick step. The air smells of roasted nuts, the street vendors parked at corners, handing bags over to paying customers. A weakness of mine, there is nothing better in autumn than enjoying a bag of candied nuts and a Coca-Cola while sitting on a park bench.

As I open the door, I see my sister asleep on the sofa, an afghan draped across her lap, an open book positioned next to her. Gertie sees the door open, moves her fingers to her lips, and gives me the "shh!" sign not to wake her. I gesture to Gertie that I am going for a walk since Essie is sleeping. I slip back outside into the New York air. When I reach Washington Square Park, I purchase a bag of nuts from the vendor and a bottle of soda. An empty bench beckons me. People stroll hand-in-hand, children play, and men sitting at tables concentrate on the chess board.

I chuckle to myself, reviewing the day: a book deal and a happy agent. Oh, how I wish my mother were alive to share in this joy. She would have been proud. She always told me writing was in my blood. I take a deep breath and watch the children chase each other in the park, their silhouettes blending into the city, completely carefree.

Dusk is falling on the New York City skyline, as the wind blows and the leaves rustle. The breeze catches my long brown hair and blows it across my face and into my mouth. Autumn is New York's most glorious season; she wears it beautifully. Nature's colors accentuate the buildings, giving the city its allure and larger-than-life quality.

Realizing I forgot to stop at the market, I leave the few moments of peace behind, the sound of the city dwarfing the sounds of my heels clicking the pavement. After I purchase groceries at the corner market, I make my way along streets that breathe life, yet prepare to open the door to an apartment that lately seems to breathe something else entirely different.

Chapter 2

A few weeks later at the newspaper, there's a man I've never seen before talking with Robert. As the editor, Robert's office is private, especially because it has interior windows that face the newsroom with blinds that can be opened or closed. Today, the blinds are open. The man is animated, his hands flailing as he tells Robert a story. The man he's speaking with must be quite amusing, because Robert is engrossed in the conversation, his eyes growing wide as he listens to the story. Laughter ensues.

I cross my arms and watch the exchange happening between the two men through the smokiness of the newsroom. I can't hear them; I can only interpret their nonverbal exchanges. I'm intrigued. I've never seen Robert wear a grin for such an extended period of time.

When Robert finally catches my eye, he moves toward the door and motions for me to step inside.

"Veronica–come in!" he says, as I walk through and face the man who has been entertaining Robert so brilliantly. "This is Perry Spada. Have you two met?"

"No," the man says. "I don't believe we have, but I know your work. Pleased to meet you," he says, as he shakes my hand.

"Pleased as well," I say. He's handsome. Italian, I presume, by the last name.

"Perry Spada is our new baseball guy. He'll be covering the Brooklyn Dodgers for us. Veronica is one of our best feature writers," Robert says. "We're on a first-name basis here at The News. No need for formalities."

Perry smiles.

"Didn't their season just end?" I ask rhetorically.

"It did, but you know, baseball never really sleeps, even in the off-season. Plenty to cover."

"Well, pleased to meet you." His eyes are not quite brown and not quite green, but a generous mixture of both, and there's an intensity to them. His brown hair is meant to be neat, but it is slightly tousled.

"Glad to know you," Perry says. "What are you working on now?"

"That's why I'm here interrupting your meeting. Robert left me word that he's got a story for me to cover."

"Yes, I do. I'm trying to keep her around, you see. She's got her head in the clouds because she's just signed a book deal with a publisher. For some strange reason, she enjoys writing make-believe stories when there are a million real stories to cover."

I feign being hurt by the comment.

"It's called fiction, and it's still real, Robert. We just change the names around to protect the innocent. Fiction's a great way to tell a story without implicating anyone." I wink.

"I would not want to be implicated," Perry says, trying to make a joke.

"Veronica, be a dear and show Perry around the place. Susanna's got a desk set up for him over near the window with the sports guys. I've got to take a call any minute from the big boss, but here's your new assignment," Robert says, handing me his notes on scratch paper about the story I'm to cover.

I know what that means. Robert's had to dismiss me many times when the publisher demands his editor's attention. He knows how to cater to the Big Man. He does it so well.

"Well, then, it looks like it's you and me, Perry," I say, as Robert picks up the ringing phone and begins his conversation.

We walk out of his office and close the door behind us, leaving Robert to speak in private. Reporters are banging away at their typewriters, smoking cigarettes, and engaging in conversations that require them to shout over the clickety-clack of typewriters.

"This is the main newsroom—world news, politics, New York news, and the like. Sports is back there in the corner. You fellas get the whole area to yourselves."

"Well, I expect we stay out of everyone's hair that way. No bothering you with stats and facts about egotistical players and ground ball rules."

"Funny," I say. "I actually like baseball. Grew up on it."

"Well, look at you," Perry says, his eyes wide with surprise. "A girl who likes baseball."

"No. I'm afraid I must correct myself. I love—not like—baseball. The Yankees, actually. Mantle's my favorite." We land at the area that will be his space and stop.

"Traitor," he says, teasingly.

He studies me for a moment and crosses his arms. A smirk runs across his face. He's well-dressed in a dark suit. He's handsome in a boyish yet sexy sort of way, and he's meticulously well-groomed. I notice how his dark hair frames those beautifully colored eyes that accentuate his youthful face perfectly. When he smiles, there's a dimple in one cheek. I like the look of him.

Daniel, a writer who covers the New York Yankees, glances up from his typewriter, and I shout to him, fighting to be heard over the noise of the newsroom, "Hello, Daniel!"

"Hello, Veronica. Lovely as ever," he says. He rises from his chair and walks toward us. Daniel asked me for a date once. I had declined the invitation, stating that I didn't make it a policy to date colleagues. It's not that Daniel isn't charming, or a nice person, it's just that I had been elevated to cover feature stories at the time, and I wanted to avoid complications like the plague. Now, he's married and has a child on the way. "Ah, Perry! Good to have you aboard!"

"Thank you. It's good to see you again," Perry says, reaching out to shake Daniel's hand. Daniel slaps Perry on the back as if they are old friends.

"We've got you all set up at this desk," Daniel says, showing him his new spot.

"Well, I believe you're in good hands now," I say to Perry. "Hope you enjoy your time at The News."

"Lovely to have met you, Veronica," Perry says. "I look forward to crossing paths and talking Mantle with you again soon."

I leave the two men to sort it out, as Daniel, at least ten years older than both Perry and me, takes him under his wing.

It would be fun to cover sports, I suppose. Nothing gruesome. No real bad news to report minus the losses or player trades. No deaths, no trials, no gangs, or creepy incidents. No sordid past stories. I wonder what it would be like to cover a team over and over again. To have the excitement of going to the games and being in the press box. The features I write don't work that way. I may write about a person recovering from losing everything in a house fire and then move on to my next story about life in Greenwich Village. It's a case-by-case, story-by-story approach. Curious folks enjoy doing this for a living. I was born curious.

Unlike the stories I write for the newspaper, novel writing offers me an escape from reality. Additionally, I enjoy writing a happy ending. In the journalistic, real world, we can't make the same promise, and features sometimes have no end, nor do they offer a promise of one. The content in news features is often more brutal than fiction could ever be. An unsolved murder. A disappearing wife. Arson at the local mill. Feature stories tend to linger, seemingly hanging in the middle, and are often without resolutions. Sometimes I don't sleep at night after I interview people who have been affected by life-altering things. But such is life. And my job is to tell the best, most authentic version of each story as is humanly possible.

Back at my desk, I take out a pad and paper and begin to jot down preliminary notes that will help me write the story Robert has assigned me. It's a case of a long, lost brother who's been found. This one may take me a while.

Robert knows that. He wants to keep me at the newspaper.

He doesn't want me to favor writing fiction over writing about the realities of the world.

Chapter 3

Essie refuses to leave the house these days. She's having one of her spells. With a mother dead for ten years from cancer and a father who remarried and relocated to New England, I voluntarily took on the responsibility of caring for my older sister who suffers from polio. Her type, the most painful of all, and the one that affects only about one percent of the population, is called paralytic poliomyelitis, and presents itself as painful episodes in her back and lower limbs. She is often riddled with fatigue from even the most minimal physical activity. However, she is getting help from an exercise doctor and has begun some new treatments, so we will see where that takes her. I continue to have hope for her.

Although it doesn't happen with regularity, there are days when I have to help her out of bed and into the bath. We have rigged the bathtub to assist with her disability. She sits and uses a hand-held device. Modesty was thrown out the window long ago. I'll never become accustomed to seeing her wince in pain. Every day I pray the medical community will invent something to lessen the bad spells.

Nevertheless, watching her manage her situation is heartbreaking.

We are lucky to have Gertie, our friend and neighbor, who

cares for Essie when she's struggling on the days when I work. I pay her a good wage, and Gertie's been the one constant since we moved into our apartment. Gertie's patience is unmatched. Her two children are grown, and she appreciates the money. Her husband, while a decent man, seems to be perpetually unemployed. We all have trials we must face in life.

I help Essie set herself up on the sofa and pull all the books she needs for the day. Somehow, she inherited a mane of long, beautiful blonde hair—my mother said it must be hereditary from my grandmother's side of the family—which she wears in a high ponytail every day. She's so petite—all of about five foot two inches—and about a hundred pounds. Pretty and petite.

Essie's an avid reader. As an older sister, she gave me my first book to read called *The Little Book About God* by Lauren Ford. I'll never forget the way she wrapped it up for my sixth birthday, with lots of red ribbons. I loved that book; it was my entre into reading and to understanding God. Apparently, she begged my mother to buy it for me. Reading allows her to escape reality, and I have become her courier, ferrying books to and from the library each week. Books make her happy and delivering them to her makes me feel as if I bring worlds and adventures to life for her to live out, if only in our modest apartment.

When I started to write stories myself in our teenage years and shared them with our family, Essie was often the one who would help me when I became stuck, offering advice. I could bribe her to help me over a cup of tea and donuts. We'd have fun with it, and then I'd read the chapters aloud to her.

"Will you have time to get me those books from the library on your way home today?" she asks me, as I settle her in and wait for Gertie to arrive.

"Absolutely. I've got the reminder right here," I say, pointing to my handbag. She nods. I'd give anything for her to have her old life back, before polio robbed her of her carefree ways.

For a woman in her sixties, Gertie has an unending supply of energy. She cheerfully bounds through the door carrying a casserole and wearing her housecoat with an apron around her waist, a scarf pulled tightly around her hair. I've been giving her extra money to help with the cost of the home-cooked meals she makes for us, since I have little time to prepare anything. Essie will occasionally take to the kitchen to make something, but it's not an everyday endeavor.

"Homemade lasagna," she says, holding the prepared dish. "Should get several meals out of it."

"Looks amazing," I tell her, leaning over the pan and taking a whiff.

"Hot out of the oven. You're heading to work, Veronica? I'm admiring your skirt!"

"Thank you. I hope it looks okay with this sweater. I'm off to interview a man for an article. I'll tell you more about it tonight." I kiss Essie on the forehead and give Gertie a hug. "I'll see you both tonight."

Thirty minutes later, I arrive at the office, where a man is waiting to meet me. He had specifically asked to do the interview at the newspaper. He is tall with broad shoulders and is slightly hunched over with a ruddy complexion accentuated by silver hair.

"Mr. Dobson?" I ask him.

"Yes." He looks nervous.

"I'm Veronica DeMarco. Happy to meet you. I hear you have a story to tell." I do my best to try to relax him, and usher him down the hallway to one of our private conference rooms I reserved for the meeting. He sits in one of the empty seats, and I offer him coffee. He takes it black.

Once we settle in, I sit down and open my reporter's notebook. "I hope this doesn't make you too uncomfortable, but I must write notes. I fear I lack a memory for the details of a good story."

"Not a problem," he says. He sips his coffee.

"Let's begin with the heart of the story. What is this all about?"

"I was contacted by a man I have never met before from Vermont, and through many conversations and lots of meetings, we have discovered that we are twin brothers who were put up for adoption fifty-eight years ago. I grew up here, in New York, and he grew up in Vermont."

My hand cannot write fast enough; I'm wondering where this story is going. I'm intrigued already.

"So, you were both given up for adoption."

"Yes." It's not difficult to see how affected this man is by the story–having to share it with me appears to be a challenge for him.

"Were there any requests to keep you two together that you know of?" Robert taught me how to ask the right follow-up questions. I'm hoping this one helps prompt more information.

"No. It was intentional to separate us." He clears his throat.

"Do you know why?" I stop writing and look at him.

"I do." He hesitates for a moment and collects himself. He takes a deep breath.

"You take your time, Mr. Dobson," I say.

He repositions himself in the chair, then leans forward. "It's because of who our parents were...are. My biological father was the famous actor Clive Crane who was married to the actress Lynette Willingham. But we are the children from an affair he had with a young showgirl named Bella Friday. Lynnette is not our mother. She and Clive had children of their own together. We were given up for adoption by Bella Friday to protect all their reputations."

My eyes grow wide. Clive Crane and Lynnette Willingham headlined the silver screen for years, tagged as 'Hollywood's Dream Couple.' They were married all their lives and were inseparable. I jot down questions that come to me as my mind races.

"If I remember correctly, Clive Crane passed away recently. Is that correct?"

"Yes. Two years ago. Cancer." I'm jotting these notes in

my notebook.

"And Lynette?"

"From what we understand, she lives in Montana with her son Larry, who would be my half-brother. She has dementia. Chances are, she won't remember anything, especially not something that she may have tried to block out, if she knew. Our lawyer looked into the situation. It's most likely pointless to talk to her. Also, there is the possibility that she was never told the truth."

I think about this for a second. "What about your biological mother?"

"Apparently, Bella Friday suffers from alcoholism and addiction. My brother and I have tried to reach out, but she refuses to see us. She has essentially denied all of it."

My hand glides across the page, messy handwriting trying to capture all of this.

"So, your adopted name is Dobson?" In some ways, I feel I am trespassing on his privacy, yet he is the one who wants to tell this story.

"Yes. Lawrence Dobson. Adopted by David and Carol Dobson."

"And what is your brother's adoptive name?"

"Frederick Lowell. Adopted by James and Valerie Lowell."

"And you are both Cranes?" I look at him feeling the weight of his situation.

"It appears we are." He lets out a long, contemplative sigh. I let it sit there for a second.

"Are you identical twins?"

"We are. That was the strangest part of all. When we found each other, it was like looking into a mirror. To think of all the time we've lost, and that we never even knew each other existed. We can't help but feel we've been cheated out of a lifetime with each other." He is shaking his head, obviously still coping with the scope of the secret that has been kept from them. And the woman who birthed twin boys refuses to see them.

"I can only imagine. It must be so hurtful. Okay, Mr. Dobson, if you don't mind, let's take this slowly and start at the beginning," I say. "There's a lot of ground to cover. Please tell me everything you have learned and how you learned it."

Mr. Dobson ends up having four cups of coffee during our interview, because it takes two hours to sort through all the details and hear his story. He is open and forthright in his storytelling, helping me to fill more than half of my reporter's notebook. As we begin to wind down, I'm humbled by how much personal information this man has shared with me. So many families are broken and filled with grief; my own has been altered since the death of my mother. I'm still affected by her absence in my life, the hole she has left behind.

"Tell me again why you have decided to share your story with a newspaper?" I ask, trying to wrap things up.

"I don't know, really. I guess because it's a bit scandalous and was kept secret for so many years, depriving me of a relationship with my brother. Maybe others can learn not to do the same to their families. Clive's dead, Lynette is not well and a recluse, and Bella Friday's a shell of who she once was, messed up with drugs and alcohol. We are trying to make up for lost time, you see. I think it's a travesty that this secret has been kept from both of us for so long."

"It reads like a film script, especially with two big-name stars at the center of it," I say, thinking about how this story is shocking and gripping at the same time. Sensational pieces sell to the public, that's for sure.

"Yes," he says, scratching his head. "It's tough to believe it's real. But in the end, I'm glad I know the truth of it, even though it's tough to forgive them." He seems genuine enough, and his story is completely believable, clearly affecting him emotionally.

"May I ask you a rather personal question off the record? How exactly do you go about forgiving this?" I ask him after becoming captivated by the story and feeling for him about all the deception.

"One day at a time," he says. "One day at a time and a lot of prayers." It's difficult not to feel hurt for this man. "And my brother is expecting your telephone call. He's happy to talk with you along with the others I named. I hope they will speak as frankly with you as I have. As for Bella, I'm not sure she's able to comprehend what this all means in her late years. When I've tried to reach out, her caretaker simply says that she is not fit to speak."

"I see," I say. This story would be even better with Bella as a source, but it still works without her, especially if Mr. Dobson's twin brother agrees to the interview. Nonetheless, I will reach out to her.

After I escort Mr. Dobson to the front door of the offices and wish him well, profusely thanking him for entrusting me to this story, I return to my desk. It's quieter in the newsroom than usual. I sit down and begin to make sense of my notes, including those I want to interview, and highlight his most important quotations. I start typing, when I feel a hand on my shoulder.

"Hi there, Mickey!"

I turn to find Perry Spada standing behind me. He smells like a mixture of soap and cologne, seemingly freshly showered in his suit. Perry's got a cheeky grin on his face, and he's holding a small package wrapped in felt with a ribbon tied around it. He hands it over to me. "For you," he says.

"It's not my birthday," I say, looking up at him in disbelief.

"It doesn't have to be your birthday to get a gift. I've got a good pal who helped me out with this."

I unfurl the ribbon, peel back the felt, and see a baseball signed by Mickey Mantle–right in the sweet spot. I'm shocked by his generosity. He seems baffled by my reaction. I struggle to find words to say.

"Oh, my! I–"

"It's okay. Gifts can be given for no reason," he assures me.

"Not where I come from. My parents weren't exactly gift

givers. I'm so touched. Thank you so much. How did you get this? He's the best player around and just won the Triple Crown!" I cannot hide my delight.

"You do know your stuff!" Perry leans against the desk and folds his arms as he studies me.

"Anyone with half a brain knows he's amazing. Wow!" I can't stop looking at it.

I run my fingers along the seams, trying not to touch the ink where Mickey Mantle signed his name.

"You like it?" He seems pleased that he's pleased me.

"Love it. It's a game ball, too. And I appreciate your thoughtfulness. I'll display my Mantle on my mantle." He laughs and appreciates my humor.

"So, what are you working on today?" he asks, changing the subject and attempting to discuss my work.

"Family 'Hollywood' drama feature. There's a lot to it. How about you?"

"Oh, just wrapping up a story about a pitching prospect. You have plans for dinner?" I'm taken slightly off guard by his boldness, yet it feels rather friendly, too.

"I actually do. Supper with my sister." It was true. I always had supper with my sister, unless an assignment dragged me from it.

"How about lunch plans? Want to grab a bite?" Perry Spada is determined, I can see that. It is tough for me to say no to him after receiving such a thoughtful gift. "What time?" I ask.

"How about now, Mickey?"

*

We walk a couple of blocks to Mo's Luncheonette, a place I've heard a lot about from fellow reporters but have never patronized. The restaurant has green walls and gold decorations hanging from the ceiling. A jukebox plays familiar melodies. Perry is a gentleman. He holds the door for me. He's telling me the story of how he came to write about the Dodgers.

"After covering the Orioles for their first two years for a paper in Baltimore, I got the break to come here. I actually couldn't believe it. I interviewed, got the job, and moved home. Couldn't wait to be back in New York. Two years was enough time to be away. There's nothing like our city, right?"

"Absolutely. Did you grow up in the city?" We find a table that faces the street. He pulls out my chair.

"Jersey City. How about you?" He settles in and takes off his jacket.

"South Orange. Well, that's where my family lived until my mother passed. I live with my sister now in Greenwich Village." I leave out the part about Essie being plagued with the after-effects of polio and how Gertie and I are her primary caregivers. I don't share this information with too many people. Not because I'm embarrassed of her or the situation, it's just that I like to keep personal things to myself.

"And your father?" Perry asks. Members of the press know how to dig in right away.

"Remarried a woman and lives in New England. We don't see him very often." Saying the words aloud makes it both altogether real and breaks my heart a little. I loathe having to explain all this.

"And how long have you been at the newspaper?" Perry asks. He seems genuinely curious.

I smile at him. "I can see why you are a good reporter," I say. "You ask a lot of questions."

"Good ones, I hope, and only when I'm interested in something, or curious about someone," he says, clarifying the statement and looking me in the eyes.

My face gets hot for a second. I've never experienced instant attraction to anyone—ever—but if I were to do so, Perry Spada may be the first. I feel drawn to him, and the conversation is easy.

"Well, I'm flattered."

When the waitress appears, we both order Rueben sandwiches. I opt for the malt as a beverage. He chooses coffee.

"How about your family?" I want to know more about this man who enjoys a Rueben as much as I do.

"Oh, pretty robust, I would say. I'm one of five kids. I have one brother and three sisters. My parents still live in Jersey City, and the youngest is about to graduate from high school. Our family doesn't have two nickels to rub together, but somehow we're some of the happiest people you'll ever meet." *Humble. Happy.* I like that.

I also feel slightly envious of the remark. I'd never call our family happy. We muddled through. Things were okay until Essie became ill with polio and Mama was diagnosed with lung cancer. I try my hardest not to picture my dad's face the day my mother passed. It's one of those images you attempt to erase from your mind. The truth is, he did love her, but more than his love for her, he has a disdain for being alone. When Sandra came along a year after my mother's death, he courted her, and I tended to Essie. After they married, Sandra wanted to move closer to her parents. I was earning a living by then, and Daddy helped set us up with an apartment in the Village. He left us to our own devices because he didn't want the responsibility of caring for Essie. It was too much for him.

"Sounds like you're blessed with a nice family," I say, pleased for him. I have the capacity to be genuinely happy for others and tend not to wallow in my own sorrows. It's just too self-indulgent. Too selfish.

"Maybe you'll meet them sometime." His tone is hopeful.

When the waitress places the malt on the table, he looks at it and smiles.

"Regrets?" I ask, picking up the malt for a sip.

"Oh sure, I have plenty. Where to start..."

"No, I mean about not ordering a malt," I say, laughing.

"I know, I know," he says, laughing with me. "I was trying to be funny."

"That was funny," I say. "Now, take a sip," I say, moving the malt toward him. "I don't want you to miss out on anything amazing."

"Neither do I," Perry says. He takes a sip, and his eyes widen. "Yum...that is a spectacular malt!" He dabs his lips with the napkin.

"I can treat you to one, if you'd like."

"No, I'm treating you to lunch. I did ask you, after all," he says, incredulously.

"We never agreed to that. We can go Dutch." Maybe I'm a bit modern, but I have paid my way all these years and have never needed someone to pay for me.

"That wasn't what I had in mind," he says, with a wink. Not an offensive wink, but an adorable one that makes me look at him even more closely. His eyes are twinkling. In the light of the luncheonette, I can see my reflection in them. "I was asking you to lunch as a date," he confesses.

"I don't date people I work with. Cardinal rule," I say, in a matter-of-fact way. Now it's out in the open.

"I did hear that."

"Did you?" I lean back and cross my arms, waiting for him to elaborate.

"Yes, that's what Daniel told me," Perry says.

"Did he? Daniel shouldn't be sharing my dating philosophies with colleagues." I pretend to be surprised by this truth.

"Why? I'm worried for you. What if Mister Perfect comes along and you happen to work together, but you're living by your own Cardinal rule? Then what?"

"I don't know. I don't wade into those waters long enough to find out." I smile. It's an honest answer, but something in his manner makes me think he knows I'm full of nonsense, and that I have a protective guard up that's difficult to breach. That may be the truth. I'm not sure. Because I have made Essie my priority, everything else has taken a back seat, and dating tops the list. Or maybe I do use my responsibility for Essie to keep relationships at bay.

"Okay, okay. I admit it. Mo's Luncheonette isn't the best spot for a first date, so I'm going to agree with you. Let's not call this a date. We're just two colleagues going out to lunch, attempting to get to know one another, you know, writer to writer, and all that," he says.

"And all that," I say, smirking.

"But I'm still paying. No argument. Now, tell me about this crazy novel Robert tells me you're working on, and promise me that I won't be a character in it," he says, as he takes a bite of his Reuben.

"I'm not in the habit of making promises like that," I say with a smile.

I'm proud of myself. I actually flirted.

Chapter 4

On pay day, I rush to the bank to cash my checks. We have bills to pay, so receiving two checks on the same day is incredibly helpful. I received one from my agent and one from The News. I have to pay the rent, the utilities, Gertie, and Martin, Essie's physical exercise coach. He comes to the apartment twice a week for an hour each time to work with Essie on her muscles. The pain sits in her joints. She's often lethargic and she sleeps a lot, so keeping her in motion as much as we can is important for the health of her muscles. I sometimes have to rouse her to do her daily exercises. She can be lazy about them.

When Essie's feeling up to it, we take the short walk to the park with the help of a cane. On bad days, she remains on the couch. On Sundays, I take her to church. She adores the parish, the priest, and interacts with members of the congregation. Plus, it allows her to spend some time outside the apartment. It makes her happy, and me, too. And undoubtedly, I, too, could use a little more faith and prayer time. As a reporter, when you hear story after story of broken people who could use our prayers, it's humbling.

Since lunch with Perry two days ago, I've accomplished a lot. I've written the first quarter of the feature story after calling Mr. Dobson's brother. He was a talker. The man gave me a ton of information, and he was sweet. Robert also approached me with another lead on something I'm intrigued to pursue. Last night, as Essie slept, I worked a little on my novel. But every so often as I was working, I caught myself doing something I don't normally do.

Even now, sitting at my desk in the newsroom, I find myself thinking about a man named Perry Spada.

I didn't have the heart to tell Essie about Perry, even though I share just about everything with her. I justify my silence by telling myself that there isn't much to tell yet. After all, how can I lead a normal life, or even think about a relationship with a man, when I fully understand my role as my sister's primary caretaker? It's been my job to look after her, and if I have to do that by writing a lot to support the two of us, then so be it. We've gotten by on my writing income for years, my father washing his hands of the two of us when I turned nineteen. Every once in a while, he floats us some money, but it's never expected nor is it a lot.

Perry is endearing, so much so that I find myself thinking of him in the middle of the day, in the middle of writing sentences. I'm flattered by his attention, though I'm not the sort of woman to give any false impressions. Labeled as someone who is direct by my colleagues at The News, who am I to disappoint them and make them think I've gone soft?

Moreover, every time I think of that autographed Mantle baseball displayed on the mantle of our fireplace, I'm reminded of Perry and his act of kindness in giving me that ball.

Somehow, it just belongs there.

*

"Veronica–get your butt in here! I want to talk to you," Robert shouts.

I'm yanked from my thoughts as I'm stringing together my feature, and dash straight to his office, where he waits for me. He shuts the door behind us.

"How's the Dobson story coming along." He's pacing back and forth along his desk, something he does when he's anxious.

"Good, yes. I'm writing it now. I may have it done by Friday." I actually may have it done later today, but I never tell him I may be done early.

"Great. I read the lead." He claps his hands together. "Strong."

"Really?"

"Yes, I hope you don't mind. The paper was in the typewriter, and I've been dying of curiosity ever since you told me about the story. I think it will sell papers."

"You are the editor. You have every right to see what your reporters are writing." It is true. And he does like to read leads. He prides himself on publishing stories that hook readers.

"Well, I'm excited to see the finished product. So, how are things?"

"Good," I say.

"How's Essie?" Robert's the only one at work who knows the full story of Essie's fragility and the time I give to her. He understands how my life has been altered, that she is my primary responsibility. He knows I give her everything she needs.

"Hanging in there. I just wish there was something more I could do for her besides what I am doing—"

"I know, kiddo. I know. But you've done so much, sacrificed so much. You are the most giving sister I have ever seen."

"She's my sister. It's my job." I mean that. Helping her has been a full-time endeavor, and sometimes, I believe, a calling from God.

"She couldn't ask for a better sister," he says, as he lights up a Pall Mall. "But you have a life to live, too, you know."

I wonder where all this is coming from.

"I know. You see how productive I am. I'm living my life."

"But are you? Your mom entrusted me to look after you,

and your dad checks in periodically wanting to know how you are. There's life outside the newsroom, you know."

"And this is coming from a man who practically lives here. Isn't your cot made up in the back of the office?" Giving him a little zinger now and then has become one of the games we play with each other.

"You've got me there. I just worry, that's all." He sits in his chair and takes a long drag from his cigarette.

"Yes, I understand, but Essie is my responsibility. And I have a novel to complete."

"Veronica, I'm talking about a personal life." He blows out the cigarette smoke and makes rings. He's proud of that talent.

I understand what he is suggesting, but it would never work. Building my own life would take too much time away from Essie. A personal life has always been low on my hierarchy of needs. Not by choice, but by necessity.

"There's some big-wig sports dinner and ball the Yankees are hosting next week for Mantle's Triple Crown, and they've invited some of the papers to attend. Connie's got me signed up for some neighborhood thing-a-ma-jig. I was wondering if you'd go with the new guy in my place, knowing your love for your hero. I have two tickets."

My eyes widen. I'm excited by the prospect of attending an event like this. "You mean you want me to go with Perry Spada?"

"Yes." He's trying to be coy about this.

"What about Daniel?"

"He can't go. He's taking vacation with his wife."

"Robert, are you trying to set me up with this guy?"

He looks guilty for a second. I cross my arms and wait for him to answer. "Remember my pledge to look after you, please. He seems like a real good one. Why not spend a little time together? And we're talking about your chance to see a Yankee great—your favorite player!"

"You're meddling in my personal affairs," I say, protesting, but smiling. He tried to set me up once before, and it didn't work out. The guy was not my type.

"Well, someone has to try to help you out," he says. "No pun intended here, Missy, but you can't keep dodging love on account of your sister."

"Ah, good one. Dodging love? I just met the guy!" I see Robert snicker at his own joke. "Truthfully, the thought of leaving Essie prevents me from even entertaining the idea of love, if I'm being honest."

"I know. I've watched you disengage from relationships over the years and come up with your own set of rules for things. Maybe just stop thinking too much about not dating and just attend this event with someone who seems like a nice fella. I've met him several times, and he seems like a genuinely nice guy," Robert says. When he speaks this plainly, I can sometimes see how ridiculous I sound. We're not marching toward the altar. I should just go to the event with him.

"When is it?

"Next Friday night."

I pause for a moment, thinking about the situation.

"You're taking too long to answer. I can get someone else to go with Perry." This is what he does when he subtly manipulates people; he tries to make up their minds for them.

"Nah, why do that? I'd really like to go. I want to see Mickey Mantle in a suit as opposed to his baseball uniform."

"Would you?" Robert laughs, pleased with himself that he's twisted my arm and I'm agreeing.

"Yes," I say. "I think I would."

*

Two weeks later, I'm slipping into a new, simple green cocktail dress with silver pumps, trying not to disturb the up-do I splurged on earlier in the day. I'm dressing in the women's room at The News because I didn't have time to go home and change. I touch up my makeup and add a splash of perfume. Perry will meet me here, and we'll take a cab over to the hotel where the big event is being held. The Yankees owner, Dan Topping, likes to throw celebratory dinners and parties. Being able to attend one in my lifetime is a thrill.

It's a mild night in Manhattan, and I wait for Perry to arrive. When he does, he looks handsome in his dark suit with a slim tie, his hair slicked back for a polished look. His shoes shine in the lights.

"You look sharp," I say as he approaches.

"Right back at you," he says, raising his eyebrows. "You look like a million bucks."

"Thanks, Perry." My face blushes slightly.

He hails a cab, and we head off in the direction of the event.

It's more like a Hollywood red carpet affair, and a lot of bigwigs and baseball noteworthy folks are in attendance. Fans are behind stanchions that are roped off, keeping them from crossing the line onto the actual red carpet that's been rolled out for the event. I see Yogi Berra, and he looks larger than life. Phil Rizzuto strides by. I'm in awe. Perry sees my expression.

"After a while, when you're around these guys all the time, you realize they're just people who play ball really well. But I can see you're in a trance." Perry's enjoying watching my eyes get bigger and bigger.

"Well, I don't do this every day like you do. Yes, it's overwhelming," I say to him as we walk side by side into the venue, desperately trying to hide my astonishment.

Perry laughs. He knows I'm giddy, and I can feel his eyes on me the whole time.

The head table is set, and I search the room for Mantle. He's only been playing since 1951, but he's made an impact on the team and on New York, and his popularity has risen. And now he's captured the Triple Crown.

"There's your hero," Perry says, pointing to Mantle across the room.

Mickey Mantle talks to people, signs autographs, and poses for photos for the newspapers. He looks good in a suit. Solid. Strong. He's being hounded by everyone around him, and he retains his boyish smile the whole time. I wonder what it must feel like to be bombarded by cameras and have people ask you questions around the clock. Ballplayers in this city are pestered by the press constantly—I've seen it firsthand, yet it never ceases to amaze me. You give up a lot to be in the limelight. The lack of privacy must be daunting when a relentless press is involved.

Perry hands me a cocktail and introduces me to some baseball folks he knows. I chat with lots of other reporters and baseball types who know a heck of a lot more about the game than I do. We sip our drinks and mingle for a while. Before the event actually begins to honor Mickey, I dash off to the ladies' room before the program begins. After I powder my nose and check to make sure the up-do hasn't started to fall out of place, I exit the restroom and inadvertently bump right into Mickey Mantle, who has just exited the adjacent men's restroom.

"So sorry," I say to him, feeling my face begin to blush for a second time.

"No worries, Miss," he says back, with his Oklahoma drawl.

I don't know if I should say anything, but I decide to, knowing I may never have the chance again. "I'm a huge fan of yours. Thank you for helping our team be great and congratulations on the Triple Crown."

"Thank you, Miss. Are you with the club?"

"No, I'm a reporter here with The News as a guest."

"Well, thank you for coming." He's actually taking a moment to talk with me.

"Good luck next season," I say. There's a man waiting for him at the edge of the hallway, and Mickey sees him motion to him.

"Thank you!"

I stand there collecting myself, shaking my head in disbelief that I just had an interaction with Mickey Mantle. Unfathomable.

I make my way back over to Perry, who has absolutely no idea what just transpired.

"I don't know what is more fun: attending this event or watching your wide-eyed expression here," he says.

"I'm stunned," I say. "I just bumped into Mickey Mantle."

"What?" Perry leans in, wondering if I'm joking.

"Smacked right into him. He called me 'Miss.'"

"Did he now? He didn't try to steal my date, did he?" I love Perry's humor.

"Don't be silly," I say, still in awe of the moment.

Perry can see I'm distracted by the meeting and a bit in shock, so he ushers me to our assigned table where he's already set our cocktails on the table. We wait for the program to begin. As the emcee takes to the microphone, I'm enthralled by the head table, the speakers, the accolades, and the larger-than-life athletes and dignitaries circulating among the crowd. The large chandeliers in the room generate reflective light that twinkles across the ceiling in the room. I can understand why Perry loves his career so much. The perks are pretty outstanding. We don't get perks like this writing feature stories. At least not this grand.

Covering baseball is certainly a lot more fun than hearing sad tales about people's lives and writing dramatic feature stories without happy endings. The benefits that come from sports writing are much better overall, I decide.

Perry raises his glass to me and makes a little toast. "To our new friendship," he says.

I raise my eyebrow, feeling a little emboldened by the wine.

"Friendship?" I ask.

"You said you don't date people you work with, so I'm just abiding by your workplace dating tenet."

"Well," I say, as I lean in toward him, "I wouldn't pay it

any mind. I may have been too hasty about that Cardinal rule," and I give him a little kiss on the cheek. He feigns surprise.

His expression tells me he's pretty pleased that I took the lead.

*

"How was the event?" Essie says when I come through the door. She knows I went to a Yankees event and was representing The News.

"It was wonderful," I tell her. "How are you?"

"Fine. Where'd you get that dress?" she asks me.

"Do you like it? I actually did buy it for the event."

"And you had your hair done," she says.

"Yes, I did. Did you have a nice time with Natalie tonight?" Natalie is Robert's step-daughter. She and Essie have become close over the years.

"We had a good time. She just left a half an hour ago." She's lying on the couch with her favorite afghan draped across her legs.

"What did you two do?" I sit in the recliner across from her, eager to hear about her night.

"She brought homemade apple cobbler and we played board games. What did you have to eat?" she's not interested in talking about her night; she wants to know more about mine.

"They served a chicken dish, but I didn't eat much. I was too excited. I actually met Mickey Mantle." I'm trying to hold in my excitement.

"You what?"

"I met Mickey Mantle. Bumped right into him outside the powder room."

"How was he?" Her eyes have grown big.

"He was very nice." Feeling the remnants of intoxication from the evening, I'm not feeling too talkative at the moment.

"Is he as handsome in person?" Essie asks.

"You think he's handsome, Essie?" I lean back in the chair and put my feet up.

"Yes, very," she says.

"Then yes, I suppose he is very handsome. I like the way he looks in a Yankees uniform." I've never thought of him as handsome or not handsome—only as a man with incredible talent.

There's a long pause, followed by quiet. Then Essie says, "Veronica, is there something you're keeping from me?" I look at her and shake my head 'no.' "Because I'm sensing you had a date tonight. Look at how dressed up you are."

I can't lie to her. I always try to protect her and our relationship, and I never want her to feel that I'm neglecting her or that she's a burden to me. But since she has asked, and because I did enjoy spending time with Perry, I share the story. It would be wrong not to tell her. Plus, he's asked me for another date this weekend.

"I did kind of have a date. His name's Perry Spada, and he's a new sportswriter for the newspaper. He covers the Dodgers."

"I thought you didn't want to date your colleagues." I can hear the tone change in her voice.

"I don't...I didn't...but he kind of fell into my lap. We have a good time together." I normally wouldn't blurt things out like this, but I feel comfortable enough with Perry to be able to share him with Essie.

"So, you've spent time with him besides this event?" I can see the way she's looking at me, wondering how much I've been keeping from her. She looks surprised and hurt at the same time.

"Only a lunch date and this event. Don't worry, Essie. We just met and are getting to know one another. Nothing will change. I'll always be here for you."

She looks at me and smiles, but her face has changed. "I know you will be," she says.

When my head hits the pillow later that night, I smile to myself, thankful that there's the faintest smell of Old Spice lingering on my skin, from when I had my arms around Perry's neck as we danced in the ballroom and laughed and laughed.

Chapter 5

Gertie shows up at eleven o'clock on Saturday to keep Essie company for a couple of hours. Perry is taking me for an autumn picnic in Central Park, and Gertie has encouraged me to go. Essie is still in her room sleeping.

"I feel so guilty even asking you for help on a weekend. Our deal is for weekdays, and I take care of her on the weekends." Gertie is holding two parcels of food. She loves shopping for us.

"Veronica, you two have become more like daughters to me. I honestly don't mind. It gives me company, too, and I feel as if I'm helping in some way. You deserve to go on a date, honey. It's okay," Gertie says.

"Why doesn't it feel okay, then?" Sometimes the responsibility overwhelms me.

"Because you have sacrificed, and you support her and you love her. Still, you owe it to yourself to live your life," Gertie whispers, unpacking the bags.

"But I feel so selfish. I wish she could be doing the same." I see my reflection in the mirror and need to dress for the day. Gertie knows what I'm saying is true, and I can tell she has sympathy for my situation.

"She does, in her own way. You just go and enjoy yourself."

I own one pair of brown cigarette pants and slip into them and a cranberry sweater. Gertie helps me put my hair into a chignon. It's breezy, and I don't want my hair in my face. I slip into the brown tweed jacket and reach for a scarf. Autumn is in the air.

"I'll be back shortly," I say to Gertie.

As I close the door behind me, I plan to make my absence up to Essie when I return home. I'll treat her to supper, and we'll play cards or Parcheesi. She loves board games.

When I step outside the door, I see Perry walking toward me. The night of the banquet, he had the taxi take me home first, so he knows where I live. We were due to meet at Washington Square Park. He's carrying a small picnic hamper and grinning from ear to ear.

"Surprise!" he says. "I figured I'd pick you up and take you out for the whole day, from beginning to end. And I've decided on a new location."

"I thought it was just a picnic," I say.

"Well, it can just be a picnic if that's what suits you." He holds out his arm for me to loop mine through.

I haven't told him about Essie and my need to return home to her, so I worm my way out of it. "We'll just play it by ear," I say, thinking that maybe over the course of lunch I'll share my personal story.

Perry hails a cab, and when the driver pulls over, he opens the door for me, allowing me to go in before him. He sets the hamper between us, his arm resting on it, and tells the driver our destination.

He opens the palm of his hand and raises an eyebrow at me, gesticulating to the open palm to place my hand inside his. We had held hands at the Mantle event, so he is expecting to pick up where we left off. I oblige. I like the feel of my hand in his. Despite the coolness of the air, his hand is warm, and he wraps his fingers around mine. My head is swirling. How did this man come so swiftly and naturally into my life? I try not to take it all so seriously—it's only our second date, since we're not counting the luncheonette as the first. I shouldn't be overanalyzing any of our actions at such an early stage in our relationship, but I'm a writer, and it comes with the job. We pay attention to nuances, phrases, and what isn't said.

I shake myself out of the trance I'm in and enjoy the feeling of my hand in his. We begin to make small talk.

"How's the novel coming?" he asks, turning slightly to look me in the eyes. I like looking at his.

"Working through the last bit. I think I'm on pace to finish ahead of schedule. What about you?"

"Oh, you know. Writing a few stories. O'Malley, the Dodgers' owner, is none too pleased that he can't get a new stadium built in Brooklyn. This guy Moses wants the new ballpark to be built in Flushing Meadow, where there's good access to the new highways. So, I'm following this story right now. We'll see what happens. He calls Ebbets Field 'dingy and in need of repairs.'"

"He may be right," I say. "A new stadium would be nice, wouldn't it?"

"Sure, it'd be great for the team, but their fan base is dropping. Attendance isn't good." I had heard this from others in the newsroom, but I didn't understand it.

"Why? They just won the World Series in '55." The taxi driver honks at the person in front of him. We both giggle.

"I think that's what they're trying to figure out," Perry says. "The owner is frustrated."

When we reach Central Park, Perry steps out of the taxi and opens my door. He pays the driver, and we begin to walk toward the park, autumn fully illuminating nature with its deep oranges and vibrant reds and saturated yellows. There's nothing like autumn in this city. New York is alive.

We find a location with a vista of the city's skyline. Perry unfurls a blanket, pressing it into shape. We get comfortable on it. He opens the hamper, and inside are a variety of cheeses and crackers, a small carafe of wine, little sandwiches, grapes, and even a few chocolate treats for dessert.

"Wow," I say, impressed with his picnicking skills, "you know how to pack the perfect lunch."

"I'm so glad you're pleased with it. I took a guess and landed on this. Hope it's all okay."

He pours the wine, and we make our plates as we breathe in the air. I put my jacket across my legs—not that it's cold. It just makes me feel cozy.

Perry holds up his glass for a toast. "I'm not really sure what to say, so I'll just keep it simple. I'm glad I've met you, Veronica. To be honest, I think I've been looking for someone like you for a while."

Flattered, I clink his glass. "Thank you. That's sweet to say."

It's too soon for me to say the same. I'm scared of where this is all going. The attraction to Perry is strong, and yet I force myself to remain slightly aloof. But he's a smart man. Maybe he sees through me. I don't like to play games, but it's often in the name of self-protection. I have to suppress the thought of Essie, of course. I will always feel responsible for her. But for today, I will only try to focus on spending time with Perry.

"Have you always wanted to be a sportswriter?" I ask him in between bites of the pepperoni and variety of cheeses.

"I love baseball. I guess because I can't play it, I might as well write about it. I loved working on my high school and college newspapers. It was a ton of fun. Made all my best friends doing that in college."

"And where are they all now?" I ask. The wine warms my insides.

"All over the country, actually. The best writers got jobs at papers, and one of my friends is writing novels like you. Yes...we all liked writing so much, we all stuck with it. We try to get together once or twice a year, but it's difficult when we've all landed in different states."

"I know. My closest friend from high school lives in Washington, D.C. She works for the government. We chat infrequently, which makes me sad. It becomes so easy to lose touch because our careers are so demanding." I do miss her. Essie never loved her; she always had something negative to say about her.

"And how did you get the job at The News?" Perry asks.

"My mother and Robert were lifelong friends. When my mother died ten years ago, my father, my sister, Essie, and I were devastated. Then, my father remarried; he'd met a woman named Sandra and moved to New England. I was nineteen at the time and Essie was twenty-two. We got an apartment that my father helped secure, which made it easy for him to relocate to New England. Because Robert works in the city and is a dear family friend, he took me under his wing and hired me at the newspaper. I needed a job. Over the last ten years, I've been everything from a Girl Friday to a secretary. I went to a two-year college and learned a little. But Robert taught me all I know about journalism, and in time, entrusted me to write stories. Don't get me wrong–there was a lot of red ink and corrections in the beginning, but I'm a fast learner, and he always said I had a knack for telling a good story. The form came afterwards," I say. I feel breathless trying to take a year's worth of life and work and mold it into one short anecdote.

"And the novel writing?" Perry seems genuinely interested.

"I just love telling stories. I had heard a story about a broken relationship, and I took that story and turned it into fiction. When I finished writing it, I sent it to an agent. It was all rather happenstance, but it ended up working out, much to my surprise!"

"A success story," Perry says. "I love hearing those. Are you working on a second?"

"Yes, that's the plan." Sometimes I'm still in disbelief at it all.

"And yet you still write for Robert?" Perry leans back, his eyes catching the light. They seem to dance with delight.

"Yes. I simply can't leave him. He's given me every opportunity, and I wouldn't be here without him. He taught me everything I know."

"A good man."

"Yes," I say. "A good man."

"Too few of them these days, if you ask me," Perry says. He sips his wine and fixes himself another cracker with cheese.

"But I'm having a picnic lunch with one such man," I say, meaning it.

Perry smiles. It's big and broad, and his white teeth shine in the broken sunlight. "Well, thank you for saying that. It's awfully kind of you."

"Well, I think it's true. We may only be getting to know one another, but I can tell that there's something special about you, Perry Spada."

He looks away when I say this, seemingly embarrassed, or perhaps it is too soon for me to say something as forward as this. I'm not sure. But I'm drawn to him like a magnet, and despite what I told myself a few minutes ago, for a second, I imagine kissing his lips.

When we finish the wine and pack up the picnic hamper, we take a little stroll back toward 5th Avenue.

"So where is your apartment?" I ask, my arm looped through his.

"Not too far from here," he says. "I rent a small basement apartment from an older fella my sister knows. He used to live in Jersey City and moved here with his wife. When she passed away a year ago, he'd been looking to rent the space, but he insisted on renting it to someone he knew from Jersey City. When I got the job at The News, I met with him. Do you want to see it?"

"Sure," I say, intrigued. "You didn't want to live in Brooklyn?"

"Nah. I'd rather live near the paper and just go to the games. I don't mind getting around by subway or cab or walking, either. Does a man good, you know?"

"Yes. It does a girl good, too," I say. "I pretty much walk everywhere I can."

We stroll the few blocks back and cross one avenue until we reach a pretty brownstone off the park. It has a black iron gate in front, and wrought iron handrails adorn the steps. It's regal looking, with potted plants helping to make a garden entrance. Perry's front door is street-level, so he searches his pocket for the key. He opens the door, and it's nicer than I expected. A little sitting area features a desk for his writing, a black Smith-Corona typewriter, stacks of books along the walls, and a bedroom in the distance. There's a compact kitchen with an icebox, stove, and counter space to prepare meals. He has a comfortable dining area, too.

"This is very nice. It suits you," I say, looking around the apartment and taking it in.

He sets the picnic hamper down next to his desk and turns to me.

"You know how as writers we're supposed to have all the words for everything?"

"Yes," I say, laughing. "Do I!"

He gently pulls me close to him, once again taking my hands in his. "That typically works best for me on paper. Not in person. I never know what to say," he says, searching my eyes to see if I, too, am at a loss for words.

His mouth finds mine, and I reach my arms around his neck. He pulls me closer, his arms wrapped tightly around me, and we kiss, the heat of our embrace making me warm all over. His lips are moist and he smells like a mixture of faded cologne and fallen leaves. He takes my face in his hands and kisses me harder, the passion building, until we are both out of breath. It's intense for a second date. I have to collect myself.

"I'm sorry," he says, as he feels me pull away slightly. "Was that too much for date two?"

I just start laughing–belly laughing. I'm convinced he can read my thoughts, and then he starts laughing, too, both of us caught up in the speed at which this relationship is moving.

"It's just, well, I haven't dated in forever, and I need to take it slowly, if that's okay," I say, after we get ourselves together, and I straighten my sweater. I place my hand on the side of his cheek to assure him I'm here, even at the relationship's swift pace. Every fiber of my being wants to pick up where we left off, but I can hear my mother's words about "decorum" echoing in my head. They seem to materialize at the most inconvenient times.

"I understand, and I'm sorry. I think I got a little carried away." He's apologizing for it, so I assure him all is well.

"Perry, don't apologize, and please don't take this the wrong way, but I'm not at all sorry you got carried away."

"You're not?" He seems somewhat relieved.

"No." I'm pretty sure he can see the glint of mischievousness in my eyes. "I did the same."

He examines me, feels the flirtation. "So, does that mean there's a third date in our future?"

I nod. "And hopefully more," I say.

Chapter 6

When I return home from my day with Perry, Essie is waiting for me in her recliner chair. I had just missed seeing Gertie because I got home a few minutes later than expected. Gertie often sits with Essie and they work on their crocheting and knitting projects. To make up for my tardiness, I had picked up supper on the way home. In the kitchen, I prepare the food and put it in the oven. Essie attempts a cross examination about my afternoon.

"Why are you all of a sudden deciding to date?" she asks me.

"It's not that I 'all of a sudden' decided to date, Essie. It's just that I met someone I actually like and want to spend time with."

"Shouldn't you be working on your books instead of gallivanting with a stranger?" It's her tone that gets to me.

Sometimes, she can be so condescending. She often feels she can speak to me this way simply because she is older than I am, in that motherly 'I know best' way. I know how to work on my projects. Work has been the bane of my existence, and I rarely take time for myself. When I'm not working, I'm with Essie, caring for her, running errands for her, making her comfortable, and earning money for our livelihood.

I turn to her, taking a deep breath and trying not to raise my voice. I don't want her insinuations to affect the pleasant mood I am in from spending time with Perry. I'm still reeling from the way I felt in his arms, his lips on mine. "Essie, I'm almost twenty-nine years old, and I know how to budget my time, including my personal life, which, you must admit, has been non-existent."

"Are you blaming me for your non-existent life? And if yours is non-existent, what exactly is mine?" she asks, pointing to herself.

"Essie, I know. No one understands your predicament more than I do. That's why I'm here for you. That's why, as your sister, you can always count on me."

"Can I? I'm not so sure anymore." Her comment stings. She's famous for throwing temper tantrums and getting huffy, sometimes for no reason except her own frustration. I can't figure out if she feels threatened or left out.

"I don't want to quarrel with you, Essie. I'm here now. I went out for a little while today, and I've brought us a nice meal to eat. Let's enjoy the food and play one of your favorite games tonight, just you and me." Sometimes it's like talking to a child.

She nods and sits down.

"And then you'll have to write." It's irritating when someone else tells me what to do and when. I'm quite adept at knowing how to get things done.

"Later, when you get tired," I say, just to quell the contention.

We begin to eat our food, and I try to avoid thinking about Perry and our date. I guide the conversation back to Essie.

"So, what did you and Gertie do today?"

*

On Monday morning, the tension is high in the house. Essie's frustration is at an all-time high; she copes with her condition and holds me in contempt. Some days, it's not her condition that keeps her down, but her mental state. She snapped at me several times on Sunday, and this morning, she fussed and chastised me for not picking up her reserved books from the library.

"I will pick them up today," I say to her. "I promise."

"You said that on Friday, and you didn't do it."

"I've been a little busy. Please forgive me. I will bring them home this evening."

"I'm sure you'll be glad to be rid of me for a few days." Essie's trip to visit our father is coming up; she's taking the train up next week to spend some time with Daddy and Sandra. The two of them will drive Essie back to the city, as they'll be passing through this way to visit with friends in Virginia.

"You know I'll miss you," I say.

She mumbles something under her breath, and for the first time in my life, I feel exhausted by displeasing her, as if all the ingratitude piqued today. I'm her mother, her father, her sister, her caretaker, her provider, her chef, and her entertainment source. No wonder she's feeling a little left out by my new relationship with Perry. I've always been careful not to make her feel as if she is a burden. I've always put her first. I'm sensing she wants me to feel guilty for spending time away from her.

Luckily, I'm off to the office. She doesn't get upset about my work schedule, at least not to my knowledge. Gertie arrives to settle Essie in for the day. I kiss her on the cheek and head out the door. The sun is shining and the crisp air feels invigorating. I walk to work and try to put Essie out of my mind for a bit, but it's difficult. She's my sister, and I know she needs me. If the shoe were on the other foot, I would hope for the same treatment. How would she survive without me?

When our father left her to my care—to which I happily agreed—I just did it and didn't think long-term. But I believe he had. Now I understand that our father did not want the responsibility of taking care of Essie for the rest of her life...for the rest of his life. That burden has shifted to me. If I did happen to marry one day, I would have to insist that Essie live with us. I never thought about it any other way or with any other outcome. And, of course, there's the possibility that she will improve over time.

Essie may have been physically handicapped by polio, but she is a beautiful woman. She enjoys getting gussied up for church. Her beauty far exceeds mine, with her porcelain unblemished skin, blue eyes, and shiny blonde hair. She blossomed into a lovely woman, despite the pains that plague her. As my older sister, I admire her. When she became ill with polio, I was incensed that the illness happened to her, telling my mother and father that it wasn't right how it affected Essie. They agreed and told me we must handle the cards we've been dealt. We've been doing that ever since.

Of course, my mother's cancer diagnosis came after Essie's polio diagnosis. She could hardly care for Essie when she became ill herself. After she died, it fell upon me to care for Essie, my father too devastated by my mother's death. He briefly wallowed in his loneliness until he met Sandra and moved away from us.

When circumstances affect your family, you have to figure out the best way to handle and cope with it. My father decided I was the one to be put in charge of Essie's care, while he escaped to New England. This is how I have been–and continue to be–her caretaker and her provider. Most days, I do it without a second thought.

Walking through the newsroom doors is like getting a shot of adrenaline. It's a welcome sound. Simultaneously, I'm energized and comforted by a place that has become my second home. Monday mornings are typically the busiest after coming off the weekend. I inhale the smell of coffee and newsprint and find the way to my desk. There's a little note on it with my name on it. I open it up as I sit in my chair.

I loved spending time with you this weekend. Have a great week. Yours, Perry.

"Veronica," I hear Robert call, "I'd like to see you in my

office."

Startled by his booming voice this early in the morning, I scurry toward his door. I never want Robert to call me a "turtle." It's a nickname he's given to writers who move too slowly on a story and the worst insult you can receive from him.

"Close the door," he says. He's wearing his red suspenders today with his tweed slacks. He looks like an editor of a newspaper; he fits the bill perfectly.

"Is something wrong?"

"No, no, my dear. I just wanted to check in with you and see how you're doing."

"I'm fine. Why wouldn't I be?"

"Just making sure."

"I'm good."

He stares at me for a second, examining me to make sure I'm not fibbing. "Honestly, I'm fine."

He scratches his head. "Robert, is there something going on?"

I can tell he's hedging on whether or not to share something with me. He sits down and sips his coffee. He motions for me to sit in his guest chair.

"Natalie told me something that I wish she hadn't," he says. Now I am rife with curiosity and fear.

"What is it?"

"Essie made some comment the other day to the effect that if she were left alone in the world, she wouldn't want to live."

I put my coffee down on the edge of Robert's desk. "What?"

He looks at me. What he has just shared is petrifying. Disturbing. Concerning.

"Do you think this is this because I've had two dates with Perry and she's worried about what will happen to her if I were to become serious in a relationship?" I ask him, genuinely.

"I don't know."

"This is horrible. How am I supposed to work knowing she feels this way? How am I going to be able to leave her alone sometimes? How will I ever be able to date anyone at all?"

We are both left at a loss as we sit in silence. Robert can see I'm becoming more and more concerned with each passing minute. I'm pacing the floor and in need of a cigarette. I motion for him to offer me one, and he hands the pack to me. I can smell the tobacco and put it between my lips. Robert reaches for a lighter. I inhale. Exhale. I feel horrible that my father has left me under Robert's tutelage and his care. I can tell that sometimes he bears the responsibility and burden for both Essie and me—and truth be told, he's been more like a father to me than my own father.

"Perhaps there's a way we can help her find something to do other than sit in the house. That will help ease your mind." It's a great suggestion, but I'm not sure how we would go about doing that.

"It would be so good for her to have a part-time job. I mean, Gertie's great, she takes care of her, but having responsibility might give her a sense of purpose and a reason to get out of the house a little," I say, thinking out loud. "Maybe she needs a diversion."

"Yes, just something as a distraction and helps her feel needed." Clearly, Robert has thought this through since hearing Natalie's comment.

"You make a great point, Robert. But whoever hires her would have to be understanding of her condition. Some days are better than others."

I sit down in Robert's chair and cross my legs. There's a run in my nylons I didn't see before I left the apartment. A run cheapens the outfit, and I'm embarrassed by the look of it. I cross my legs and try to hide it by folding my arms over top of it as I sit up straight.

"I'll see what I can find out," I say to Robert.

"Your mother would be so proud of you, the way you take

care of your sister. That's true love, right there. She raised you right."

I smile at Robert. He always says the kindest things about my mother, and the mere mention of her name today makes me feel sadder than I've felt in years. I miss her dearly. If she were here today, I know I'd have her unbridled support. Had my mother not become ill, I also know she would be the one taking care of Essie. She would never have allowed my father to let this fall to me, even though I volunteered, and even though Robert has been charged with keeping tabs on us.

I stand up and Robert motions for me to come near him. He's not typically an affectionate man, especially not at work, but today he pats me on the arm and tells me it will all be okay.

When he says that, I believe him.

Chapter 7

Perry smells like musk and sweat. He's wearing trousers with suspenders, a shirt, and a vest with loafers. He looks adorable. He reminds me of the late James Dean. Sexy and casual.

"Hello, Mickey," he says to me when he sees me looking at him. He's taken to calling me Mickey at work, which is funny and cute at the same time, and I don't mind it at all. Mickey Mantle brought us together, after all.

"Where have you been?" I ask, moving closer to him.

"I've been running all over Brooklyn trying to get interviews. News is breaking about O'Malley's push for a new ballpark. Not sure where this is going to go, but I am verifying sources."

He pours himself a cup of black coffee and brings me a cup, too. We stand near my desk looking at one another with smiles on our faces. Seeing him makes me forget about all the other responsibilities, like deadlines and book sales and Essie. I could fall into him right here and would love to have those arms wrapped tightly around me. He feels like a safety net to me, even after only knowing him for such a short period of time.

"After I take a shower, because I clearly need one, I'd love to take you to dinner. I heard about this little dive place on 9th Avenue that has the best calamari—"

"I can't." I breathe deeply.

"Why not?"

"Trouble at home I have to take care of. I'd love a rain check, though."

"Trouble at home? Do you live with your family?" he asks, realizing he knows the location of where I live, but we haven't discussed my living arrangements yet. I don't want to lie to him. I have to explain.

"It wasn't that I was trying not to share this aspect of my life with you, but it was nice to not have to talk about it, if only for a bit. I live with my sister and she's handicapped. She has polio."

I see his face drop, a look of concern taking over.

"I had no idea. I'm sorry."

"Don't feel bad for me. I volunteered to take it on. We share the apartment, and I've been caring and providing for her ever since."

I can see his worry deepening. "That sounds like a lot to handle."

"I have help. I pay a woman down the street to help me take care of her while I'm working, and sometimes she helps me out on the weekend, as she did when we went on our picnic date. It's just that it's difficult to manage my free time, because she relies on me."

"I understand," Perry says, rubbing my arm. "You don't have to say another word. I won't put pressure on you. I'd love to see you, but I get what commitment means."

I appreciate the way he is responding to my situation with empathy and understanding.

"You let me know when you'd like to come to dinner with me, or, if you're open to it, I could bring dinner to you and your sister—"

He's reaching for her name, but I had never shared it, so I help him out. "Essie."

"I could bring dinner to you and Essie."

I realize I'm in an office, the office where I get paid to work, but I pay no mind to my surroundings. I reach up and hug him and kiss him on the side of the cheek.

"You are special, mister," I say, feeling myself become a little emotional from his generosity and gentle manner.

"We all need to eat, right?" he says, as we let go of each other. He winks, trying to make light of it all. I appreciate his humor, and I realize it's just his way of saying he wants to see me.

On the record, I desperately want to see him, too.

"Let me check with the boss and see if she's up for it," I say to him.

"I'm here whenever you need me." He leans in to give me a little peck on my cheek, and I like the way it feels.

All of it.

*

When I return home that evening after a long day, Gertie has food warming in the oven, and Essie is in her normal position on the couch. She tosses me a quick hello, and then gets back to reading her book. Sometimes I feel as if we're two strangers dancing around issues that neither one of us chooses to discuss. The death of our dear mother, the disappearing act of our father, the irony of the aloneness we both feel here together. It's sometimes heartbreaking to see the way she's recoiled from the effects of her condition. It also must be challenging to see me moving forward with my life.

"We're going to church on Sunday, right?"

"Of course. Have I ever not taken you?"

She rolls her eyes at me. "Just confirming, in case you have plans." Sarcasm and bitterness at its finest.

I make her plate of food, wanting to tell her that Perry has offered to bring us dinner, but I choose not to say anything at all. She's not up for this kind of discussion, and I'm actually looking forward to some solitude this evening—just my typewriter and me—getting down to some creative business. I've got loads to do and the pressure is on. Deadlines drive my world, and I've never missed one yet. I don't plan on missing anything in the near future, which is why I could use the quiet time tonight.

When I clear Essie's plate and get her settled for the night, she tells me there's a pie in the icebox that she wants. I cut her a slice and heat the teakettle. Her evening routine: always tea, preferably Earl Grey, and whatever sweet nibble we have around the place. I steep the teabag in water and add a little cream to it—just the way she likes it. I bring it to her on a tray without so much as a word of thanks for serving her.

It's just the way it is, disheartening as it may be. We get used to routines. Our responsibilities trump our desires, at least that's how it works in my life. But it doesn't have to be that way for the characters in my fiction; I can give them something happy. In the imagined book about my sister and me, Essie would be cured, she'd go out and live a happy, pain-free life, marry, have children, work in a library or teach at a school, and grow contentedly old with her husband. I'd love to be able to write that story for her in real life, to see her waltz off the couch. Life isn't fair, that we know.

I grab my own cup of tea and sit at the small desk in my room that faces the window. Outside, it's a cool night, and the lights from the street help illuminate my room. I begin to peck at the keys, allowing the story to take over as a welcome escape. It's a way to transport myself into someone else's life, someone else's situation, and to bring those people to life on the page. I'm typing away, working into the very late hours, when I finally stop typing.

The apartment is quiet; the city has become a little sleepier; and I just want to sleep for days.

Chapter 8

I manage to get Essie in the cab and out of the cab without too much trouble. She's dressed up in her best skirt and blouse with a cardigan, and her hair is pulled into a high ponytail. She typically likes to sit in the front pew, so that she doesn't have to be seen limping to receive communion. Mass is very crowded. We take our place in the front row, and she lowers herself into the seat and straightens her skirt.

"I'll be right back," I say to her, leaving her to sit by herself for a few minutes.

I walk toward the back of the church, where I grab the church bulletin. I like reading news, what can I say? I want to know what's happening at church, especially if I can get Essie out of the house to attend an event or two.

Returning to the pew, I genuflect and sit beside Essie. The altar is adorned with colorful mums. The organist begins to play *How Great Thou Art*, my mother's favorite. We try our best to make it to church every week, my mother having instilled a strong faith in her two daughters. I'd like to think she would be pleased to see us here together, praying. I wish I could thank her for introducing me to God.

As I peruse the church bulletin, I see the HELP WANT-

ED section. It reads: *Part-time individual needed in the office to work two half-days a week helping Father Brannon. Flexible schedule. Call Janice in the Parish Office for more details and to apply.*

I wonder if this is a job Essie can handle. Perhaps it would give her a sense of purpose to work two days a week for the church. It may bring her joy. I fold the bulletin and place it in my purse, hoping it might be feasible.

After mass, the incense still floating in the air, the light streaming in through the stained-glass windows, Essie and I make our way down the aisle. A man I've seen before but have never met approaches us and says hello to Essie.

"Hi, Essie," he says. "It's good to see you."

"You, too, Malcolm." They are on a first-name basis? I find this interesting.

"Are you going to be able to come to the church bazaar on Friday?" he asks her.

Essie glances toward me, and I raise my eyebrows at her, indicating that it is she who should answer the question. With a soft breath, she turns back to Malcolm and says, "I'm hoping so."

This is news to me. She has never mentioned Malcolm, nor has she mentioned wanting to attend the church bazaar, but I smile as if I'm keen on it all, and say, "She wouldn't miss it."

Malcolm seems intent on having a conversation with Essie, and so I excuse myself for a moment and give the two of them some privacy. Turning into the church office, I pull the bulletin from my hands, ready to ask about the opportunity. A woman with cat eye-glasses in a bright, red dress and matching red lipstick approaches me and smiles, bearing her contrasting white teeth. I see her at mass all the time but don't know her name. "Can I help you?" she asks.

"May I ask about this opportunity you have here for a part-time employee?" I point to it in the bulletin.

"Yes, of course. Are you interested?"

"Oh, no. Not me. I was inquiring for my sister."

"What would you like to know?"

"I was wondering if it would be feasible for someone with polio to hold that position. My sister's legs don't work as well as they used to, but her mind is sharp, and her arms and fingers are unaffected. She has pain that comes and goes, but I'm thinking she needs a reason to get out of bed each morning instead of sitting around the house all day waiting for me to come home from work. A couple of days out each week may do her quite a bit of good."

"Do you mean the young lady who is seeing Malcolm Flannery?" I'm caught off guard.

"Yes," I say, my own reply feeling a bit feeble.

"He is tremendous. Such a brilliant financial supporter of the church."

The woman moves behind her desk where she retrieves paperwork out of folders in the desk's drawer. It takes her only a minute to get it all together. She turns to me and says, "Here are the application papers. I think it sounds like something that might be a wonderful fit for her."

I take the papers from her hand and thank her. My mind is jumbled. *The young lady who is seeing Malcolm Flannery.*

"I'm Molly Jones, should you need any further assistance. And you can return all the paperwork to me, as well," she says.

"Thank you, Molly. My name's Veronica DeMarco, and my sister's name is Essie."

"We will look forward to hearing from Essie, then!" She smiles encouragingly at me.

Completely baffled by Essie's connection with Malcolm, I return and find them sitting outside the church on a bench, engaged in a conversation, laughing. I stand back from them where they cannot see me. Like a fly on the wall, I observe their interactions. Essie is talking and smiling; Malcolm is leaning in towards her. He has a receding hairline and a long face, reminiscent of a young Fred Astaire, and he's wearing a herringbone jacket. He looks like a college professor. I wonder how the two of them know each other, and moreover, how well they know each other. Father

Brannon, the pastor of the church, approaches them, and they engage with him in conversation. She's keeping something from me.

I watch Essie's animated face as she talks. She looks almost unrecognizable and unfamiliar to me, like someone I've never met before. Tossing her head back, she laughs, a hearty laugh that I haven't seen or heard in quite some time. Her eyes twinkle. Miffed by all this, I stay hidden until Father Franklin walks away, and then walk toward Essie and Malcolm.

"Well, shall we get ourselves home for some lunch, Essie?" I ask.

Malcolm seems none too pleased that I am about to take her away from him, but Essie mumbles "sure." The cane she uses is next to her, and I hand it to her.

"I guess I'll see you, Malcolm," she says, as we begin to walk away.

"Take care, Essie. Hope to see you Saturday."

Essie nods, and we continue walking until I am able to hail a cab that will take us back to our apartment.

*

Once inside, Essie settles into the dining table, keeping mum about Malcolm. She has not uttered a word. I make the standard Sunday meal: spaghetti and meatballs with a salad and an almond cake for dessert. Fearful to broach any subject that might alter Essie's current good mood, we talk of the homily and the flowers at mass.

"Do you remember the church we used to go to with Mama when we were little?" Essie asks me.

"Sure. The one with the marble altar and the green leather bench coverings?"

"Ah, you do remember then."

"Yes," I say. It was tough to forget the putrid green color. Even as a small child, it stood out among all the white and tan colors of the old, steepled church.

"I miss going to mass there," she says. I thought she might cry as she said the words, which made me feel my mother's absence just as much.

"It's hard living life without her. I suppose it always will be," I say.

"I know it hasn't been easy for you, having to care for me, but you've done the best you could, really. I'm sorry if I don't always show my appreciation." Essie's comment seems sincere, and I feel as if I've been relinquished from all the guilt I carry around all day. I start to cry.

Then, I start to sob.

Essie is watching me like you'd watch a train wreck. She keeps saying she's sorry for bringing up Mama, but the truth is, I'm crying because for once I don't feel like I'm useless at caring for her.

"It's okay," she says, patting my arm, "it's all okay."

"No, it's not. I feel as if I'm failing you."

"You're not failing. We just came upon unusual circumstances," she says. It's a rare moment of humility for her.

I dab my eyes with a napkin, taking deep breaths and trying to bring myself back into the moment of joy and not of regret and worry. She pours the wine, and we both take a sip.

"To new beginnings," she says.

"Indeed." I raise my glass. We sip our wine.

"So, how do you know Malcolm?" I ask.

"We met at a daytime function that Gertie took me to one day," she says matter-of-factly, avoiding elaborating on it.

"I see."

We continue to eat our food when I decide to broach the subject that I want to discuss. "Did you happen to notice the 'help wanted' notice in the bulletin?"

Essie shakes her head "no" as she twirls her spaghetti.

"I looked into it for you—I hope you don't mind. There's a

job that's been posted for a part-time person two days a week, and I didn't know if it's something you may be interested in applying for." I place the church bulletin in front of her. She reads the job description expressionless. She chews her food, sips the wine, but doesn't answer me. "Any thoughts?" I ask.

"Interesting," she says, in a very non-committal way.

"Interesting good or interesting bad?"

"Neither."

"Is it something that sounds like it would be enjoyable for you, just for a change of scenery a couple of days a week?"

"I just worry about my condition, you know. What if I wake up one day and can't manage to get to work? What then?"

"I don't know," I say, "maybe that's something we can discuss with them."

She cuts her meatball and takes a bite of it. She's morphing into to the Essie I've become well acquainted with over the last many months—the aloof one who doesn't want to talk.

"Let me think about it," she says. "And let's not talk of it any more today. I'm tired."

Essie's great at ending conversations. She just dismisses me and says the conversation is over, just like that. We finish our lunch together, and I ask her if she would mind if I go for a quick walk. She says it's fine, that she wants to lie down on the couch and take a rest. She turns on the television, and I change into pants and shoes to stroll.

I need to walk the blocks of Greenwich Village. It's the best place for me to clear my head. Yet even the calm of the Sunday streets cannot stop me from wrestling with the question that plagues my thoughts: why is my sister shutting me out of so many conversations, including one involving her relationship with Malcolm?

Chapter 9

On Monday morning, after I get Essie to the train for New England, I drop off the paperwork to the church. Essie had filled it out with minimal fussing. Maybe she's embracing the idea of working. She also said she would like to go to the bazaar at the church. It takes place annually before Thanksgiving, and it will give her something to do on Friday night.

Perry greets me at the door to the newspaper offices with a smile on his face. He looks mischievous and holds his hands behind his back. He's smiling as I approach.

"Please tell me you're free on Saturday evening," he says. His eyes sparkle in the morning light.

"Well, you're in luck. I haven't had plans on Saturday night for several years now," I say, making light of it.

From behind his back, he presents two tickets to *My Fair Lady* on Broadway. "Any interest?"

"I'm a sucker for musicals."

"Well then, dinner and a show? And then, afterwards, perhaps a night cap?"

"Sounds dreamy," I say.

"I was hoping you would say that. And I'm giving you plenty of notice to work out assistance for Essie?" I love that he not only remembers her name, but calls her by it in our conversations, as if we are all old friends.

"Seeing as how she has a little date of her own for Friday night, I don't think she'll mind."

"Does she?" Perry's eyes widen.

"Yes. There's a fellow who wants to meet her at the church bazaar, so I'm taking her on Friday night. She comes home from visiting our father on Thursday."

"I'm wide open on Friday night. I'd be happy to join you. A double date, perhaps?"

"Let me check with the boss, but it sounds like fun," I say, meaning it.

*

Essie's absence allows me to get some things done while she's away. I clean the apartment from top to bottom. I make myself a quick meal, and then I sit down to write. I have a lot to catch up on with the novel and need to spend some time polishing it. My mind drifts to Perry. I seem to be doing that a lot these days, and as I listen to the ticking of our clock, the quiet feels unusual. Essie is rarely not here.

I don't know Perry well, but what I do know so far, I like a lot. He is kind and understanding. He goes to great lengths to add an element of surprise and care to the relationship he's building with me. He's empathetic about my situation with Essie and adds no additional pressure to the circumstances. These are all amiable qualities, in addition to the fact that he's close with his own family, and talks of them—and visits them—frequently. *A man who loves his family is one to cherish*, my mother always said.

As my eyelids grow heavy, I get ready for bed and tuck myself in, the absolute quiet of the night lulling me to sleep immediately. There's an unusual sense of peace in the apartment in Essie's absence.

*

Daddy is driving Essie home today. After the success of the Dobson story, Robert has assigned me a new one about a female mob leader who was arrested last year in New York for crimes against humanity. The woman–Rosa Manetti–has been sentenced to life in prison. According to Robert, she's agreed to be interviewed for a series of articles. It's the first time I've had butterflies about writing a story–and I've never interviewed a crime leader.

I look through stacks of articles that have been written about her over the years. Stories that begin with bold headlines such as "Heartless Mafia Princess..." and "Morbid Manetti..." and "No Regrets Rosa..." are strewn across my desk. I take the time to read each one in order to get to know my subject. Plucking away at the typewriter keys, I make a list of questions I want to ask her. The interview is scheduled for tomorrow. How does one approach an article about a woman whose been convicted of running a mafia ring? She's been involved with so many illegal schemes over the years; countless accusations fill her file, from trying to bribe and influence politicians, to perhaps the murder of a rival family godfather, to dark situations within her own family. Knowing what I do from the stories of Al Capone, this woman frightens me, but at the same time, she's undeniably intriguing.

"This one's going to take you a while, lady," Robert says, as he sees me working at my desk.

"Tell me about it. You sure you want me writing this series?"

"You help us sell papers, so there's nobody better," he says with a wink, and he disappears to the kitchen to pour himself his fifth cup of coffee. Sometimes I count his refills; one day he ingested ten cups of coffee.

Even with this massive undertaking, I can't stop thinking about Essie. I'm hoping she receives a call from the church about the job. I know that some days her pain can be debilitating, but maybe if she has something new to focus on, a diversion that includes work and being at the church, she may find a sense of herself that's been lost for so long.

After reading article after article, I strive to know as much as I can regarding all the crime lady's nefarious activities. When I finish crafting the preliminary list of questions, I have one overriding thought: she's going to be intimidating. She seems ruthless. I wonder what it will be like to be face-to-face with someone that maniacal.

After I've tidied up my research and stuff the questions in my briefcase, it's time to go home. Perry's coming around the corner.

"Can I walk you home, Mickey?" His coat is already on.

"Well, that sounds like a treat, if you ask me," I say, obviously flirting with him.

"Does it?" He looks pleased with himself.

"No one ever walks me home, so yes. I'll enjoy the company."

"As will I," he says.

He helps me with my coat. I can feel the warmth of his skin touching mine. I'm so glad he was hired by the newspaper. Life feels so much brighter and lighter with Perry around.

We step outside the office and onto the streets of New York City. The wind kicks up between buildings, as we watch leaves scurry across the avenue. Without hesitation, Perry reaches for my hand, and I squeeze his, as we walk together, staying in step. No doubt Perry could out-pace me, but he moves in time with my own strides as I walk in heels.

"So, are you open to me accompanying you tomorrow night to the Christmas bazaar?"

"I am. I just want to make sure Essie's okay with it. She should be back from her trip when I get home," I respond. I haven't ever really explained the capricious nature of living with her on a daily basis: the mood swings, the frustration levels, the impatience with me.

"I understand," he says. "After you mention it to her, will you call me later and let me know?"

"Of course." He slips his card with his home phone number on it into the pocket of my coat.

We turn the corner and arrive at a flower shop, where he stops and tells me to wait outside. I tell him this isn't necessary, but he tells me to hush and vanishes inside the entrance. As I wait outside, I watch people walking their dogs, taxis roaring by, and vendors soliciting customers. How can anyone not love living in this city? Moments later, Perry returns with two bouquets.

"One for you and one for Essie," he says.

I reach up and kiss his cheek. "You are unlike anyone I have ever met before, Mr. Perry Spada. You are the most thoughtful person I know."

"I guess my mother taught me right. And my sisters used to sit on me until I did something nice for them. Sometimes you learn the hard way," he says, laughing.

"I'd like to meet this family of yours."

"You will soon, I hope."

The pace at which I have fallen for Perry and see his goodness, combined with the potential of what we could be together, sometimes makes me feel off balance. Whether he is trying hard or not trying at all, it doesn't matter. I am smitten. He has brightened up my life.

When we arrive at the apartment, we stop outside in front of the stoop.

"Would you like to come inside and meet Essie?" I ask Perry, as dusk falls on Manhattan.

"I'm not sure that would be fair to her. She just got home and is not expecting me. But I'd like to meet her if I come to the bazaar. Just tell her the flowers are from me, and that I look forward to meeting her properly tomorrow."

"Yes. Wonderful. I will check with her and will call you

later."

I reach up to kiss his cheek, and instead he turns and kisses me on the mouth. It's a sweet kiss, lasting several seconds, as he pulls me closer and my imagination runs wild for a moment. I wonder what it would feel like to wake up next to this man, feel his skin next to mine, to be with him morning, noon, and night. To take care of each other for—

A car honks and startles us both, and the driver shouts something out the window at us. We look at each other and laugh.

"I'll see you later, then, Mickey," he whispers, and I watch him go down the block before I turn into the house.

"I'm home," I shout.

"Hi," I hear back. Essie is coming from the bedroom hallway.

"Where are Dad and Sandra?" I ask. They had said they wanted to say hello to me before they continued on to Virginia.

"You're so late. They had to leave." She is right. I am later than I expected to be, but in fairness, I wasn't exactly sure what time they were to arrive.

I walk toward Essie and give her the flowers from Perry.

"For me?" she says. "Why in the world would your boyfriend buy me flowers?"

"Just because. Flowers for both of us. Wasn't that kind?"

"Yes, but I still can't understand the reason why he would buy me flowers."

"Esther Joanna DeMarco! Honestly! Do you have to analyze everything? He was just doing something nice."

"Out of pity," she says.

I turn and look at her. It takes everything I have not to want to scream at her and tell her she's acting like a ridiculous child. I breathe for a second before speaking.

"Okay, if that's the case, then he pities me, too. It was not out of pity. He was simply doing something kind."

"Why?" Essie is fussing with the wrapped flowers, looking

carefully at each one.

"No reason." I feel the frustration building, but I try to keep it at bay.

"There must be a reason," she insists.

"Well, I don't believe there is, but he is very much wanting to join us tomorrow night for the bazaar. Like a double date." I look at Essie, waiting to see how she will respond.

"With Malcolm?"

"Yes...Malcolm wants you to go, right?"

"But it's not a date."

I stop and look at her in all her naivety. I know it's a date. She knows it's a date. She's just too pig-headed to admit it. "Well, date or not, Perry wants to join us tomorrow. You don't have a problem with that, do you?"

She mumbles something under her breath. It sounds like she's mocking me: *"You don't have a problem with that, do you?"*

I feel myself wanting to react to her comment, but I refrain from lashing out. I turn my back to her and walk into the kitchen and place my flowers in a vase. I do not offer to do the same with her flowers. Then, bouquet in hand, I proceed down the hallway to my bedroom, where I place the vase full of flowers on my dresser. Essie's room is ajar, and I see four stacked boxes in her room.

"What are those boxes?" I yell from the hallway to the living area.

"They were Mama's. Daddy gave them to me. I think it's the last of them and he wanted me to have them."

I place the vase on the nightstand next to my bed, noticing her choice of words: that Daddy wanted her to have them, not us.

I walk toward the living area so that I don't have to shout to her. "Would it be okay if I looked at them at some point?"

"I suppose. But let me go through them first. I'm the one who is here most days by myself. It gives me something to do. They are a mess and definitely need to be organized."

"Okay," I say. She has a point. I just wish she would speak

kindlier toward me. But she is right: she does have more free time than I do.

I walk back down to my room, slip out of my shoes, and flop on the bed and stretch out. I close my eyes and make the sign of the cross, saying the words I pray most often: *Lord, help me navigate my relationship with Essie. Give me patience.* Then I pray for my mother.

Thinking of her still makes my heart ache.

Chapter 10

Prisons are eerie, no matter what time of day you visit them, even at ten o'clock on a sunny, picturesque fall morning. Arriving promptly for my appointment, I'm scheduled to meet the warden who arranged the interview with Rosa Manetti. She spent her first six months in solitary confinement, but now she's in a cell among the prisoners, at least that's what the warden explained over the telephone. From the photos in the newspaper, I can see she's a hard looking woman, with dark features and embedded, dark circles under her eyes. She just turned thirty-eight. But photos can be deceiving.

I'm processed through the visitation area, where the warden, Martin O'Sullivan, meets me. He's tall and broad, with a crooked smile and square jaw. His eyes are deep-set, and his voice—a bellowing baritone with a Long Island accent—tells me to follow him to a room where Rosa is waiting. The cinderblocks along the corridor are peeling paint. When I arrive, she is in shackles sitting at a table, two armed guards on the opposite side of the room. It smells damp. The starkness of the room adds to my nervousness.

"The guards will remain in the room for the duration of the interview. You have an hour, as requested. If at any point you'd like to terminate the interview, simply tell the guards, and they will escort you out. If at any point you feel threatened, afraid, or off-put by the prisoner, let us know. Again, we will escort you out," O'Sullivan says.

"I am in the room, O'Sullivan. I can hear what you're saying," Rosa Manetti says, rolling her eyes. Her voice booms; her New York accent is thick.

I nod. Uncomfortable doesn't begin to describe the tone of the room. The whole process is intimidating. I've never set foot in a jail, let alone interviewed an infamous criminal before. My eyes meet hers in a cold stare that lasts a few seconds before I sit in the chair opposite Rosa Manetti. She looks younger in person and has dark brown eyes and flawless olive skin that's mostly hidden by her prison uniform. Her hair is unkempt, a deep chestnut brown. I can feel her eyes upon me, as I reach into my bag to retrieve the reporter's notebook. The warden remains at the door until we begin.

"Ms. Manetti, my name is Veronica, and I'm from The News. Thank you for agreeing to be interviewed for this series."

"Your last name," Rosa Manetti demands, and not as a question. She clenches her fist on the table.

"My last name is DeMarco. Veronica DeMarco."

"Italian."

"Yes." I click my pen and open to the first page of the notebook. My previous one had run its course. I'm starting with a fresh page.

"A nice, good Italian girl," she says, almost mockingly.

I'm not sure how to navigate this interview. She's immediately combative. This isn't going to be easy, so I simply meet her head on with the same level of inquiry. "This interview isn't about me, it's about you, Ms. Manetti. So, shall we begin?"

"I need to know who I'm dealing with. I need to know more about you, girl," she says, leaning back in her chair and examining me.

"Okay, fair enough. What do you want to know?"

"Gimme the basics. Your background and all that."

"I'm from New Jersey but live in New York City with my older sister. Our mother died ten years ago, and I took care of my sister after my father remarried and moved to New England not long after my mother's death. I still take care of her because she has a handicap. Anything else you need to know?"

"*Men*," she says, mumbling the word under her breath.

"Excuse me?" I ask, not sure of her meaning. Does she want me to tell her about the men in my life?

"I said '*men*.' It figures your father would leave you to the dirty work of caring for your sister. And at such a young age. How old were you then?"

"I was nineteen."

"Too young," she says.

"Is that what happened to you? That you had to do the dirty work?"

I've struck a chord, and she mellows, but only slightly. She lifts her head to look me in the eyes. "You get stuck doing everything for everyone else and don't get a chance to do anything for yourself. Things were expected. My father didn't have a son, and so I got involved with the family business. The business did a lot of bad stuff, and I ain't no saint, but we all have choices to make in life to survive, at least that's what they tell us, until you realize that you ain't really got a choice at all. So, I became part of the family business. Then I became the head of the family business after Pop's murder. He was no angel, Pop, and he put me up to things. And now I'm here, rotting away in this hellhole for the rest of my life. There. You got your story. Makes it short and sweet."

I'm writing down her comments word for word, so it's taking me a minute. Maybe I should have learned shorthand.

"Any other questions, writer?" she asks, impatiently.

"Oh, lots, actually. I want to know more about you—"

"I bet you do."

"Are you willing to continue?" I ask her, clicking the tip of my pen.

She hesitates for a moment, and for a second it's dicey; she either wants to lambaste me or cooperate. She takes a deep breath in, glances at each side of the room where the guards remain standing, and then exhales. "Ah, shoot, sure. I'd like to take them down—take all them traitors down—for lettin' me end up in here. Nobody gives a rat's ass that I'm in here. You see anybody tryin' to get me out? No. We do the interview. What the hell else do I have to do today? I'd rather be sittin' here with you than in that dank cell. Ask away, writer. We've got fifty minutes left."

I ask her a stream of questions about her family, her father, her role as a female mafia leader, and inheriting the business. She tells me about the rival families and how they're all out to get one another. She reveals how being in charge of 'the family' affected relationships among family members. She discloses the names of some of the other mafia families; apparently, her only chance at parole hinges on some key blanks she has to fill in for investigators. Her tone tells me that she's mad at the world, and she wants to squeal.

"I'm gonna die in this stinkin' place. And for what? A bunch of two-faced family members who sacrificed me at the altar of the damn family name? My cousins have left me here. They say they don't want nothin' to do with me. Why? All for power. All in the name of power. And when you step back, you realize it doesn't last long. Power is fleeting, and you don't need it to have a good life. So, what's it all for? I've had a lotta time to reflect in here. Makes you go crazy—you think crazy thoughts. I wish I knew then what I know now. I would've moved my ass to Tahiti and never looked back. You ever been to a tropical island, writer girl?" she asks me.

"No, never," I say.

"I went once, only once, with a fella I loved who never loved me back. Come to find out the two-faced son-of-a-bitch ran off and married my sister instead. But get yourself to an island before you die. You've never seen such beauty. Makes you know God is real. New York, it's a joke—all cement and buildings. A sunrise on an island? Perfection. God's handiwork. Why I stayed in this godforsaken city, I'll never know. I shoulda never come back from that island. Everything went wrong when I did."

"And you and your sister...do you still have a relationship with her?" I'm writing and talking at the same time. The guards seem to be listening intently. I wonder if they have some sort of an employment agreement, whereby they can't repeat things they hear in prison. Makes you wonder.

"No," she says flatly.

"She doesn't come and visit you?" I've stopped writing and lean in to hear Rosa's answer. I know the answer. I saw it in my research. I just want to see how she responds to it.

"She can't," she says, fiddling with the link on her cuffs.

"They won't allow her to visit?" It's like pulling teeth; she's not giving me the story I need here.

"Oh, they'd allow her to visit, she just can't, 'cause she's dead. They both are, the pair of 'em, she and my ex." She fidgets when she says it.

Finally. Now I can ask the question. "Did you have them killed?"

The look she gives me is a blank one, unreadable. Then she says, "I'm not at liberty to say whether I did or I didn't, but they ain't here no more." A chill runs up my spine. I write down her reply word-for-word, my hand shaking a little more than it did moments ago.

The guard tells us time's up. Before she leaves, she adds: "In my line of work, you gotta watch your back. I'm glad you're writin' my story because it's a damn life lesson. What do you call it? A metaphor—or somethin' like that—for life? People you don't expect will turn on you. When you get wounded in the heart, you wish you were dead, because then you don't have to feel no more pain in your heart. So keep your guard up, writer girl, because it's the ones closest to you that kill you slowly, allowin' you to draw just enough breath to suffer over and over and over again."

Chapter 11

Essie wears a dress I bought for her from Macy's. It's a pretty brown shade with a plaid collar, and it looks lovely on her skin tone. But no matter how many times I compliment her on the dress and her hair and makeup, all she wants to do is talk about the ugliness of her shoes. The result of having polio is that she has to wear brown Oxford shoes, one with a lift in it to even out her stride and help balance out her limp. She despises everything about them.

"These are not stylish at all. I feel like a clodhopper." Her face twists as she says the words

"Whatever a clodhopper is," I say, trying to make light of it. She has no interest in my sense of humor at the moment.

"How can this outfit be the least bit pretty when I have to wear these horrible shoes?" she asks, trying not to look at them.

"Well, I know a man at work who says he doesn't give a lick about women's shoes. He says he never even notices them. He goes straight to the eyes, and you have gorgeous eyes," I say, doing my best to quell her anxieties about her appearance.

"Well, I think he's lying about the shoes," Essie says, and she stands next to me. "Why, just look at my shoes next to yours! You can wear those glorious pumps. You look like you belong on the cover of a magazine." She's never been one to let things go.

"Hardly," I say. "Your face is as pretty as a picture." Ever since we were small children, I'd known she was the one who has been blessed with a perfect face—big eyes, a slender nose, perfectly formed lips, and shiny, bouncy, golden hair. My dark brown wavy hair can't compete with hers.

"Well, I envy you wearing those shoes," she moans.

"But a man doesn't kiss your feet, darling. He kisses your face because he loves the person you are, not your shoes. Men don't care about feet or shoes or brown Oxfords. They have other things to focus on. In the end you'll see I'm right," I say, finally trying to put an end to the debate.

By the sound of our conversation, you would never know that Essie is older than I am. Perhaps that immaturity comes from being constantly fawned over and protected. Not being out in the world and having to fend for yourself, but rather relying others to do it for you, leaves you in a perpetual child-like state. Perhaps I've done it all wrong. Perhaps I've enabled her to be the way she is sometimes.

"Oh," she says in a cavalier way, "I forgot to mention that the church called earlier. I got the job."

Standing in front of her with my mouth wide open, I clap my hands. "And you're just telling me? That's wonderful!" I say. "You don't seem the least bit happy."

"No, I am excited. It's just going to be different." Maybe what she means is that she now has a responsibility—a commitment to keep—something she's not used to doing.

"In a good way," I say. "Oh Essie, I'm so proud of you."

She rolls her eyes and pushes me away when I attempt to hug her. "Let's just focus on getting ourselves to the bazaar. Are you ready yet?" She's never been able to show affection comfortably.

"I think I am ready...just need to grab my bag." I navigate back down the narrow hallway toward the bedroom to turn off my lights and collect my purse. I stop for a moment at the closet.

I hear the doorbell ring and brace for their meeting. Essie opens the door and Perry is there. I listen to their exchange from the bedroom door.

"You must be Essie," he says, taking off his hat to meet her.

"I am. And you're Perry. Come on in," she says, opening the door wide for him to step inside.

I adjust my shoes, allowing them to interact for a moment without my interference. Not that I'm trying to influence their relationship, but I just think it will be better for the two of them to get acquainted without me staring at them for the first few minutes.

"What a charming apartment," Perry says. "It suits the two of you."

"Thank you," I hear Essie say.

"So, tell me about this bazaar. Is it any fun?" Perry's voice is friendly, as it always is, and he's not kowtowing to her.

"Oh yes," Essie says, her voice lilting a little. "There are games and desserts and coffee, a live band, and even some merchandise vendors. It's festive."

"I like festive," Perry says. "And it sounds like the perfect thing to do on a Friday night. Thank you for letting me tag along."

"Oh, it's no problem," I hear Essie say, turning on the charm. She can do it when she wants.

"Hello, Perry," I say, as I enter the room. It's strange having a man in our apartment; typically, the only men who ever visit are Robert, who periodically checks on us or comes for an afternoon tea when he's working at the newspaper, and Daddy. Daddy only visits three times a year.

"You look lovely," he says to me, then turns to include Essie, "well, you both look lovely. May I escort you two stunning ladies to the bazaar then?" he asks. Essie looks at my feet and notices that I changed into my own tan Oxfords.

He extends both of his arms for Essie and me to take. She actually smiles, grabs her cane for good measure, and then loops her arm through his while I take the other.

Then, we're off.

*

Malcolm is waiting for us at the entrance to the church hall. In dark-rimmed glasses that sit on the bridge of his nose, he looks distinguished and is nattily attired in his slacks, coat, and tie. His clothing looks rich; it smells of money. His face lights up when he sees Essie; I only wish I could have seen her face when she spotted him.

The four of us meander into the main room where a small group of three musicians begins to play music, throwing in a Christmas carol now and then. Though it is weeks before Christmas, it's lively; the bazaar is one of the church's biggest fundraisers and kicks off the Christmas season. There are handmade crafts, games booths, and books for sale in the corner; two Christmas trees are decorated with ornaments; and three women in the back have a booth with knitted scarves, mittens, blankets, and sweaters for sale. People peruse the food and gift tables.

Essie is walking straighter than I have ever seen her walk. If you didn't know her like I know her, you'd say she was the most charming person in the room. She turns on that million-dollar smile of hers, and the polio vanishes. Her eyes twinkle when she talks. Malcolm is standing next to her as she speaks with a few members of the congregation. He is erudite and full of knowledge when he speaks. Perry and I sip on hot chocolates, as we step away from the discussion giving Essie and Malcolm their space.

"Your sister is charming," he says. "But you two look nothing alike."

"I know. Apparently, she looks like my father's mother. She was from northern Italy. She got the looks in the family, that's for sure."

"I mean no disrespect to Essie, but I beg to differ. You, Miss Veronica DeMarco, are gorgeous." He kisses me on the cheek. I feel myself blush. "It's just that you don't look related. It's funny that way. One of my brothers and I look nothing alike either. I think he got the genes from my dad's side of the family, and I seem to favor my mother's side. Anyway, she's sweet," he says.

"Give her time," I say, "she'll show her true colors soon enough." Instantly, I feel remorse for saying something negative about my sister. And at a church function, nonetheless. I should know better. Perry looks surprised by what I just said out loud. I'm ashamed of myself. I shouldn't have said it, even though it's true. Sometimes I allow her to wear me down. I don't know what's gotten into me. "I'm sorry," I say. "That was uncalled for."

"I will not judge. You live with her, I don't. It's just I can see she has a sweet side to her."

"That she does," I say, trying to make amends for my behavior. "I just don't get the opportunity to witness it too often, especially not with me lately."

"Well, I can imagine her condition may make her a little bitter. But getting out of the house like this will do her good." Perry's observant and honest. He makes me feel even worse for the condemnation I offered about her.

"Yes," I say, bringing the hot chocolate to my lips to blow on it, "and she got the part-time job here at the church I was hoping for, so that's progress."

"Good. That may do you both a world of good. A little distance never hurts. You know what they say—spending too much time together with someone is not always best for the relationship."

I stop and look at him for a moment, wondering if what he's saying is in reference to my relationship with Essie or a foreshadowing of what a relationship with him might be like.

"So, what you're saying is that you can spend too much time with someone?" I'm looking him in the eyes.

He catches my drift, then swiftly amends his previous statement. "Not if it's with you, of course," he says flirtatiously, which makes me wonder what his true meaning is. In any event, the comment sticks with me for the rest of the night, whether it should have or not.

Later, as I've lost sight of Essie, and after two hot chocolates and a bit of dancing with Perry, I excuse myself to use the ladies' room. The band is playing The Christmas Waltz, and the dance floor begins to fill up with couples. I turn the corner toward the washrooms, and beyond the double glass doors, I see two figures standing on the patio. As I move closer, I realize it's Essie locked in a kiss with Malcolm, his hands on the backside of her skirt. I quickly dodge into the Ladies' Room and catch my breath.

You can live with people your whole life and still not know them, I think to myself. Exactly how long have these two been communicating? Involved? Kissing...or more? I feel foolish for not knowing, and it makes me wonder what goes on during the day when I am at work. I also question what Gertie knows.

I flush the toilet and wash my hands. I catch a glimpse of myself in the mirror, noticing the look of shock on my own face. Moreover, I'm unsure as to how to proceed with her knowing what I now know...and what I have seen with my own eyes.

When the band stops playing and the people gather in the church to talk, I see Essie and Malcolm re-enter the main room, a little smirk on her face, her skirt slightly askew. She catches my eye.

"There they are," Perry says, and I nod and begin to walk toward them.

"This was such a great time," Malcolm says. "I wish the evening didn't have to end."

I'll bet you don't, I think, not in contempt, but just fully attune to the fact that my sister has been keeping things from me, while simultaneously giving me grief about my relationship with Perry.

I feel Perry slide his arm around my waist. It's a comfort. No longer will I feel guilty about further developing my relationship with Perry. Clearly, my sister has a relationship of her own that she is unwilling to discuss.

The question is...why?

*

Two weeks later, Perry invites me over to his apartment on a Saturday. I tell Essie I have to go to the newspaper for a bit to finish up a story, because I don't feel like having to tell her anything. Ever since she returned home from the trip to see Daddy, and certainly since the bazaar, she's acted strangely and has kept to herself, answering me with one-word answers. I don't know if she knows I saw her with Malcolm in their intimate embrace or not. I keep my distance, and that means keeping my own relationship to myself for now.

Perry opens the door when I arrive, and I fall into his arms easily. I've been thinking of him nonstop. At work, we do our best to get our jobs done, but on breaks—and even for lunch—we try to see each other.

"Finally, you're here," he says, whispering it in my ear.

I know I'm falling in love with him—perhaps even already in love with him—and the ease of it, of being with Perry, feels so right. I keep wishing Mama had lived. I know she would have adored him. Daddy might even like him, too, though I do not seek his approval. Even when I try to find a flaw with Perry, I simply cannot. He is beginning to mean the world to me.

He takes my face in his hands and kisses me, shutting the door behind us with his leg. For some reason, I hear my mother's voice in my head, a word of warning about a woman's sense of decorum. We stand there for a moment, locked in a kiss and a warm embrace. He kisses my forehead when we separate. His warm hands hold my face as he kisses my lips and the tip of my nose. It's like a sanctuary here—a place to get away from everyone but Perry.

He sits on the couch and motions me to sit next to him. I snuggle in next to him, placing my head on his shoulder. The relationship comes so naturally, and I've tried my best to block the word "decorum" from my vocabulary, because I'm letting my heart guide every step I take as I attempt to move in sync with Perry.

I've never felt this blissfully happy or secure in my life, so I block out the decade old rules of dating that my mother told Essie and me to heed and allow myself to enjoy every minute of this courtship.

Chapter 12

"Is that Manetti story almost done, Veronica?" Robert calls from his office chair. He's lazy sometimes and shouts instead of actually getting up on his feet and walking to the door.

"Yes," I shout back, mimicking him. I rip the paper from the typewriter and gather the rest of the pages together. Luckily, I remembered to number them, so I put them in order and hustle into his office.

Taking the pages from my hands, Robert says, "This first installment is coming along nicely. I'm glad this is a series. She is fascinating."

"Manetti, fascinating? Scary, more like it!" I say. "She's petrifying. Does that mean I have to go back to the prison and subject myself to all that again?"

"It might," he says, reading the lead again for the fifteenth time and marking it with his pen. "You should go every week if you can get stuff this good." His eyes glaze over as he continues to read my writing. I sit in the chair opposite his desk and wait. That's typically what I do when he's reading my copy. My blood pumps a little harder than it typically does when he's in the throes of it. I can barely focus on anything but his facial expressions as he reads each page. Call it insecurity or the desire to please. Either one works.

"This is something here," he says. "Tell me again why you want to write fiction when you're so damn good at this?"

"Because I love it," I mumble.

It's the truth, even if he doesn't want to hear it. The fantasy world has always been a place for me to turn when things are bad. My mother dying. My father's remarriage. Essie's illness. Escaping into novels is where I find my imaginary friends—characters who experience things I can only imagine. When I fell in love with reading, I started to write. I was inspired by other writers to become a storyteller. When Robert offered me the job at the newspaper, I figured this is where I'd get my start. Hemingway began as a journalist. So did Dickens. It's the best way to practice the craft. Learn the ropes. Write powerful content consistently. And so, I did.

I counted my lucky stars that Robert had room for me at The News, and as well, had the time to tutor and mentor me. Every day under his guidance is a learning experience. He's a brilliant editor and the epitome of a successful newspaper man. I have the utmost respect for him.

"Seems to me you can escape into real-world crap, too," he says, with a wink, bringing me back to the conversation. "There are a lot of weird, fascinating, crazy people in this world that will give you all the stories you could ever want." I smile at him. I treasure our relationship, the way he looks after me, and the way he advises me.

"We're running this in Sunday's edition. It's going to sell some papers," he says, proud of himself. "So, you and Essie are coming for Thanksgiving?" he asks me.

"I think so, if the offer still stands."

"When has it not? We love having you both," Robert says. I know he means this. Some people just say things; Robert means what he says.

"Yes, we'll be there. What can I bring?"

"Just yourselves. We look forward to having you," he says,

handing my story back to me. "And take this to the copy desk. It's a go. Can't wait to see it in print."

*

It's a good thing we got the invitation from Robert, because Daddy had telephoned telling me that he and my stepmother wouldn't be making it to New York City for Thanksgiving, but that he was hoping we could come to New England for Christmas. At least he invited us. Last year, we were on our own. My relationship with him isn't as good as the one he has with Essie. Although, I do believe she resents him a bit. Deep down inside her, she has trouble forgiving him for not caring for her and for leaving her with me. She's never said as much directly, but she always infers it.

I imagine I'd feel abandoned, too, if the shoe were on the other foot. I already feel neglected by him, despite being an independent sort who can figure things out. If I had a condition, it might break my heart. That said, even in my earlier years, I knew I never wanted to be grown and living with Daddy. I yearned to be out on my own. It just happened that I also felt responsible for my sister, too, and told Daddy she could live with me. He never once fought me on it. I felt it was my duty to care for her. Mama expected it.

With my work complete in the newsroom, I decide to run a quick errand and make my way home early. I've got some chapters to work on, and Essie's probably already returned from her job at the church. She works on Tuesdays and Thursdays now, and she takes a cab or gets a ride from someone who works at the church. I pick up a few things at the market and begin the walk back to our apartment. It's a cold, blustery day in the city, and there's a chill in the air that knocks at your bones. I stop and put my gloves on and pull my hat a little closer to my head. Most days the walk feels short; that's not the case today. Fighting the wind, I turn the corner onto our street.

I see Malcolm dodge out the front door of our apartment, look both ways, and then head in the opposite direction from me. He didn't see me.

Once again, I'm treated to a new reality that my sister is living a life that she is keeping a secret from me, for some reason unbeknownst to me.

*

I unload the items from the market and begin to make dinner. Essie sits in her chair with her feet propped up on the stool she sets in front of her, the afghan draped across her lap. Her hair looks slightly messy. The television is on, but she's not really paying attention. Her nose is in one of the books I brought home from the library. I don't mention seeing Malcolm, but I ask her how her day was to see how she responds.

"Same as always," she retorts, with a tone of disgust as she sits twirling her hair. I can see her profile from the kitchen. She doesn't look up, nor does she ask me about my day.

Come to think of it, she rarely asks me about my day. If she did, I would tell her that Robert loved my piece about Rosa Manetti and said I have a real knack for telling dramatic stories; I'd tell her that Perry brought me a jelly donut and a coffee this morning just because he cares for me; and I'd tell her that I saw the most beautiful dress in the window in our favorite shop on Madison that I'm going to splurge on for the holidays. Perry has asked me to spend New Year's Eve with him. I assume Miss Tight-Lip will want to spend her holiday with Malcolm. She hasn't said as much, it's just a hunch.

I'd also tell Essie I passed the pet store on the corner and saw a puppy that looked exactly like Petals, our family dog when we lived in New Jersey. My mother adored that dog. I'll never forget how hard Mama cried when the neighbor accidentally hit Petals with her car in the dark one night and killed her. I'd never seen my mother cry like that before. My father, on the other hand, never liked the dog. "Having an animal in the house is disgusting. They go to the bathroom outside, bring their dirty selves back into the house, and then proceed to get comfortable on the sofa. It's unsanitary," he would tell my mother. He didn't even join us as we buried Petals.

I often wonder what it was that brought my mother and father together. She was such a kind and gregarious soul. She had the disposition of a saint. She was patient and even-tempered. Her smile lit up a room, although some people said her teeth were too large. Her big smile was her best feature, and I inherited a mouth similar to hers. My mother glowed. She beamed with joy at Essie and me. She loved her girls. Why was she taken so soon? It makes you think about life in a whole new way. If you knew you would only live to the age of forty-one, what choices would you make differently? Ever since her death, I've kept this thought in the back of my head. Life is too short not to live it as fully as possible.

Essie breaks my trance as I finish cutting up the vegetables for dinner. "Did you say we're going to Robert's for Thanksgiving?"

"We are," I say, as I slide the veggies into the oven. "Why?"

"No reason." I sense there's more to it, but I let her statement sit there while I finish frying up the chicken.

Chapter 13

On Thanksgiving Day, Essie and I dress to spend the day with Robert's family in Montclair, New Jersey. We take a cab to the train station. On the ride, Essie says nothing of Malcolm or what he's doing for Thanksgiving but asks me about Perry. I tell her Perry's with his family in Jersey City, where he'll spend the day with his parents, brothers and sisters, and nieces and nephews. He invited me to come, but I'd already accepted Robert's invitation.

Essie's pain seems much better these days. Even her walking has improved, and I'm not sure to what we owe that blessing. Perhaps the fact that she moves more and is working instead of being so sedentary is helping her muscles and her mood. We board the train and find our seats. Essie always brings her cane with her, even when she doesn't need it. She relies on it a lot, plus it helps people to stay out of her way. Robert will meet us at the other end at the station and drive us to his house. He keeps an apartment in the city for weekdays when the days are long at The News and goes home on the weekends. His wife, Connie, is a nice woman. Sometimes she can be a little fussy, but she always has good intentions. They married later in life, and Connie has children from a previous marriage. Her grown children will be there today—Alan, Rosemary, Natalie, and Victor—along with their spouses and children. It's always nice to see them, to get a taste of what it's like to belong to a big family.

"There are my favorite girls," Robert says as we approach. He's carrying a large umbrella as the rain has just started to fall. Luckily, it's only supposed to last for a short while. He makes us feel special and opens his home to us, no matter what. Robert's been a family friend for ages, always willing to help us at every turn. He's hosted us at Thanksgiving for the last six years. I wonder what my own father is doing today. He didn't even call us this morning to say hello.

"Hi Connie," I say, walking through the door and giving her a hug. "Here's Milo's best bread, just as you asked!"

Connie takes the bread from my hands. "Let's pray this man never goes out of business. It's the best bread in all of New York City!" I couldn't agree more. It's my favorite bakery, and I'm a regular. Milo knows me by name.

Within minutes, the family arrives, and there's more food than we can eat. Connie's turkey is always done to perfection, and Rosemary makes a savory turnip recipe. The children look adorable in their Thanksgiving outfits, and Robert insists on taking a group photograph before we sit down to eat. He's finagled the camera on a tripod and tries his best to get us all in the frame. He's always loved photography, ever since I can remember. After several minutes, we finally snap a few photographs before the children tire of posing for the camera, and we settle at the dinner table. Natalie says grace, and we begin to eat the elaborate meal.

When we finish eating, the older children play games in the den, and I stay behind to help Connie and Rosemary clean up. Essie has turned on the charm and is reading a children's book to the two little ones curled up on the sofa. Natalie sits by her side. I want to freeze this moment for her; she looks so happy and content.

"So how are things at The News really?" Connie asks me. "Robert is just drowning in work. I feel like we never see him anymore."

"I know. I feel bad for him. Being the editor of a major

metropolitan newspaper is the most demanding job. Never offer it to me. We writers, we just want to tell stories and hit our deadlines and go about our day," I say, trying to make light of it.

"Is it really as busy as he says?" she asks me as I dry the large platters.

"It really is. It's constant. And he has so many people to look after. His office is a revolving door. It's a wonder he can take the day off. Putting out a newspaper every single day is quite a feat, and he's the best at his job."

"Well, thankfully, he put Ted in charge for the day," Connie says. Ted is our assistant editor. He lives alone and his parents and extended family are in Detroit. Deciding not to go home for the holiday, Ted volunteered to cover for the weekend. Robert promised to bring him a plate of leftovers as a sign of his gratitude.

As we clean up and organize the desserts, the phone rings. Robert answers it, and I hear him talking, wondering who it is on the line. I hear him laughing and wonder if it's Daddy calling to check on Essie and me and wish us a Happy Thanksgiving.

"Yes, she is. Hold on just a moment," he says, placing the phone down and walking toward me.

"It's Perry. He wants to chat with you," he whispers. He puts the receiver down and motions for me to follow him to his office.

"Perry, huh?" Rosemary says with a smile. Maybe Robert has told them I'm involved in an office romance. I feel my face become warm.

"Don't pay attention to the gawking," Robert says, as we walk down the hallway.

I follow him down the hall to his beautiful library that serves as his home office. It's filled with books that cover every inch of space on the elaborate built-in bookcases. The large, paned, cottage-style window looks across to the immaculate gardens in the back; the smell of books fills the room. I can imagine being quite inspired writing in here. "Here—you can talk in private," he says, lifting the receiver and then tiptoeing out the door, closing it behind him.

"Hello," I say to Perry after Robert has left. I make myself comfortable in Robert's leather swivel desk chair. I hear a click and the background noise disappears as Robert hangs up the other extension.

"Hi-ya, Mickey," he says. Every time he says this to me, I smile. I don't know why I love it so much. "Happy Thanksgiving. I just wanted to wish you a good day and tell you that I wish we could be together." I hear lots of chatter in the background, and the sounds of music coming from the stereo.

"That's a lot of wishing," I say, teasingly. "I miss you, too, and I just saw you yesterday."

"Feels like forever ago, though, doesn't it?" The sentiment is sweet, and I know exactly what he means. "Let's plan to do something sometime this weekend."

"It's a date," I say. "How's your family?"

"Everyone's good. They look forward to meeting you."

"Well, I look forward to meeting them, too," I say. The way he has described his family to me, I feel as if I already know them. I can't wait to see them in person.

"I'll call you tomorrow when I get home. Be safe getting home tonight. I love you," he says, as if he's said it his whole life.

These three words have not yet been uttered between us to this point. I've known that I love him, too, but neither of us has said it until now.

"I love you, too," I say, the words spilling out of my mouth freely. "Give my best to your family."

We hang up, and I sit there in pleasant shock. I've always wanted to be in a relationship where there's no need to play games—to be able to say exactly what I mean, feel what I feel, and for my significant other to be able to do the same. There's definitely something magical about this relationship I have with Perry, and I never want it to fade. If I could write this relationship into one of my books, it would play out exactly as it is right now.

I twirl around in the chair and look around at all of Robert's books. He's accumulated quite a collection, even though he loves to badger me about writing fiction all the time. He's one to talk; his shelves are filled with fiction, from Hemingway to Austen, from Shakespeare to Gaskell, from Steinbeck to Bradbury. I walk over to his copy of *Pride and Prejudice*, my mother's favorite book, and select it from the shelf. It has a red spine and red cover with a drawing of the main character, Elizabeth Bennet, on it. I begin to leaf through the novel, because it has become one of my favorite books as well. I open the cover and see an inscription inside. It reads: *To Robert–You'll always be my Darcy. Love, L.*

It takes me only a moment to realize this is my mother's handwriting. I would know it anywhere. I've kept a collection of her handwritten notes that she wrote to me over the years in a box in my room that I cherish. And the "L" is for her first name–Luisa. I sit in the chair holding the book, and the reporter in me attempts to put the pieces together of what this could possibly mean. Robert married Connie after my mother died, about eight years ago. He'd been a bachelor up until that point. Could it be that my mother loved Robert? How did my father fit into this equation? Did he ever know? Did my mother love my father?

My brain feels jumbled, and I'm desperately trying to make sense of it. Does Robert take good care of us because he loved my mother? Maybe my mother knew my father wouldn't watch over us, that he wasn't capable of it, as he has so aptly proven. I want to know the truth, but I can't ask Robert, can I? And I can't ask Daddy, because what if he didn't know about the two of them? How will I approach this? What can I possibly say to Robert? *Did you love my mother?*

All of a sudden, I feel lightheaded. Perhaps Robert looks after Essie and me because of guilt, because it is the only way he can atone for being in love with my mother when she was married to my father. And then the cancer. And then her death.

I wonder who misses her more? Who misses her most? Who loved her most?

I feel cheated that I cannot ask my mother these questions directly, and even more cheated that she never shared any of this with us. I lift the book to put it back on the shelf when a photograph falls to the floor from the inside of it.

I bend down to pick up the picture off the hardwood floors and hold it in my shaking hands. There, in black and white, is my mother and Robert, sitting on a stoop in New York City.

*

The rest of Thanksgiving at Robert's is a blur to me. I'm able to smile and eat pie and play charades with everyone, but on the inside, I'm tormented by the discovery in the library. Twice Robert asks me if I'm okay; everyone is wondering if I've had some sort of spat with Perry, despite insisting that we did not. It's unfortunate that the elation I felt hearing Perry tell me he loves me has become mingled with the tragedy of finding out there's some strange history between my mother and our family friend, Robert. Additionally, because Essie and I have a relationship that has deteriorated into something unrecognizable, I can't speak to her about it. I refuse to speak with her about it. If she can't share with me that she is having a full-blown relationship with Malcolm, then I am not inclined to share this shocking revelation about our mother with her.

You will always be my Darcy, my mother had written. This sentence echoes in my head as Robert drives us back to the train station that evening. Her own copy of the novel was on the shelves in our home in New Jersey. What happened to it? I haven't seen it in years. I hug Robert goodbye, and it feels as if there's a chasm between us. Essie and I ride side by side in silence on the train. Lost in thought, I prop my head against the window, staring at all the lights and feeling the rhythm of the wheels on the tracks. My imagination is running wild with images I wish not to imagine. Just what kind of relationship existed between my mother and Robert?

Chapter 14

On the Saturday after Thanksgiving, my father calls and talks to Essie on the phone. He's asking her if we're coming for Christmas.

"Veronica isn't going to be able to make it this year," Essie says matter-of-factly into the phone. "No, no—it's just she has a lot to do for work. You know the newspaper business. She's covering a story and she's also on deadline with her novel that's due in January. I'm able to take off a few days and come and visit," she says. I notice she says nothing about Perry.

The tenor of her voice makes her sound pleased that I will not be joining her on this getaway. Maybe it's because she gets my father and Sandra all to herself without me for seven days, and they'll spoil her rotten. My father is good like that—he may not have been able to handle the day-to-day rearing of my sister and me, but he's excellent at hosting short visits. Sandra loves to cook, and she's quite fond of Essie.

As for me, I will get the pleasure of spending Christmas with Perry. He wants me to be there, and honestly, so do I. Because our relationship has become much more intimate, our conversations and affections growing more important to the two of us each day, I can't imagine not being with him for the holidays.

For the last few weeks, I've been looking for clues that may shed more light on what I learned about my mother and Robert. It's one of the reasons I don't have the fortitude to see my father and Sandra right now. I have so many questions I want to ask. There are so many questions.

I've been reluctant to share what I've learned with Perry, too. I'm leery to involve him when there are no leads save two—the written inscription inside Robert's copy of *Pride and Prejudice* and the photograph that fell from the book. The problem is that he's our boss, so I rationalize that involving Perry is not what's best right now.

When Essie hangs up the telephone, I ask her the question I've wanted to ask her all morning. "Essie, is there any chance I can look through those boxes of Mama's now? Are you done going through them?"

"Why?" she says, looking up from her knitting. She's making a scarf, and I wonder if it's for Malcolm.

"I just don't have many pictures of her, and she kept all those old scrapbooks and loose photographs in those boxes. Can I look through them and reminisce?"

"You don't need my permission, Veronica. They were Mama's, not mine. I don't need them anymore."

It's an odd thing to say, and she says it bluntly. Does she just enjoy being ornery?

"But they are in your room, and I don't want to trespass."

"So take them to your room," she says.

Trying to remain calm on the inside, perhaps inside those boxes is a clue to the puzzle I am trying to solve, but I try not to get my hopes up. And yet, there must be something that will shed light on my mother and Robert that she never told me. I've been losing sleep over it, and I haven't brought up anything to Robert.

I move the boxes into my room and plan to take inventory on what's in there when I have time. For the next several days, thankfully, I will be distracted by the holidays. The only thing I should be focusing on is Perry and spending time with him and meeting his family. I treated myself to two new dresses for Christmas Eve and Christmas Day. Perry and I decided to spend Christmas Eve at his place and then the whole day on Christmas with his family.

When I get to my desk, I rifle through leads that have been left on my desk for me. As I'm talking to someone on the telephone, Perry stands next to me watching me, smirking as I work. When I finish the call, he kisses my forehead.

"How are you, Mickey?" It has become my office name. In private, he calls me Veronica now.

"Good, you?" He looks infinitely happy.

"Perfect," he says. "Just perfect." He looks dapper in his new coat. We picked it out together at Macy's last weekend.

"I'm happy to see you, too. What shall I get your family for Christmas? I have absolutely no idea."

"Food is the way to their heart. Jellies, jams, chocolates—no need to fuss. We prefer to spend time with each other instead of spending lots of dough on gifts. Something little is just perfect," he says. "They are very excited to meet you." He gives me a wink.

"I'm excited to meet them," I say, as I reach for his hand and give it a squeeze. We play it cool at work and keep our affections to a minimum.

"And Robert doesn't expect you for Christmas?"

"No, he knows I typically spend it with my father. I think Essie's thrilled to have Daddy all to herself. Besides, she and I could use a break from each other, I think. Something's happened to us over the last several months, and I can't quite put my finger on it."

"Sister trouble, I call it. My two sisters are always at each other's throats. They quarrel about the most ridiculous things. It drives my mother nuts," he says, taking a bite of the apple he is holding in his hand. What he's saying is true—sisters can have that dual love/hate relationship. I just wish that wasn't the case with Essie and me. We'd always gotten along swimmingly, and she knew she could trust me, and that I would take care of her. But there has definitely been an inexplicable shift. A deafening silence.

Gertie calls it growing pains, at least that's what she said to me last week when she brought us another homemade chicken casserole. She says that as people age and mature and begin to find love of their own, resentments about outside relationships set in; relationships can often fall apart until they fall back together. She's a wise woman, that Gertie.

One thing I know for certain: I couldn't have found Perry at a better time. God certainly works in mysterious–and beautiful–ways.

"Well, I'm off to get some work done," Perry says, lightly tapping my shoulder.

"Oh my," I exclaim. "I have to get going! I'm going to be late to see Rosa Manetti!"

"Be safe," he yells to me as I stride toward the doors.

*

On the way to the interview, I stop off at the Italian Bakery on 9th and pick up two boxes of cookies and one bag of sweets. I figure I'll try to give them as Christmas gifts, even though I'm not sure they'll let me take them in.

The warden has become used to seeing me; this is my sixth time visiting Rosa Manetti. And while she's been a tough nut to crack, she's softened slightly. I've shown her the clips of the two articles I've written so far, and she seems pleased with them. At least that's the meaning I ascribe to "not bad" after reading the pieces.

"Good morning," I say to O'Sullivan as he processes me through security. "These are for you and your staff, I say," handing him the two boxes of cookies. "Merry Christmas."

I see a little smile form on his lips as he utters "thank you" and takes the boxes from me. I have the small bag of cookies in my purse and don't want to keep that from him.

"I brought this small bag of cookies to share with Ms. Manetti. Would it be okay if we have them in the interview room?"

I can tell he wants to decline my request, but in the spirit of the holidays and his appreciation of my gift to him and the staff, he just nods. "But she can't take them out of that room," he says to the guard as he inspects the bags, just to make sure we know who is in charge.

"Thank you very much, sir," I say.

Rosa is already in the room when the guard opens the door for me. She looks like she's just showered; there's no stench in the room when I enter, and her hair has been combed.

"There she is, our writer girl," she says. "I'm starting to look forward to our visits." I pull the chair out to sit across from her in the stark room, the two guards standing stoically in the room, positioned slightly behind and on either side of her.

"I brought you a treat." I hand her the bag of cookies, placing it on the desk that sits between us. "Mr. O'Sullivan said we can eat them here, but he won't allow you to take them back to your cell."

"Ain't that kind of him," she says, and she opens the bag. "Merry ho-ho-ho to him, too."

She puts her nose inside the bag and inhales. Surprisingly, I see tears begin to form in her eyes. She just sits there, taking in the smell of the cookies. She collects herself, remembering there are others in the room. "My mother used to work at her parents' bakery. I spent many days as a kid in that place. It's just bringing me back, is all."

I hadn't expected to see a softer side of Rosa Manetti. Sure, she sometimes becomes a little less hard when she speaks of the past, of growing up and her childhood before her innocence was shattered, but this is the most vulnerable I've seen her.

"You're allowed to eat them," I quip after a few minutes.

"Might make me feel too sad, writer girl," she says. "How

will I bounce back after this? Some days I just want to be dead. I wish to be dead. I'm hoping one of the other family guns comes in here and takes me out. Would you wanna be in here? I mean, you can only dream of Tahiti so much before you realize you ain't ever gonna see Tahiti again—or godforsaken New York City for that matter."

"I thought there's a chance of a reduced sentence if you cooperate," I say, trying to sound hopeful.

"Yeah, that's what they say, but do you know how many people are manipulative? They talk in whispers. I'm not sure who to trust, especially in a rat-hole like this."

"Well, your lawyer should help you sort it out, right? I'm sorry if the cookies upset you. I just wanted to give you something for Christmas. Making you melancholy wasn't my intention."

"Why are you so nice to me? We've been together several times, and I've told you a lot of crap. I ain't no angel. Why on earth would you bring me cookies? Cookies for Rosa Manetti, the dangerous criminal?"

"Because no matter what you've done or what you've been involved in, you're just Ms. Manetti to me, and you've never treated me badly. So, in turn, I am doing the same. And I have every intention of telling your story to the best of my ability—all of it."

"Well, you ain't done me wrong yet, kid. It's the Italian girl in you. You're one of the good ones. You've kept your word to me, so in that case, I'll have a cookie for you. Here, you have one, too. And stop callin' me Ms. Manetti. I told you to call me Rosa, eh?"

I smile at her, reach in and grab a powdered raspberry cookie, and she takes a bite into an amoretti cookie. I watch her eat it, savoring every bite. She's enjoying it, and when she's done, she simply says, "Heaven."

"I'm glad you liked it. Now where do you want to begin today? It's the holidays, so we can start there. Is there anything you'd like to share with me about your holidays?"

There's a moment of silence before Rosa answers. "Yes.

These cookies remind me that I miss my mother, especially at the holidays."

I hear one of the guards shift; even he wasn't expecting that tender answer. I glance up at Rosa and look her in the eyes. "That, we have in common. I miss my mother, too."

"What happened to yours?" she asks, not afraid to meet the question head-on.

"Cancer. I had just turned eighteen. Yours?"

"Pills, most likely. Dead, right there in her bed, and I found her not too long after my father had been hit. Maybe she was scared she'd be next. But she sure as hell didn't think about her children before cuttin' off her own life. And I'm sorry about your mother."

My own mother died in the hospital; I can't imagine finding my mother dead in her bed and at her own hand as Rosa did.

For a minute, the only sound in the room is my pen inking the page. Rosa watches me write my notes. "I wish my mother hadn't always covered for my father. I wish she coulda talked to me instead of me having learn everything the hard way. Maybe if she'd stuck around, my life woulda been different, ya know? But I don't think she was a strong enough person to fight for me, or to get me out of that life. In any event, at least I'd have known the truth about my family and the difference between what was real and what wasn't." She sighs.

"I understand," I say, writing as furiously as I can.

"Turns out, she kept a lot of things to herself. I wonder if she was ever truly happy, or if she ever knew happiness. I tasted happiness for a moment there. Makes you understand why it's so addicting. But my mother never shared anything. It's probably why I talk too much. She never badmouthed my father, even when he deserved it. I never saw too much love toward him, come to think of it. I rack my brain trying to imagine a tender moment between them. Nothin' comes to mind. Makes you wonder if they even cared about me or my sister or if they were too wrapped up in their own drama. The truth is, after my father died, even though

I was technically 'head of the family,' it was my Uncle Joey who ran everything. I was the scapegoat. And my mother, God rest her soul, didn't protect me from any of this. Granted, she killed herself shortly after my father's death, but I was a pawn. They all hid behind me doin' the dirty work."

Sometimes when Rosa's speaking, I forget to write. I take a bit of a pause here, trying to catch up with my notetaking.

When she sees I've stopped writing, she continues: "And my sister, she was no help either. She was only a year older than me, but the girl had no sense. No sense at all. And she was callous. Didn't care who she hurt, as long as she got her way. She was always wrapped up in her own selfishness."

I pause for a moment when she says this and reflect. Essie's the same, at least right now she is. I keep jotting notes.

"Somethin' tells me you got a story to tell, too, writer girl." Rosa folds her arms and leans back in her chair. She examines me and waits for me to respond.

"Someday, Ms. Man–, Rosa. But for now, let's focus on you and get this third story out there."

"If only the ghosts could talk, right Veronica?" It's the first time Rosa Manetti calls me by my given name, and I'll never forget how much I agreed with what she said, and that her insights got me thinking about my own family.

Chapter 15

Perry's family home on Christmas is like walking into Radio City during the holiday season: it's chaotic, festive, and filled with spirit. Tinsel is everywhere, and the blinking tree in the front window is dwarfed by all the ornaments; you can hardly see the branches. I giggle with delight. The house is a bit cramped and disorganized, a far cry from the way my family's Christmases were. Mama always had everything neat as a pin in our New Jersey home. It wasn't a big house, but compared to this tiny row home, it was the Taj Mahal. And yet despite the smallness of it, the Spada's home feels absolutely perfect.

Perry's three sisters—Cici, Maria, and Donna—all tend to me, making me feel at home. Cici, the youngest one who will graduate from high school in the spring, is attached to my hip, and I see Perry looking at me from across the room while he chats with his brother, Dean. He had warned me. "I hope you know what you're getting into coming to my house for Christmas," he had said many times. Maria and Donna, both homemakers and married, ask me questions about what it's like to work for a newspaper as a woman. They are fascinated by my accomplishments as a reporter and novelist.

"We know what Perry tells us about his job writing about

sports. But you're writing about Rosa Manetti! That's amazing. Were you scared? She's legendary in the Italian circles."

"At first, I was intimidated to interview her, not now. We can relate, even though the things she says can sometimes send chills up my spine, I won't lie. But I see some goodness in her, too. After spending so much time interviewing her, I'm warming to her."

"But she had her sister and her lover killed!" Maria says.

"She has not admitted that to me," I tell them honestly.

"But you know she probably did it. It was a crazy love triangle!" they insist. In my heart, I don't want to believe it's true, but I shrug my shoulders as if to say I'm not sure.

Perry's mom calls us in for Christmas lunch, and there's so much food, I'm not sure my stomach can handle the vast platters of an all-encompassing Italian meal that appears as if it came straight from the tables of Italy. My own family may be of Italian descent, but we never stuck to traditions. It just wasn't Mama's style. Daddy wanted to let go of Italian traditions and position himself as an American, without any ethnicity attached to it.

"I hope you came hungry, Veronica," Perry's dad says to me.

After lunch, we gather around the Christmas tree and engage in a frenetic exchange of presents and laughter and hear stories of their childhoods while Christmas music plays in the background. There's nothing too expensive exchanged: sweaters, record albums, books, toys for the kids, and of course, the jellies and chocolates I give to the Spada family. Wrapping paper is all around the small family room, but the glow of the tree illuminates the happy faces of this family.

With his arm around me on the couch, Perry squeezes my shoulder. "Everything okay?"

"Yes," I say. "Just perfect."

*

Later, back at Perry's apartment on Christmas night after spending the day with his family, we cuddle up on the couch and turn on the television. This is the first time I haven't spent a holiday with any member of my family, and I'm glad to have Perry all to myself. I wonder how Essie is faring. I called in the morning to wish them all a Merry Christmas, and I spoke to each one of them on the phone. My conversation with Essie was curt. She couldn't get off the telephone fast enough.

Robert had called me right after that to wish me a Merry Christmas. He seemed thrilled to know I was spending it with Perry. I don't know why he has such affection for Perry, but I'm happy for it.

"I think you were a huge hit tonight," Perry says, sitting next to me, his arm around my shoulders.

"I loved spending today with your family. They're all so sweet and welcoming."

"We don't have much, but we have each other, and that's all that matters." Perry touches the ends of my hair.

"You're so right," I say. "And I feel like that's what's missing in my life."

"Don't despair—you still have your sister," he says, turning to face me.

"I know you're right, but my relationship with my sister is not the same as the relationships you have with your sisters and brother. Everything feels so light and airy with you all. Loving. With Essie, it's like walking on eggshells. Nothing's perfect, I realize, but I desperately miss my mother, Perry. She was the glue that held our family together." I find myself beginning to get weepy.

"But you have your father and stepmother and Essie still... you still have a family."

"I do, but it's not like yours—yours just seems so comfortable, and mine, well, it's just uncomfortable, awkward, and a bit in shambles."

"Everything comes and goes in waves, don't you think? Sometimes things are great, and other times they feel as if they're falling apart. You and Essie have a good relationship—it's just bumpy right now. You'll get through it. You know how I know? Because you are kind-hearted, Veronica, and full of love and patience," he says, trying to calm me. "Now, take a deep breath. It's Christmas, and there's no time for sadness and worry. Besides, I got you one more present."

"But you already gave me a sweater and a beautiful purse. Just spending the day together was a gift," I say. Sometimes there's just no point debating with him.

"Well, I can't have my best girl feeling sad on Christmas. So..." He reaches into the drawer of the side table and pulls out a small, square box. It's wrapped nicely with a little bow on top. "This is for you."

I open the box as Perry wipes away my tears. Inside, there's a gold necklace with a heart charm on it. "Oh, Perry, this is beautiful," I say, and I reach over to give him a kiss and hug.

"Wait, it's inscribed," he says, "look at the back."

I turn it over and read the inscription. "Us. 12.25.56," it reads.

I'm so touched by the gift, and I feel horrible that I didn't get him anything as meaningful. He can see it on my face. "I wanted you to have this. No worrying, remember?"

"Thank you, Perry," I say. He fastens the necklace around my neck. My own family life may be strained, but I find comfort in this relationship and vow to make it the best it can be.

It's what matters now.

Chapter 16

I shove the pages into my new leather briefcase, a gift from Robert for Christmas that will replace the old one my father gave me years ago. It's been getting dual usage as a journalist and a novelist. But today, the bag contains the edited two hundred and seventy-eight pages of my new novel. The editing is complete, thanks to working around the clock. Robert's been patient with me at the paper during the last few weeks and has lessened my load. I've appreciated it. Plus, the Rosa Manetti series is a hit.

Perry's been equally patient with me, although he's been busy gearing up for spring training and keeping up with all the Brooklyn Dodger news. There's a lot of buzz about the Dodgers this spring. Rumors have been rampant about the team and a new stadium, and Perry's stories have become quite popular. People are wondering what's going to happen with the new ballpark that's been proposed. Ebbets Field is in a state of disrepair. According to Perry, the place is shabby, and the owner desperately wants to build a new ballpark. Negotiations are at an impasse, at least that's what Perry's been reporting in the paper. I've been hanging on his every word; he's a beautiful writer and his words–his writing–makes me love baseball even more. It's not the Yankees and Mickey Mantle, but I've started to follow the Dodgers more closely because of

Perry.

Essie's now working three days a week. The church is appreciating her efforts so much, they offered her more hours, and she agreed. She must be enjoying the job for her to take on the additional day. The combination of her therapy, the new medication the doctor has prescribed, and her newfound sense of purpose have helped her both physically and mentally. She seems to be getting stronger each day. She's a far cry from where she was. Maybe 1957 will be one of the best years for her. I pray each day that's the case for her.

Before I go to bed at night, I open my mother's journals and scrapbooks. I've been combing through them a little at a time, but it's all been in vain. My mother didn't write anything about Robert, at least nothing I've read so far. There is no trace of the words she inscribed in his book about him being *her Darcy*. But I'll keep looking. My mother, it seems, was also someone who kept everything. Her scrapbooks were put together pretty well, but other boxes just contain miss-matched things, scraps of paper, sketches, and strange knick-knacks. I think I've learned that my mother was quite eclectic, and maybe a bit of a Renaissance woman. She seemed to have been interested in so many things–literature, theatre, painting, sketching, and music. I miss the sounds of the piano in our home when she would sit and play for hours. Funny that she never taught either of her girls to play.

Malcolm's taxi arrives. Lately, he's been escorting Essie to work. She's finally fessed up that they are "more than friends."

"He's here," I call to her, as I slip into my coat. There's a visible shimmer to the road and sidewalk; the precipitation appears to be a mixture of snow and ice. Essie and I gingerly make our way to the waiting taxi. I hold her arm because I don't want her to slip on the black ice. "We may go out to dinner after work if the weather cooperates," she says. "I just wanted to let you know."

"Sounds great," I say, hailing my own taxi. "Have a good day. I'll see you later tonight."

Malcolm exits the taxi and helps Essie get in comfortably.

"See you," Essie says, as he closes her door.

When she told me about Malcolm a couple of weeks ago, of course I wasn't the least bit surprised. I feigned that I was. I didn't want to let on that I already knew the big secret. I told her Malcolm seemed like a great guy, and I think he is. She seemed surprised to know that I liked him. She's my older sister; I want what's best for her.

I hop into my own cab as the driver navigates the slippery streets. Maybe it's a little icier than I initially thought. I don't think about my safety, or what could possibly happen, because I'm a few minutes late for my appointment with Alice Hawthorne, and if there's one thing Alice Hawthorne hates, it's lateness. And one thing she hates even more than lateness is a missed appointment.

For a moment, I feel panic rise. I brace myself in the back seat. I don't think about the taxi swerving and hitting another vehicle or being smashed by a bus. The last thing I remember hearing is the screeching of tires and the sound of metal crunching.

*

I wake in a stark room, the smell of antiseptic rousing me. Engulfed in pain, a woman in a white uniform is trying to speak with me.

"Ms. DeMarco, can you hear me?" she says, as she's rubbing my arm.

I nod.

"You've been in an accident. We're tending to you now. We've notified your family. It's a good thing you had your emergency card in your briefcase, Ms. DeMarco. Very resourceful of you. I can't tell you how many people don't carry that card." She's fiddling with the line that is attached to my arm going into my body.

"Perry," I say.

"I'm sorry, what is that Ms. DeMarco?"

"My boyfriend, Perry. At The News. Perry Spada."

"You would like us to call him?" she asks as she leans in to hear me.

"Yes, or the editor, Robert. Robert Barone." I'm whispering the words the best that I can. The nurse writes down the names on her pad of paper.

Within the hour, Perry and Robert arrive at the hospital. My leg is broken, my face is scratched with glass, my left arm is in a sling. The nurses are tending to my injuries. Perry sits down beside me and grabs my hand. He looks as if he might faint. In my haze, I see Robert standing at the end of the bed, his face white, as he wrings his hands. It's a habit he's had ever since I've known him.

"What happened?" Robert asks.

"The last thing I remember was the taxi sliding and seeing a bus. The taxi slid, I heard a crunch, then, nothing. Is the taxi driver okay?" My speech is slow, steady, slurred. They're giving me a lot of pain medication.

"Yes. The taxi was hit on the passenger side. They told us he's already been released from the hospital."

"Alice," I say. It's taking every ounce of energy to talk. Perry sits and rubs my hand.

"Yes. I will call her." Perry says, reading my mind. He knows all about Alice. I keep him up to date on everything.

"The pages."

"I know. It was your final manuscript. We have it. It's a bit mangled, but they took your briefcase from the taxi with your wallet inside."

I look at Robert. He's highly concerned. "Just try not to talk and rest. We will stay with you."

"Essie?"

"Yes, she knows. And your father. He wants to come, but he's worried about traveling. The snow is too thick up there. He'll get here when he can," Robert explains.

I nod. I beg forgiveness for the thought, but everything about my father always seems to be on his time.

Feeling the warmth of Perry's hand holding mine and knowing Robert is here, I drift off to sleep confident they will take care of things.

*

Two days later, Essie shows up to visit. The doctors are weaning me off the pain medications, but they want to keep me in the hospital for another few days. It feels like an eternity. The smell of the hospital makes me sick; it reminds me of Mama and death.

"Well, now look at the pair of us. How will we ever get along with two of us as invalids in the same house?" Essie says. She's removing her gloves and sitting in the chair beside me. I can't tell if she's attempting humor or if she means what she says.

"Clearly, you should not refer to yourself as an invalid, Essie. You are working and seem to be enjoying life as an independent woman. Look how far you've come."

She can't deny it. She knows she's made tremendous progress these last several months.

"Did you see the bus hit you?" she asks.

"No." I look out the window. The sun is shining, hopefully melting the snow that accumulated. I'm not sure I'll look at winter weather the same way again, or if I'll have the courage to get into a taxi again. I'm also wondering when Daddy will show up.

"Do you remember anything?" Essie's hands are folded properly on her lap. For a second, her demeanor reminds me of Queen Elizabeth, all formal and proper, though she looks nothing like her. I liken her more to Grace Kelly.

"Nothing. I just remember being late to meet Alice and wanting to get to her office as quickly as possible. The taxi driver didn't realize how the cab would slide on the black ice."

"They say you could have died had that bus hit you two seconds sooner."

I swallow, understanding full well the gravity of my good fortune. I have thanked God in prayer for looking out for me. "Well, let's be glad the bus driver wasn't in a hurry then, right?"

Essie reaches inside her bag and pulls out a couple of magazines. "I brought you these, well, to bide the time."

"Thanks, Essie. I can't wait to get out of here. Are you okay at home by yourself?"

Essie looks at me as if to say she's not by herself, so I ask again. "Is Gertie checking in on you?"

"She brought groceries over today." Essie refuses to answer the question. Perhaps Malcom's staying at our apartment. I'd really rather not know.

"I'm so sorry you have to ingest this food," Essie snickers, examining the food on my tray and showing complete disdain for it. One might go as far as to say that she seems to be enjoying the role reversal, of seeing me incapacitated and miserable.

"You're going to be on crutches for a while," she says, "maybe a couple of months." I take a deep breath. "But maybe you'll finally know what it feels like to be me," she finishes.

Her words sting and wound me. The comment infers that I've had no empathy for her over the last many years, when in fact, I believe I've always had incredible empathy for her. I'm the one who has taken care of her all these years. Her insensitivity is alarming. It's all about her, even as I lie in this hospital bed trying to recuperate. Nearly killed. My blood pressure rises, and all I want is for her to leave. I close my eyes and try to imagine I'm anywhere but in this hospital bed. Anywhere but here. I try imagining what Rosa's Tahiti looks like after hearing her description of it. I think of Perry and his beautiful, warm eyes. I think of the kindness of his family. They make me laugh. There's nothing that leaves me feeling unloved or scrutinized when I'm with them. Being with them is easy and fun. Being with Essie is the opposite.

"Essie, what exactly is going on here—between us? What's happened to our relationship?"

She gives me a cold stare, then looks beyond me and out the window. "Nothing," she says.

"Nothing? Feels like something to me."

"It's just maybe this will teach you to stop looking down your nose at people and pitying them."

"And by 'people,' you mean you. Is that what I do? Truly? With all your heart, you actually believe this?" She refuses to answer me.

I want Essie to leave the room. I have nothing left to say to her, but I don't muster up the words to ask her to leave. Luckily for me, she beats me to it. She rises from her chair.

"Well, I've an awful lot to do, so I must be off," she says flatly. "Malcolm's waiting for me outside."

"Is he? Had I known, I wouldn't have kept you," I say.

"It's no problem. He doesn't mind waiting for me," she says, an air of arrogance attached to the words, as if men worship the ground she walks on.

"Well, I appreciate you coming." I say this even though I will never forget that it took her two days to visit me or what she just uttered to me moments ago.

Treat people as you would have them treat you. Love one another. Bestow kindness as kindness has been bestowed upon you. Such reminders are necessary, I know.

The nurse returns to remove my supper tray and saves the day.

Essie moves toward the door. She is without her cane. I can't remember seeing her without it.

"Bye," she says, giving me a dismissive wave.

I watch her walk away wondering what on earth I have done to be subjected to her bitterness and cruel words.

Chapter 17

March is cold in the city. When the wind whips, it hurts your skin to step outside, which is lucky for me, because I've been stuck inside. Still healing from the accident, my leg remains in a cast. Robert's made it possible for me only to work at the office when needed, and Alice has sent Melvin over a couple of times with last-minute page questions. The novel should be on the bookshelves by May if all goes well.

I'm missing Perry terribly. He's in Vero Beach for spring training covering the Brooklyn Dodgers. I can tell he misses me, too. He's written me three letters that I read over and over again, just to hear his thoughts and his voice through his writing. He calls me in the evenings, too, before I go to bed.

Essie's relationship with Malcolm has kept her occupied; he seems to be incredibly smitten with my sister, and they spend a lot of time together. The minimal bit of time I've spent with him has been nothing but pleasant. He dotes on her, and she loves it. He has a kind disposition. I hope she treats him well, better than she treats me.

My father was able to visit for a couple of days with me. He came on his own after the snowstorm, left Sandra behind, and booked accommodation in a hotel. I got to see him for about twelve hours total. Like Essie, he's become much more distant with me, and I'm not sure why. Some moments spent alone are downright awkward. It feels like a transactional experience trying to communicate with him, like buying an oven or a car. I try not to dwell on it, because it only makes me sad. Maybe it has something to do with missing my mother. I accept the fact that Essie's his favorite, and always will be. Their demeanors are so similar.

Alone in the apartment, I open one of my mother's boxes I haven't had time to tackle yet. Photographs are tucked into a small paper bag. They look old and ragged, and I realize these are pictures from her childhood, of her own parents. I begin to sort through handfuls of black and white photographs, trying to identify the people in the images. My father's parents live on the West Coast of Florida now, and we exchange cards for birthdays and holidays. My mother's parents are both dead, and I have only a few memories of being with them when I was quite young.

Photograph after photograph portray a very happy childhood for my mother: photos of her sitting at the beach with her favorite doll; standing on the boardwalk in a seaside Jersey town; playing at a backyard party. She never put these memories into albums, however. Perhaps there were just too many. In one picture, she is wearing a striped bathing suit, standing at the edge of the ocean. Looking at her expressions in the photographs, I wonder if she could have guessed how short her life would be.

And then I come across a wrinkled and worn photograph. If you take away the grey hair and imagine him without the lines on his face, a very young-looking Robert laughs with my mother in a park-like setting. My mother and Robert are facing each other and laughing, looking into each other's eyes. *Her Darcy.*

One photograph.

I know it sounds unfathomable, but even in this still photograph, the eyes tell what the words cannot say.

*

How do you know when to broach a subject with someone when it could potentially alter the strength of your current relationship? How do you decide to bring up the past without taking a risk that your relationship may never be the same again? Furthermore, the mere mention of it could not only affect the relationship but affect the course of your career and future.

Your life.

I pour myself a glass of red wine. Everything I've seen suggests that Robert and my mother had a relationship. Clues would tell you it's all adding up. The book. The inscription. The photograph. How intimate and long-term was it? In some way, I feel cheated by this knowledge. What exactly was the nature of their relationship?

Perry's been gone for days and days. I'm missing him and am ready to share what I've learned about my mother and Robert. I want to tell him all about it now, but I don't want to do it over the phone.

Should I call Robert? I'm petrified of learning more than I want to know. I'm frightened that should I confront him about what I've uncovered, our relationship may never be the same. I love my job, love working for him. I respect him so much. How can I ask him? It will be so awkward.

The night seems endless. I am wide awake, unable to get physically and mentally comfortable, the leg cast bothersome and itchy, as my thoughts swirl inside my troubled head.

*

The next day, I meet the warden and sign in to see Rosa Manetti.

"You're all banged up," he says as a statement rather than a question.

"I am. Taxi accident."

"Looks like you got the raw end of the deal. Did the taxi

driver come out unscathed?"

"Pretty much," I say. "We hit black ice."

"You got lucky."

I nod in agreement.

As we make our way to the interview room, the warden walks slightly in front of me as I hobble behind him, trying to keep up with his pace. The jingling of his keys echoes throughout the hallway. Funny thing, those keys. They are either keys to freedom or keys to hell. Bring a few prospective lawbreakers in here and let them hear those keys. They might make someone think twice before engaging in any criminal activity.

Rosa Manetti smiles her crooked smile when she sees me in a cast with crutches as I struggle to get into my seat. Only two more weeks and I'll be out of it, I tell her.

"What the hell did you do to yourself? Did you get hit by a bus?" she asks me, thinking she's being funny.

"How did you know?" I ask, placing the crutches next to me.

"Writer girl, you're kiddin'," she says.

"I am not kidding. I was in a taxi and was hit by a bus during that snow and ice storm a few weeks back. Didn't you wonder where I've been?" I ask, getting comfortable.

"Holy moly, writer girl! I was only teasing. I didn't know something happened to you. I guess it wasn't your time to go, eh? The Good Lord was looking out for you. I can't say I know anyone who has actually been hit by a bus. A train, yes, but not a bus." She looks at me, and I understand her attempt at dark humor.

"Well, now your life is complete, Ms. Manetti. You can say you know someone who was hit by a bus and lived to tell the story."

"Rosa," she says grinning, imploring me to call her by her first name.

"Rosa," I say, correcting myself. "I'll also have you know it took great courage on my part to get back into a taxi to come see you."

"I appreciate that you didn't let your fear stop you."

I hand her the bag of cookies I picked up from the bakery, and she raises her eyebrows. "What are these for? Have I helped sell some newspapers?" Her eyes widen as she looks inside the bag, delighted by its contents. She's in a lighter mood today. Our relationship has become much less suspicious. We are moving along into some other realm, though at this time, I can't exactly say what it is.

"Your story has sold a lot of papers," I tell her. "Thank you for all your help."

"You're welcome," she says. "So this is not an interview today, I take it?"

"Nope. Just a visit." I say it that way intentionally to shock her. She looks bewildered for a moment when she realizes I am just visiting her...because...call me crazy...I like these interactions I have with this woman. She provides me with something I can't quite put my finger on. Plus, apparently the carrot dangles in front of her; if she cooperates with investigators, she may get a reduced sentence. She shared as much with me the last time I saw her. It's certainly lifted her mood since she was presented with the deal.

"So, how's lover boy?" she asks me. I had told her when I visited the last time about Perry, and she probed me for details. While I didn't share everything, I did share a few little nuggets about him.

"He's good. In Florida covering the Dodgers."

"Not my team," she says. "Always loved the Yankees. I try to stick with winners."

"Me, too," I say. "He's been gone a while, so I miss him."

Rosa looks concerned. I bat back tears, take a breath.

"What's happened, writer girl?" A motherly tone comes from her voice. Her question makes me sadder, because a thought pops into my head that I wish weren't true: *this woman may actually care more about me than my own sister.* Which may be why I'm here.

I begin to tell her about my mother and Robert. About Essie. I start talking, and I tell the criminal everything I know.

At this point, the guards have softened a bit, probably because I bring them sweets, too, so they no longer rush me out the door. They let me have this conversation with Rosa Manetti. Halfway through, I wonder what I'm doing, why I'm sharing all of this with her, and I realize why. Rosa's a good listener. She may be Italian mafia, she may break laws, she may even be off her rocker, but she listens intently as I speak. I think she's thankful to have someone who visits her to take her mind off other things.

"So, did you swipe the book with the inscription?" she asks me.

"No. It was on Robert's bookshelf. I couldn't steal it." I reposition myself, as the cast can be very uncomfortable.

"Actually, you could have. I would have." She smirks, raises an eyebrow.

"I know you would have, Rosa. But what if he were to look for it? He knew I was in the library."

"Have you found any other letters or clues in the boxes?" The roles have reversed. She's interviewing me now.

"None. Just that one picture and what I know from reading what my mother wrote inside the book."

Rosa has no idea who Mr. Darcy is from *Pride and Prejudice*, so I have to fill her in. I tell an abridged version of Jane Austen's story. I don't think Rosa's ever read a novel in her life. The newspapers, yes, but a novel, no. She can read; she's no dummy. She's sharp as a tack.

"There's no beating around the bush then," she says, pointing her finger at me and leaning toward me as she speaks. "You're gonna to have to ask your boss about his relationship with your mother. You're going to have to ask if you want to know. See if he squirms when you ask him. Watch what he does. You gotta understand body language, writer girl, and I know you do, because you have to in order to write the stories you write. Even when you ask, you can't expect answers. Believe me, I would know. That's why sometimes you've got to use force or threaten 'em with..." Her voice trails off, and the room grows quiet.

The guard shuffles, and I see him look our way, as he listens to Rosa. I shake my head to her to indicate that we should probably not use the word "threaten" in this prison. Inside, I'm smirking.

Rosa smiles. She enjoys getting people riled up. She definitely thrives on being a troublemaker, but I try not to focus on that. If you remove the questionable dark nature that makes Rosa who she is, she is a clear thinker who offers sane commentary about situations. When you misjudge someone's intellect on the basis of what they do for a living, you're making a judgment about someone. And it could be very wrong. Rosa is smart. Savvy. Still, I wonder if I should be taking advice from someone who is behind bars.

"I'll try to muster up the courage. I just don't want our relationship to change. He also adores Perry, and I don't want anything to affect his relationship with Perry. He does work for him." This I mean, wholeheartedly. It's why I'm so tentative to bring it up.

"Sometimes the risk is worth the reward," she says back. "It was my father's favorite saying. If it's the truth you want, then you gotta think about it that way."

She takes a bite of her second cookie and looks at me pensively. "I'm not sure this batch is up to the usual standards, you know?"

"I–" she interrupts me before I can answer.

"Oh, and another thing, smarty pants. I have read books. I'm reading the Holy Bible right now. I'm allowed, if you can believe it. No offense to your book, but it's a pretty good one. Not sure either of my parents ever read it. If they had, maybe things woulda been different. I'm up to Isaiah. That prophet had a lotta good insight. He knew Who was coming down the pike. He knew our souls could be saved. Gives you some kinda hope and comfort, right writer girl?"

I nod. "You do know Saint Paul wrote his best letters from

jail. Maybe you'll be inspired by him," I say.

"He's New Testament. I ain't there yet. Don't spoil the ending for me, writer girl." She winks when she says it. "And you'll be glad to know I've learned some new words, like *emulation* and *purloining*. Did you know that *husbandman* meant farmer? Mighta been easier if they just said farmer."

"I'm just glad you're reading it," I say.

"Me, too. Some Catholic I was. I'm not sure what took me so long."

This is why I have to keep coming back to visit her. I can't bear the thought of her being in here with no one coming to visit her. Ever. It troubles me—truly it does. I find some comfort knowing she is studying the Bible, and it makes me realize I should do more of that, too. As well, it dawns on me: in some incomprehensible and unfathomable way, we need each other. We have an unusual bond. I'm pretty sure the guards have picked up on that.

*

Malcolm sits across from me at the dinner table. Essie is in her room changing from work. He picked her up, and we're all eating supper together. Since the church bazaar, we haven't done anything, just the four of us. It's especially not going to happen because Perry's still in Florida. He's due back early next week. The Dodgers' opening game is April 16. I've already taken off work to attend the game with Perry's sister, Maria. She's a huge baseball fan, and we've got two tickets to see the game, thanks to Perry. The best part is that my cast will be off by then. I'm looking forward to walking the streets of New York like my old self, or an unstable version of my old self. We'll see what happens when the crutches are gone.

The words Essie uttered to me in the hospital that day—that maybe I will understand what it's like to be like her, to see how she lives in this permanent state—still sting. But I have to say, now that I have lived this life for a certain number of weeks, I probably understand it even better than before. It is a burden for her. I understand that—always have—but living with an injury certainly does ratchet up the empathy.

Essie's going to live with polio all of her life. And while there have certainly been strides made and her pain seems to be improving, I understand why she's bitter about it. She wants to feel normal, like she did before the polio got her. She was only twelve when it struck her. Somehow, I came away unscathed. Mama always blamed herself.

"So, do you think the Dodgers will be good this season?" Malcolm asks me. He's got a crooked smile, and he speaks softly, in a kind and measured way. There's something hypnotic about the tone of his voice.

"Perry thinks they may have a shot, so I hope so. But you know I like Mickey Mantle and the Yankees, right? So there may be a lot of arguments over the course of the baseball season," I say, teasingly.

"I like the Yankees, too. My father used to take me to games when I was a kid. We'd have so much fun cheering them on."

"I didn't know you liked them, too." I get up off the chair and head over the fireplace where I grab my cherished signed baseball and gingerly bring it over to Malcolm. "Can you read that signature?" I ask.

"Wow! That's Mantle," he says looking at the ball, then looking at me. We are both admiring it, being careful not to touch the ballpoint signature. Essie enters the room and sees us huddled over the baseball.

"Well, don't you two look cozy," she says sarcastically. I hope Malcolm is taking note of how she can turn on a dime. She's often nasty for no reason. We're looking at a baseball, not a diamond ring.

"Your sister was just showing me—" he begins, but she interrupts.

"Oh, I know what she was doing. Beaming over her favorite keepsake from Perry."

I look at her as she says this snide comment. I'm not going to let her win. "That's right. It is my favorite, and I will cherish it forever, not just because it's Mickey Mantle, but it's what brought Perry and me together. I love it," I say, returning it to its rightful spot. "Dinner should be out in two minutes," I say, changing the subject, because that's what works best with her. Don't discuss anything for too long, or she will take issue with something. And clearly, she didn't like me getting too close to her boyfriend.

Just then, there's a knock at our door, and we all look at each other. "Are you expecting someone, Essie?" I ask her.

"No, but maybe it's Gertie," she says. I hobble toward the door. *Just two more weeks of this cast*, I think.

I unlock the door, and as it opens, I hear the words, "Surprise!" Perry is standing there holding a bouquet of flowers. "I'm back!"

He leans in to kiss me, and I kiss him back, throwing my arms around him, almost losing my balance. It feels good to have his arms around me. His face is nicely tanned, his skin warm to the touch from all that Florida sunshine.

"Well, don't just stand there at the door, it's cold. Join us for dinner, Perry," Essie says in a congenial tone, turning on the charm. I'm so happy to see him. I can't let go of him.

"Okay, lady, let's get you to the dinner table," Perry says, taking the flowers and escorting me to a chair and pulling it out for me. "I'll put these in water."

He's home. All is right in the world.

Chapter 18

Perry's lifted my spirits since he's been back from spring training. And while he's incredibly busy reporting on the team and working around the clock, at least he's back in the city. We spend as much time together as we can despite our busy schedules. Essie hardly needs me for anything anymore; she's got Gertie and Malcolm tending to her around the clock. Lately, she and I are in and out of the apartment. Two passing ships in the night, they call it. I'm not complaining. I love seeing Essie become more independent.

I still don't mention anything about my mother, Robert, or the inscription and photographs to Perry. He has enough on his mind. Baseball season is taxing. There are so many home games and Perry will be in the press box every day writing his stories. I haven't broached the subject with Essie yet, either. But I've decided to discuss the subject with Robert. I can't keep it to myself anymore. I am becoming more miffed every day as to why my mother kept things from us. I exhale and remind myself that I was just a teenager then. What did I expect? For her to tell us the story of her life on her deathbed? She could barely speak at the end. The cancer had spread so quickly, and she had become a shell of herself.

"Morning, Veronica," Daniel says to me as we collide at the doorway, both of us running a couple of minutes late.

"Hi Daniel," I say, walking through the doors of The News.

"Looking better with that cast off," he says, holding the door for me.

"Why, thank you! Unfortunately, casts haven't become the fashion hit of 1957 that I was hoping for, so I let it go," I say. We typically enjoy exchanging this type of banter. It's benign and surface talk. And there's always that underlying truth that he asked me out and I turned him down. We're far past that now, despite that I said yes to going out with his colleague and have an intimate relationship with him. He must think I'm a complete hypocrite.

"There's still time," he says. "It's only April. You may need to invest in another cast soon."

"No chance of that. I'd burn the crutches at the stake if I didn't think I'd get arrested for arson in New York City." He gives me a look, and I give him one back.

"Maybe your pal Rosa Manetti can help you dispose of them without leaving a trace," he says. Clearly, he's been reading the series I wrote about my favorite mob lady. I wonder what she's up to today. It's probably a good thing I never saw her in her element, but only as a vulnerable woman behind bars. Outside of the bars, who knows what she would be like.

I see Robert smoking like a chimney inside his office. One hand's holding the phone, and the other one is flicking ashes into the ashtray. I pour myself a cup of coffee and wait for him to get off the phone and stand in his doorway. My heart is racing, but I've talked myself into this. I'm going to do this today.

"Any chance you're free for lunch?" I ask him, peering at him through the doorway.

"Lunch? Since when do I take a lunch break?" Everyone knows Robert doesn't take lunch, so, sure, it's a little odd that I'm asking him this, but I'm also hoping it makes the point that I need to speak with him. And that it's urgent.

"Yes. Today you need a lunch break. I need a lunch break. The truth is, we both need a lunch break. Together."

He snuffs out his cigarette and looks at me. I wonder if he knows I know.

"I can go, but it has to be early. I've got a meeting with circulation at one-thirty. Do you want to go at eleven-thirty?"

"Sure," I say. "Maybe it's more of a coffee and donut outing, then," I say.

"Either way, I'll be ready at eleven-thirty." He tries to hide that he is surprised by my mention of this. We are close and we have a wonderful relationship, but the truth is, we don't typically have lunch together.

No matter what, I've got the photograph in my purse, and I'm ready to hear the answers. But it's no bother. I've only been keeping this to myself since Thanksgiving.

*

We walk to the little corner place four blocks away from The News. It's a short distance from the paper, but it's not a place where many of our staff go for lunch. I picked it for that reason.

We both order soup and a croissant, just the right balance of breakfast and lunch, with coffee and tea, respectively. There's an odd sort of silence that hangs between us. I've known Robert Barone my whole life, and I've never felt this awkward with him. But there it is. My palms begin to perspire.

"So, I suppose you're wondering what this is about," I begin.

"You could say that," he says, fiddling with his croissant. He's trying to cut it in order to lather it with butter.

"I just want to say that no matter what, I don't want our relationship to change. I hope that my asking you these questions doesn't get me into trouble with you." I keep my eyes focused on him, watching and examining him all the while.

He looks up, and seriousness clouds his eyes. "Well, you're a good reporter," he says. "I would expect you to ask only the *right* questions."

I can't tell if this is a welcoming statement or a cautionary prelude. Nonetheless, I proceed.

"Do you remember when Perry called at Thanksgiving and I sat in your study to take the call?"

He nods 'yes.'

"Well, I don't know what possessed me, but I opened up your copy of *Pride and Prejudice* because it was my mother's favorite—her absolute favorite—and it is also mine. I saw an inscription in my mother's handwriting. I would know her penmanship anywhere. And then I saw a photograph of you and Mama sitting on the front steps of a house somewhere. I'm just wondering..." I pause, trying to get the words out.

There's silence as we both stare at each other. He places the croissant on the plate, sips his coffee, and then leans in to speak.

"Your mother and I were just good friends. Really good friends. That's why I look after you and Essie," he says, trying to brush it off.

"A good friend who calls you 'her Mr. Darcy?' You have read the book, have you not? Mr. Darcy and Elizabeth were not 'friends.' They were madly in love with each other."

"They grew to love each other," he says, correcting me.

"Is that what happened between you and my mother? You grew to love each other? I want to know the truth, Robert."

"We just...we were just...friends," he says.

I reach into my purse and find the photograph from my mother's box, the one of Robert and my mother in the park, laughing. I hand it over.

"I would beg to differ," I say to him, placing the photograph in front of him on the table. Either he had never seen it before, or it's his favorite, because I can see Robert swallow hard as he looks at it. "You were a bachelor for a long time, Robert. Did you and my mother—"

He stops me there and hands back the photograph. "We

were the best of friends, Veronica. We just had a close relationship."

"But is there something more? Is there something you're not telling me? Something that has to do with my dad?"

Robert wipes his mouth with his napkin, and I stare at him. He's not angry, he's not upset, he just wants to set the record straight. "Look, I don't know how else to tell you this: I made a promise to your dad to look after you and Essie when he married Sandra. I want to keep my promise to him and honor your mother by doing this and keeping things as they are. You mustn't try to assume things."

"I'm not assuming," I say, "but the photograph says a lot, doesn't it? As does a heartfelt inscription in a romantic book. Is there a story that hasn't been told?" I ask.

"Well, I can't tell you what to believe, but I can tell you that I've done what I promised to your father, and will continue to do so, provided you're okay with that. And I've kept a promise to Luisa, my dear friend, your mother. I'm not sure what else you want me to say."

"I just want to know what my mother's state of mind was, who she loved, everything about her. She was my mother, and I was a teenager when she died. I feel like I have nothing left of her. To be honest, I feel quite cheated—" I fight back tears. Robert sees my state. He's having trouble looking at me.

"Life doesn't always give us the hand we want, but we have to play the cards anyway," he says to me. "And we need to remember her as she was and her wishes. She asked me to help look after you girls. How could I say 'no?' We'd known each other since we were children. She's gone, God rest her soul. Your mother was a wonderful woman—kind, gentle, and a great mother—and I was blessed to know her."

I realize then that he's not going to tell me anything. He's not going to tell me more about his relationship with my mother. I must learn to accept that she is gone and there's nothing any of us can do to change that. Learning more about her and her life and passions isn't going to bring her back.

We pay our bill, and we walk in silence toward the newsroom. He puts his arm around my shoulder.

Nothing has changed between us.

And yet I can't help but feel that something has changed between us.

Chapter 19

The Brooklyn Dodgers opened on the road in Philadelphia on April 16. Two days later, Perry's sister, Maria, and I are in our seats at Ebbets Field trying to wave to Perry in the Press Box. After several attempts, he finally sees us and waves back. A big smile runs across his face.

"He's smitten with you, you know," Maria says, getting comfortable in her seat. The weather is disgusting, cold and misty. The antithesis of perfect baseball weather.

"As much as I am with him." I don't like to hide my feelings from his family. I want them to know that I adore him.

"I'm so glad he found someone who suits him. The girls he dated in high school—all trouble, I tell you."

"Well, I'm not sure I want to know," I say, laughing. "It's probably better if I didn't."

"Oh no. It was nothing like that. It's just, he never seemed to find the right person or connection. Not like I have with Eddie. Eddie and I have always felt like we belonged together. We were connected even when we weren't, if that makes any sense."

While I don't ask for her to explain it, I do understand what she means. I've dated some duds, too. And then, of course, I dated no one for a long time, because I felt like dating no one was preferable to dating someone who wasn't right for me.

"Well, anyway, between us girls, I hope you two last forever. I love the way you are with each other, and I want to see my little brother happy."

She hands me the popcorn to share. It's fun being here, even though we're bundled up together in the rain with a bit of fog, but we don't care. Baseball season is upon us. And while it's not the Yankees or Mickey Mantle, I'm happy to be rooting for Perry's Dodgers today.

Because I've always been Essie's caretaker and have spent so much time at home with her, I'm truly lacking in the good girlfriends department. There are a few women I get along with well at work, but I haven't had a best friend since high school. Essie had filled that role in our younger days. Until last year, we were thick as thieves. I'm hoping Maria will help fill that void. She's sweet. She reminds me of Perry: laid back, kind, and pleasant to be around. I love her black hair that she wears in a cropped bob. Her eyes are a hazel gray. She and Perry definitely got the looks in the family. They are both striking in their own way.

When the Dodgers win the game, 6-1, we are cheering with the rest of the fans who have stuck it out until the end. Perry is taking us for pizza after he finishes his story, which he promised to write along the way and complete as soon as possible. As a fellow writer, I never put pressure on him to write quickly. Sometimes these things take time.

We wait for him to finish, and when he's done, we hail a cab and find Nunzio's, a family-style pizzeria that he's wanted to try. Since the accident, taxis feel claustrophobic. It isn't always easy to put the accident out of my mind. Perry seems pleased that Maria and I had a good time together at the game, and he tells us we look pretty, even if our hair is a little damp and frizzy due to the weather.

"Mantle had two walks, a triple, and scored two runs today," Perry whispers to me. He loves to tell me about Mickey Mantle. He keeps tabs on him because I love him. But I think he loves him, too. I think he is "our" favorite player.

"How can anyone not like Mickey? I mean, he's just terrific," Maria chimes in. Perry looks at me funny and chuckles a little.

"Maria, have you actually seen Mickey Mantle play?"

"Not in person, but Eddie listens to the games on the radio all the time and we see the pictures in the newspaper. He's tough to avoid." The cheese on her pizza is slipping off the pie as she directs it into her mouth. We end up staying at the restaurant for an hour, talking about the game and having a few good laughs.

Afterwards, we walk Maria to the subway to get back to Jersey City. She kisses her brother, envelops him in a big bear hug, and thanks him for the tickets.

"I had fun with your girl today," she says, and then she leans over and gives me a hug and kiss on the cheek. "Let's do it again soon, Veronica."

We watch Maria descend the subway steps, and she turns to give us a wave. Perry hails a cab. "So, what's the latest on your book?" he asks me, as we slide into the backseat of the taxi. Perry gives my address to the driver. He reaches for my hand and holds it.

"May eighteenth release date, they tell me," I say, as I snuggle into him in the taxi. Alice had told me as much the other day. I'm hoping this is still the case.

"That's wonderful. Am I coming to the launch?"

"Of course. You're my date. I have to read a passage." I notice how fast the taxi driver is going and do my best to focus on my conversation with Perry. He senses my anxiousness and squeezes my hand as a sign of comfort.

"That sounds like fun. Do you know what part you're going to read yet?" He's doing his best to distract me from my thoughts, I can tell.

"No," I say. "I haven't selected it yet."

"Is The News going to cover it on the society pages?" he teases.

"I don't know, but they better give me some acknowledgement somewhere." I'm grinning at the thought of it. Robert had mentioned that they would, I just don't know who is writing the piece.

"And what's your latest assignment? No more Rosa Manetti?"

"I'm not sure yet. Robert may want to do more stories. Things are unfolding each day about the crime families."

"You like her," he says, hearing something in my voice. "I might even say you like her more than just as the subject of your stories."

"I do, but only if I don't think of her as a criminal."

"She led a mob family," he says, glaring at me intently wanting to see my reply. "It's an interesting choice for a friend."

"I know. She's definitely shrewd. But she's also funny, and she's caring. I know, I know. It's difficult to comprehend. But sometimes I just look at it as she was protecting herself and her family."

"Jeez," Perry says, rubbing his hair. "You really do like her."

"You would like her, too, if you met her. Especially if you didn't know she was...well...a mafia dame. She's kind of quirky and says what she means. She's a good listener. And she likes you."

"She likes...me?" he asks, leaning back and turning his body to look me squarely in the eyes.

"Yes, she told me as much."

"And just what does she know about me?" There it is. That smirk. That little devilish smirk.

"We talk."

"I'm not sure I want her knowing anything about me or my family. What if she gets out and decides she doesn't like our kind in Jersey City?" He's teasing me, so I humor him. He enjoys talking about Rosa.

"Don't be silly. You have to trust me on this. Just bring her cookies from a good Italian bakery, and she'll love you for life."

He leans over and kisses me. This conversation is all in good fun, and we both know it. Our senses of humor jive. We've talked about Rosa Manetti many times. He seems especially concerned for my well-being. Time and again he has worried about my interactions with this woman. And time and again, I tell him that she would never do anything to anyone unless she was provoked. Underneath all that criminal behavior is a woman who longs to get out of the whole business of it; I can tell she yearns to be loved. She also is someone who wants to be left alone to live her life. I tell Perry about her reading the Bible. She's the perfect example of *"If I could do it all over again, I would."* I know what Rosa's answers would be. Walk away from it all. Become reborn. Reinvent yourself. Don't get suckered into the menial and trivial nonsense...

The taxi pulls up in front of my place, and Perry hops out to open the door for me. "Are you growing as weary as I am of being apart and saying goodnight at the door? I love you, Veronica," he says, and he kisses me. "You and I both know that we can't do this forever. At some point, we're going to have to figure this relationship of ours out."

I nod and begin to speak. "It's just...Essie—" and he puts his finger gently to my lips as if to say, *let's talk about this another time.* He kisses me goodnight, and I give him a big hug.

It's definitely a conversation for another day.

Chapter 20

My sister is unusually chatty as we dress for my first book signing. I'm a little surprised she's attending, to be honest. Her behavior toward me hasn't been too kind as of late. Nevertheless, she's wearing a very stylish outfit that Malcolm purchased for her, a teal dress with a white sash that shows off her curves and her voluptuous chest. Essie says nothing about her shoes, which Malcolm had custom-made for her. They are better looking than her usual ones. I think she feels relieved that she can wear such a pair.

Essie will be sitting right next to me as I sign books at Brentano's Books on Union Square. Alice has a love affair with this place. Brentano's, Alice says, made her fall in love with literature. For that reason, she's intent on partnering with the bookstore to launch her authors' books here.

"We've got to support the ones that support us, Veronica. They are working hard for us," she had said to me in her office when I saw the final proof and held it in my hands. I felt like crying. *Pushing Through* is a novel about two lost souls who find each other in chaotic New York City, having uprooted themselves from Italy with no more than $100 to their name. It's a story that encompasses adventure, careers, and falling in love. I got the idea for the novel after interviewing a sweet couple for a feature story. Afterwards, I let my imagination run wild, filling in the blanks to tell this inspirational and timeless story

The bookstore is busy when we arrive. People are milling about, and I see Alice from across the room. She waves me over. Essie tries to keep up. I'm anxious. I'm excited. I'm feeling overwhelmed.

"Well, here's our author now," she says. Not a hair out of place, Alice Hawthorne looks like she stepped off of a movie set. Her pink suit is beautifully tailored with a large brooch on the lapel. Her chin-length blonde hair is curled and styled to perfection. And Alice never goes anywhere without her red lipstick.

"Darling, this is Ned, the general manager of the store. He's going to get you situated. Hello, my dear Essie–it's so good to see you. So good of you to come out and support your sister and see the inner workings of life as an author!" Alice knows how to interact with people so well. She is the ultimate public relations guru who masquerades as an agent.

"Good to see you, too, Alice," Essie says. They kiss each other on the cheeks, as if they are old friends.

I barely have time to read the room, because Ned is giving me an overview and the line is beginning to form. It's not a long line, but a decent one, so it will be nice to chat with people as they come through to have their books signed. Interacting with people comes naturally to me, and I love to hear the stories people share as they connect with the characters and plot lines. I'm looking forward to meeting people and hearing their stories. All you have to do is listen. People love telling stories, and if you listen closely enough, maybe you'll be inspired by another idea for the next book. At least that's what I tell myself.

By noon, I am signing books. Women tell me they are excited to read my novel. A few people connect me with the Rosa Manetti stories that have been in the papers. The chatter begins, and I answer their questions. "Was Rosa Manetti scary?"... "Did you enjoy writing that series in The News?"..."Will there be a book about Rosa Manetti's life?" I do my best to answer their questions. "My journalistic writing is very different from my fictional writing," I tell them. "I'm not sure, but Rosa does have a trove of stories to tell." The chatter continues.

I sign a total of 108 books in the span of an hour and a half, and then leave behind a stack of 30 signed copies. Alice whisks us away to the next bookstore, Scribner's on Fifth Avenue. We have an hour before we have to get settled at the bookstore, so we dash into a coffee shop for a quick bite to eat.

Essie is along for the ride on this. I can't tell if she's enjoying it or hating it. At times, she seems proud to be with me; at other times, it seems I am taking her away from something. She's mentioned in the book in the credits, where I wrote: *With special thanks to my dearest sister, Essie. I couldn't have written this book without you.*

I've often wondered if Essie would enjoy writing her own book. She has the time to do it, as her hours are still part-time at the church. And she's such an avid reader. We've never really spoken about it, but for some reason, it dawns on me now. But would she be able to take the rejection that comes with it? Sometimes she can be mentally fragile, and I worry for her. It took loads of rejection letters before I found Alice Hawthorne.

Suddenly it dawns on me as I sit in this dingy coffee shop off Fifth Avenue, that I cannot protect my sister my whole life. I can't do it, nor should I try. As her younger sister, I've been her keeper since the polio—and I will probably instinctively be this way for the rest of my life. But I can't shield her heart from love or rejection or from herself, even. She is a grown woman—turning thirty-one this year. I've been with her every step of the way and will continue to do so as I am needed, but I wonder sometimes if I need to let go. Maybe just a little at a time.

"So, you'll start with Chapter twelve then? I think it's the most riveting opening chapter, Veronica," Alice says to me, interrupting my thoughts, as she pays our bill. "We have to go."

We walk across the avenue to the bookstore. Alice thrives

on scheduling two signings in one day. The second one begins at four o'clock. I'll read first, then sign books. Both Malcolm and Perry had said they would be here. I take a quick scan of the place. Everything seems to be in order.

The bookstore has erected a podium with chairs in rows in front for shoppers to sit. Nigel Ferris, the book specialist and events person, will host the event, including the question-and-answer session. My palms perspire. I can feel the pulse in my neck. I look around. As I approach, I see them. Some of my friends from The News are in the audience, and I'm touched. Daniel, Perry, Susanna, and Robert are in the front row. I'm tickled pink to see the support. I feel my voice begin to quiver. Essie sits next to Perry, and a few minutes later, Malcolm arrives and sits on the other side of her.

Alice appears pleased as punch at the turnout. When Nigel Ferris introduces me, I stand and walk toward the podium. I open the book.

And then, I begin to read.

*

"What made you want to become a writer," a woman in a red dress asks. She is taking notes. I wonder who she is.

"It was a place for me to go with my thoughts," I say. "My sister and I both lost our mother young; she was twenty-one and I was eighteen. I had always kept a journal, and after my mother's death, it was a place to write daily, with no judgment. I love to read. I love the art of storytelling."

I see the woman scribble down what I'm saying into a notebook. Not a reporter's notebook, though. Not the ones Perry and I use at The News. It's a regular notebook.

Next question.

"With all of your experiences as a journalist and all of the feature stories you've written for The News over the years, I was wondering if your characters are based on people you have interviewed or people you know?" I see Robert shift in his seat. He can barely make eye contact with me during this part of the program. Perry is all smiles, and he nods encouragingly to me.

"Sometimes," I say with a smile. "They are often a composite of many different people I have met or interviewed along the way."

"Do you have a forever love like your main character, Sophia, had in your book?"

I feel bashful. I wasn't expecting that one, and Nigel seems to want me to answer it. I look at Perry, and I make a split decision. It would be foolish not to acknowledge him. "I have a lovely boyfriend, and we've been together for eight months so far, so we will see..." The audience giggles with delight.

I'm hoping Perry is okay with that answer. He winks at me.

"I notice your sister is thanked in the book. Is she your muse?" another woman asks.

Essie offers a little smirk. I'm going to give this all I've got, despite our strained relationship. She is my sister after all.

"My sister is my best friend, my roommate, my family, and part of my blood. She and I have navigated life together—the two of us—especially over the last nine years after the death of our mother. I absolutely couldn't do any of this without her and her willingness to help me brainstorm and get organized. She used to scold me when she knew I should be writing." That gets a chuckle from the audience.

Essie seems to bat back tears. She can't look at me and keeps her head down.

Maybe sharing this in public will help us get back to normal.

*

At the end of the event, after conversations and the book signing, it's time to go home. Essie tells me she will go home with

Malcolm. Alice kisses me goodbye. Perry and I walk outside to hail a cab. I notice how the city is sparkling today. Everything looks fresh and new in the springtime. Being happy makes everything look better.

"Well, you should be proud of yourself," Perry says. "I'm proud of you."

"And I'm proud of you," I say.

"I didn't do anything." Perry puts his arm up and hails a taxi.

"Yes, you did. You were there, and that means the world to me."

We climb inside the cab and hold hands. Knowing that one hundred and fifty people bought books at that signing makes me incredibly happy, but even more so than that, having Perry as my number one supporter is unmatched. I know how truly blessed I am to have him by my side.

Chapter 21

"There's a call for you," Susanna shouts to me from across the noisy newsroom. She sits just outside of Robert's office and has been his assistant for years. She's in her late thirties and dresses to the nines. I get a lot of my fashion sense from watching what she wears to work. I'm thrilled she took the time to attend the book talk on Saturday.

"Ok," I say, taking my coffee with me.

I see her fiddling with the telephone. "You're going to have to take it here," Susanna says. "Somehow it came to my phone instead of yours."

Susanna's desk is immaculate. No wonder she keeps Robert so organized. Everything is labeled and in neat piles. She hands me the receiver.

"Hello," I say. "This is Veronica DeMarco."

"Just the writer I was looking for," the voice on the other end says. I'd know that voice anywhere, the huskiness, and the thick New York accent.

"Ah! You got phone privileges?" I shout. Susanna looks at me, hanging on my every word.

"Is it THE Rosa Manetti?" she mouths. I nod. She leans in to hear more.

"Well, you miss seeing me, writer girl, so I had to call," Rosa says, teasing me. I imagine her sitting there in her prison uniform with a mischievous grin on her face. "The powers that be let me have a call now that I've squealed. There may be a big story breaking, and I wanted you to know."

"Are you giving me a tip?" I ask her.

"Indeed, I am, writer girl. I'm giving you a very big tip for your newspaper."

"Why?"

"Because we're gonna take them down. I ain't that nice to say I'm doin' it all for you."

I snicker. At least she's honest. "So, what have you got?"

"Well, it looks like they may have enough from me to finally get the DeCarlo family. I just may have let some names slip accidentally, along with things they've done, you know, gambling, illegal smuggling, racketeering, and the like. My father hated Tommy and his family—hated him to the core. I figured, what the hell? Might as well give you some real reporting instead of writing those fluffy books you dream up."

"Yes, well, I don't do investigative reporting."

"You will now." It's said as a command.

Rosa knows how to play her cards. She's smart. It makes you wonder what her life could have been had she not turned to crime. Unfortunately for her, it wasn't the line of work she could leave behind easily.

"I see. So, I am to follow the trail of Tommy DeCarlo to see where it leads?"

"That's right. Got it? Something may break soon. Be on the lookout." I hear noise in the background, from wherever it is she is calling me.

"You're not going to get me killed by writing this story, right, Rosa?" I ask, half jokingly, half seriously.

"Naw, you ain't gonna get killed, kid. You're gonna get famous! Now, they're gonna rush me off this phone. Tell your editor to get on this. I only got to make this one call 'cuzza good behavior. Don't forget...Tommy DeCarlo. They may nab him. Maybe soon."

"I'm on it," I say.

"Aw, come on! I'm talkin' to my friend, here, Ernie...," I hear Rosa say, putting her hand over the receiver. The guard is rushing her off the phone. She was only allowed a few minutes.

"Thanks, Rosa..." I begin to say, "I'll let the paper in on your tip."

The line goes dead.

*

I tap on the doorframe of Robert's office. His face is inches away from a story he's editing, holding his pen, making marks on the copy. I hate to disturb him, but he needs to know.

"Yes–" He looks up and sees me there. His tone softens. "Hi, Veronica. What can I do for you?"

"I just got the strangest call from Rosa Manetti. She's telling me that Tommy DeCarlo may be next to go."

"Killed?"

"No, investigated. Taken down. Apparently, her tongue slipped and she ratted him out, but don't tell anyone."

"You want this story?" Robert's eyes grow wide, and he claps his hands.

"She wants me to write it. She put it in my lap, but I don't normally write this stuff."

To be clear, I typically only write features, some more intense than others. But the truth is, investigative journalism is something I've never explored. I've never done it. It belongs to someone on that team. Spending my time writing about people, places, things, and events is where my passion lies. But, I'm happy to help in any way I can.

"How about you co-write this one," Robert says as more of a direction than a question. "Now, tell me everything you know so far."

*

Sitting with Perry at an Italian restaurant on 49th Street, I fill him in on what's happened. "I'll be writing the article with Bill Brandy. Do you think that's strange?" I ask Perry.

"No, not at all. It's done all the time," Perry says. He's right, of course, it's just that I've never co-authored an article before. Robert says I'll bring the feature-style to the hard news type of reporting that's required of investigative journalists. I'm looking forward to working with Bill on the piece. He's been around for many years at The News, and I know it will be a great learning experience. He's a real pro.

Perry and I sit in a corner of the dim restaurant, the candlelight illuminating the place with a soft glow. With wood walls and limited artwork, it's a far cry from Italian restaurants where the walls are decorated with paintings and pictures of Italy. Someday I'll get there, to Italy, and see the countryside for myself. It's a dream I've had for years. Mama had described it with such clarity. I've been drawn to the idea of visiting ever since she painted a visual image for me of Italy through her stories.

"What's new with the Dodgers?" I ask. "I hear there's real talk of leaving town."

"There is real talk of the team leaving town. It worries me that I may be out of a job."

"Ah, silly. You won't. You're too talented for that."

Perry reaches for my hand and kisses it across the table. I smile at him. He gives my world a sense of contentment and calm, grounds me in goodness, and makes me want to make him happy every single day. I'm in love with him. I'm in love with all of him, everything about him. I never knew I could feel this complete with another person. I always wondered what it meant when people would say they found the person they wanted to share their life with. Prior to meeting Perry, I'd never felt this way about anyone. My outlook has changed over the last months. Now, I can't imagine not having him in my life. I know he feels the same way.

"Thank you for saying that," he says. "I'm so glad we found each other."

"Me, too. I thank my lucky stars every single day."

Chapter 22

Bill Brandy and I sit across from each other at the local donut shop reviewing what he's found out about the DeCarlo family. He's sketched a family tree, and we're studying who's involved in the crime ring. It seems no one is free from the name one carries. All those involved could be arrested for something. Bill and I organize our subjects and figure out a strategy. He got a source to go on the record about his dealings with the DeCarlos. If one word can sum up their entire mafia organization, the word would be "ruthless."

For my part, Bill wants to see if Rosa will talk to me again—give us more details—so, I schedule another visit to the prison. Bill hands me all the notes he has so far, and we agree that I will assemble the piece using his notes and documentation and the information that I have gleaned from Rosa. He will revise and edit the article before we present it to Robert.

Afterwards, I hail a cab to get to Alice's office as quickly as possible with the pages I have completed so far for the second novel. I typically share segments with her, and I want her feedback on how I'm progressing. Hurriedly, I walk up the three flights and greet her receptionist.

"Unfortunately, Alice is in a meeting, Veronica," Lila, Alice's secretary, tells me.

"No problem," I say. "She's not expecting me. I just wanted to surprise her with what I've got so far. Is it okay if I just wait for her?"

"She's meeting with your sister, so you can go right in."

The look on my face catches Lila off guard. She quickly realizes she has shared something that was meant to be a secret.

"I'm sorry," Lila says, nervously wringing her hands. "I shouldn't have said anything."

"It's not your fault. I had no idea." I'm dumbfounded and hurt.

And then I remember what Rosa had said to me all those months ago: *It's the ones closest to you that kill you slowly, allowin' you to draw just enough breath to suffer over and over and over again.*

In that split second, I recognize the depth of my hurt. Essie and I have fallen away from each other. Can I pinpoint the demise of our relationship to the timing of the publication of my first book? I wasn't sure. I wasn't sure about anything anymore. My mind is doing flip-flops as I stand there in a momentary stupor. It's as if I have been hit over the head and awakened from a fantasy that my relationship with Essie is made up of two loving sisters. I have given and given, sacrificed and worked hard for the two of us, and trusted in her without fail. It seems unfathomable that she would shut me out of her life. That she wouldn't share whatever is going on behind that closed door.

And yet, she is doing just that.

First with Malcolm and now with Alice.

I feel my face redden, and I'm jolted back to reality. And then I remember what Alice said to Essie the day of my book signing. I remember thinking it was strange at the time. She said, *"So good of you to come out and support your sister and see the inner workings of life as an author!"*

I retrieve the pages out of my briefcase and hand them over to Lila. She takes them from my hand, and she can clearly see I am shaking. "Please give these pages to Alice."

I'm desperately trying to hide my emotions—those of disbelief, shock, and disappointment. What would my mother say about this predicament? I start to feel a lump in my throat. I miss my mother desperately. I was forced to become a woman without her and kept the promise I made to her to care for Essie. But right now, I feel as if I have failed them both.

"I will, Veronica," Lila says, looking down at the manuscript pages I handed her, as she arranges them neatly on the desk.

"Thank you," I say, barely choking the words out of my mouth.

I exit the building as fast as I can, in awe of my sister's secretive nature. The deception is mounting. What has transpired between us that has led her to keep so much from me? She tried to hide her relationship with Malcolm, and now she is hiding the truth about writing books for Alice. How long has this partnership been in existence?

My feet are taking me faster and faster toward our apartment, while my brain attempts to catch up. When I arrive, I put the key in the door and fling it open. I have no idea what I'm looking for; I just need to feel close to someone in my family. My mother is dead, and yet I still feel her presence. Wanting some clue or explanation as to why my own sister is pulling away from me, keeping secrets, I toss my coat and purse onto the chair and begin to rifle through my mother's boxes once again. I haven't spent as much time digging around as I should. I've been preoccupied with other responsibilities.

I organize the contents on the floor in my room. Box after box, I peruse my mother's keepsakes and belongings. Pictures of Essie and me as kids...artwork that we made in school...a photograph of my father...recipes bound by a rubber band...a few copies of books.

What am I looking for? I ask myself. *What clue would help me understand my own sister's turn of behavior?*

I look at the clock and wonder how long I have before she returns home. A bead of perspiration drops onto an old photograph. I stomp my feet and let out a moan of frustration. There are so many things here, but nothing is leading to the answers I'm seeking.

Leaving the mess of the boxes on the floor of my own room, I get up and open the door to Essie's room. It is neat as a pin. Nothing is out of place. She likes things tidy, Essie. She has a fit when I leave a pair of shoes or a book in the living room. Her shelves are impeccably kept. Books are organized by title and nothing is out of the ordinary. Snooping as I am, I decide to go ahead and further investigate by opening her drawers to see what's inside. The first drawer of her small desk is nearly empty, and the second holds blank sheets of paper. But when I get to the third drawer, I see it: a copy of a handwritten manuscript bound up with a ribbon, secured with a knot that I know I cannot redo in order to read what she has written. I try not rifle through it, knowing that I must keep it intact, keep it as it is.

In this moment, I realize she has been writing. She has been writing and not sharing. Choosing not to use a typewriter, she has handwritten every page to keep it from me. Pens don't make noise like typewriters, and I recognize that she has been writing privately so that I would not know. She planned to keep it from me entirely.

I share everything with her—everything. I have counted on her for things as my big sister. I let her read every draft of my writing, every page. She has always wanted to be a part of it all, and I have allowed her to be. She has seen me go through the trials and tribulations of becoming an author. She has watched me stress and rework and revise things. She has seen what it's like to put your work out there. Her eyes have been on me the whole time.

And now it all makes sense. She wasn't just along for the ride.

She has been in training.

*

When I calm down and put everything back in order in the apartment, I call Gertie. She's around Essie a lot, especially during the day when I am not, at least that's what I'm given to understand. I just want to see if she will share anything with me.

"Oh, hi Veronica," Gertie says, as she picks up the telephone.

"Hi, Gertie. I was wondering if I could ask you something in confidence...about Essie."

"Sure, of course," Gertie says. She's about an amenable a person as you could meet. Honest. Hard-working.

"Have you noticed anything different about Essie lately?"

"I can't say that I have," she says. "Well, just that she spends an awful lot of time with Malcolm."

"Really?" I don't know why I should be surprised. Nothing should surprise me at this point.

"Yes. Sometimes when I come over, I'm only there for a bit, and then she sends me off. These are on the days when she's not working, of course. I would never leave her if Malcolm didn't come calling."

"I see. So how many hours a week are you actually with Essie?"

"Maybe a few. Should I have told you? She told me you knew."

There it is. She is manipulating Gertie, too. I don't want Gertie to feel bad about it, and I still want to be able to count on her, so I don't make a fuss over it.

"It's okay, Gertie. I just hope we can keep this between us for now. I'm a little worried about her, but I'll let you know if anything further develops. Thank you so much."

I end the call and sit there for a moment. She's hardly using Gertie's services, which I pay for, and she didn't' tell me that, either.

After a few moments of considering this newest development, I call Perry to see if he's available to meet me for a drink. I need to talk to someone. He's on his way to the ballpark, but says he has a few minutes for a quick meet up.

We choose a location near the office, a small restaurant with excellent hamburgers that's open until eight o'clock. When he sees me, he can tell something's askew. "What's happened, darling?" he asks me in his sweet Perry way.

"It's a long story. I feel awful for taking you away from your job."

"Not at all. Tell me. I'm here for you." He takes my hand in his and pulls it to his lips, giving me a sweet kiss.

"Everything with Essie is a mess. You and I both know something is going on with Malcolm and that it's probably been going on for far longer than either of them lets on. And just now, I went to Alice's office to drop off my manuscript, and Essie was meeting with my agent behind closed doors. She didn't tell me."

The frustration has piqued. It's been building up for weeks now. Essie is pushing me out of her life. I feel it. I feel it in my gut. I know it. The hurt is mounting. Of course, I don't say these words to Perry, but I know they are true.

"It's probably just a phase, sweetheart. It's probably just that she's asserting her independence now that she has a job and a boyfriend. You want more independence, too, right?"

"Yes," I say to him, "but I want it without secrets and contempt."

"Do you really think Essie—your own flesh and blood—has contempt for you?" Perry looks at me, his glare piercing my soul as he says the words.

"I'm sorry, Perry, but yes, I do. Something has inherently changed, and I don't know what it is."

"It's called growing up and away. Perhaps she will marry Malcolm and he will be the one to take care of her, not you." There is kindness in his eyes when he says it. "Have you tried talking to her about it?" Perry asks.

"Yes," I tell him. "She won't open up about anything with me. I'm at the end of my rope."

Why is she so closed off? I have thought about this over and over. Did I think Essie and I would live together for the rest of our lives? I don't really know, but I do know this: I would never leave her on her own unless that was what she wanted. My door would always be open to her.

"She's also spending a lot of time with Malcolm and not sharing that with me, either. She shortens Gertie's time with her so she can be with him. That's what Gertie told me in confidence. I'm not upset about her moving on, spending time with Malcolm, or even potentially becoming engaged to Malcolm. I'm upset that she doesn't share her life with me at all, not to mention that I am paying Gertie and Essie dismisses her. My relationship with her is not what it was. We are no longer the sisters we were at one time."

"How would you have described your relationship before all of this?" Perry picks up his coffee and blows on it, the steam rising in front of his nose. I'm realizing he drinks coffee around the clock.

"As a loving, caring, sister relationship. We looked after one another."

He pauses for a moment. "How did she look after you?" He looks up from his coffee and stares at me waiting for the answer. It's an innocent enough question. He's just being curious. It's the right follow-up question.

It's just that there isn't a good answer.

I think for a moment and shrug my shoulders. "I really don't know. We were just there for each other after Mama died. We were two peas in a pod. When Mama was sick, we bonded, because we had no choice but to look after one another. Watching your own mother die changes you, Perry."

"Has your mother's death altered her?"

"Maybe. And before that, the polio." I say the words, recognizing my own vulnerability. There are words you can't just say to anyone. It stings to unleash the thoughts.

"But you weren't the cause of her polio."

"No, but I didn't get it. Maybe she resents me for that." I pull the straw to my mouth and sip my Coca-Cola. "But she did get the beauty genes in the family."

"She is very pretty," Perry says. I look at him, and for the first time, his words are not helping, but rather making me irritated with him, and he knows it. He corrects the statement before I jump all over him: "She is pretty, empirically. But you, my darling—you are stunning. There are no other eyes I would rather look into than yours, and there is no other soul I want to love. Do you hear me?" Living in a state of vulnerability takes its toll after a while.

"Yes," I say, but I can't help but feel wounded by his remark and a little angry at myself for doubting his love for me.

"Do you believe me?" He leans in and grabs my hand, wanting to be sure.

"Yes."

"You know I love you, right? More than anything in the world. And I'm not going anywhere. I'll always be right here." The sun has lowered in the sky, and a ray of light touches his brow.

"I'm sorry," I say. "I feel the same way."

He moves from across the table and sits next to me, hugging me and pulling me tightly to him. I've come to trust him more than I trust anyone on this planet.

When he pulls away and kisses me on the forehead, I look into his eyes. "Thank you," I say, touching his cheek.

"Do you want to come to the ballpark with me? It'll take your mind off things." He's pulling dollars out of his wallet and leaving them on the table for the waitress.

"I can't. I have to work on this article with Bill and then get up early to visit Rosa tomorrow. I have to be there at eight in the morning, and it takes me a while to get to the prison."

"I'm sorry you have to go back there. It doesn't bring me

any comfort knowing you're at the prison."

We stand to leave and walk out the door, Perry's arm around my waist. I'm glad he cares about my wellbeing, but the truth is, right now, I'm looking forward to seeing Rosa. Her directness and honesty is refreshing, and in some inexplicable way, her take on people and things seems to be something worth listening to at the moment.

I actually need her.

Chapter 23

The birds are chirping outside the window, the morning light streaming in through the curtains of my bedroom. Standing in front of the full-length, ornate mirror, I look at myself. Am I pretty at all? I take a step closer and inspect my nose, the length of it, the way it's a bit too large, and, upon closer examination, that it's also slightly crooked. When I'm tired as I am now, I notice the dark circles under my eyes. Hereditary. My mother had the same, and yet she always had an ethereal look to her. To my own detriment, I can't block out the comment Perry made last night, which is factual and blatantly obvious: Essie is beautiful. Her nose is perfect—the epitome of daintiness. An ounce of envy percolates. It's an unappealing virtue and a sin, and I dislike myself for allowing the thought to take up residence in my brain. Envy never gets anyone anywhere, this I know. But sometimes we cannot control our emotions any more than we can control our hearts.

The apartment is quiet, and I assume Essie is asleep. I ate my dinner late and alone last night and then tucked myself away in my room, working to organize the research for the story about the crime families. I heard the apartment door squeak open a bit after eleven o'clock, and then I heard Essie close her bedroom door.

Styled in women's trousers and a chiffon blouse, I walk to

the corner and hail a taxi. I climb in and we begin the drive to the prison. I wonder how Rosa copes with the confinement of waking up in a small cell every day. I'm relieved to be leaving my own little prison—my apartment—that lately feels like a punishment. The silence between Essie and me haunts the place, the tension lurking in every room. We have neither had a shouting match nor a loud verbal disagreement. The dynamics of living together has become increasingly more awkward and lonely. Knowing the isolation this brings, the thought of the never-ending solitude that Rosa must feel daily eats at me. I try not to think about it, but sometimes I can't help myself. Isolation can disturb even the sanest of us. It's no wonder she decided to cooperate. It's the only hope she has.

I pay the taxi driver and walk up the sidewalk to the usual bleak entrance. The place gives me the creeps, even after all these visits. Today, I am without cookies or any sort of refreshments for the guards and Rosa. I was too tired last night to make the walk to get them. I will promise to bring them the next time I visit. I did bring my novel for Rosa to read. She didn't ask for it; I just figured she might be interested, if only to quell the feelings of utter isolation. We'll see what she says.

The warden greets me at the door.

"Well, it's been a couple of weeks," he says to me, his hair yet to be combed. "No cookies?"

He is teasing me, and I enjoy it. What makes someone want to be a warden? I suppose you've got to find some thread of humor to work in a place like this, otherwise you harden.

"Unfortunately, Warden, my day was full yesterday. I will be certain to bring some next time. But I do have this book for Rosa for you to inspect."

"Okay, but I'm holding you to it," he says, stretching and yawning. "They're getting Rosa and bringing her to the room." He inspects the book, then hands it to the guard to check.

"Thank you," I say, and he signs me in and escorts me down the hall to our usual spot. Two guards are already in the room waiting. I choose my regular seat and sit down. Moments later, the door opens, Rosa's booming voice shouting, "You're getting to be my favorite visitor."

I laugh. She's shackled as always, but her face is bright. Her uniform looks like it could use a wash, and her hair is wilder than normal–past her shoulders and incredibly wavy. "Where the hell are my cookies?"

"I'm so sorry," I say, feeling guilty about my lack of effort. I should have known better. "Time got away from me yesterday. I promise to bring some next time. I did bring you this, though." A second guard inspected the book, so it made it through.

"Ah, writer girl brought me her book!" Rosa says, proudly showing it to the guards. "Look at her name right on the cover. A little diversion!"

"Hopefully," I say, smiling at her. "And, hopefully, you'll think it's good."

"As good as that Darcy book you were telling me about?"

"No," I say, laughing. "I'm no Jane Austen."

"Maybe she woulda been a better writer had she been born Italian like Michelangelo," Rosa says. "Italian women feel with depth, ya know? You gotta feel with depth to write good stuff. And the next time you come, maybe you could bring me a cake. It's been a long time since we've had a good cake, eh guards?" I can see her dark eyes fade into a memory, reminiscing. She's taken to charming the guards now.

"Is there a particular favorite you'd like?" I cross my legs and lean in for the answer.

"My father preferred pie. He loved Ricotta pie."

"And what Italian cake do you like, Rosa?"

"To me, there is nothing better than Italian cream cake. My mother made it from scratch. The bakeries in New York can't make it as good as she made it. The smell was intoxicating. When I remember the happy times at home, I always think of the smell of that cake."

I begin to write this down, as Rosa continues: "You're surprised I used the word 'intoxicating.' You didn't know my vocabulary has grown." I chuckle. "But seriously, Missy, you ain't gonna write about my favorite cakes. It doesn't go in the article, or I don't talk. No one can think I'm soft," she whispers.

"Yes, I know," I say, looking at her with a grin. "I just want to try one of these cakes later, or try to make them. My mother cooked, but never baked sweets."

"I'm sorry for you," she says. "You didn't grow up a true *paisan*, even though you are of Italian descent."

"Well, I did–"

She interrupts, holding up her handcuffed hand. The chains around her wrist make a noise, and I see the guards watching her every move. "It's okay that you didn't have a traditional Italian upbringing. I'm well aware of that by now. But I think your Perry did. You'll learn from his family's traditions, and you gotta keep up the traditions. They're important. Families know they have to pass 'em down, or they get forgotten, erased. It's our job to keep our families alive, and we do that through our stories–good and bad–and our traditions."

I pause for a second to look at her. Rosa has so many bigger problems to think about, but right now she's worried about my lack of Italian culture and cream cake and insists that I keep traditions alive, probably because she knows her chance of doing so may never be possible.

Of course, I don't write down our exchange per her wishes, but I'll always remember what she said. She's looking out for me in her own way.

"So, fill me in on Tommy DeCarlo," I say, ready to hear the latest.

*

After thirty minutes of Rosa explaining the mob and how the integral players all connect, we finally get to the heart of the matter. "Your father and Tommy DeCarlo knew each other since birth?"

"Born days apart," Rosa says, wiping her brow. For some reason, the holding room is hotter than usual. Even the guards are uncomfortable. I can feel myself perspiring underneath my blouse.

"And what was the problem between them? What made them such enemies?" I've learned how to ask questions the right way with Rosa, and then how to ask a follow-up to get what you need for the story.

"Well, you know, power...and my mother." I'm trying to write legibly. She's talkative today, stretching her memory into the past, diving into her family stories.

"Your mother?" The statement forces me to pause.

"She was a real beauty, my mother. She had it all—good family, pretty face, a figure like Elizabeth Taylor, sweet disposition, and the smarts. She had the smarts, Missy. She was a package deal." Rosa sighs thinking of her late mother, and I see her drift away from the conversation for a moment.

"And your father loved her." This seems to be a fact, so I state it as such.

"Yes," Rosa says, "he did. But I don't think she ever loved him."

"What?"

"You heard me." She knows she's shocked me with this statement.

"Are you kidding me?" I ask.

"Why would I kid about love? I don't do that, writer girl."

"Who did she love, then?"

She lets out a big sigh, purses her lips, and then says, "Tommy DeCarlo."

Understanding the dynamics of this mob story, I finally have the missing piece of the puzzle. Hidden among the mafia vendettas and power plays, I start to see the Manetti and DeCarlo families' hostility and hatred for one another—what connected them and what made them mortal enemies. Is it possible it all came down to a love triangle? Could Rosa's father have been married to a woman who loved the head of another family, Tommy DeCarlo? And when Rosa's father was murdered and her mother committed suicide, was it a Shakespearean tragedy? As I continue to barrage Rosa with questions, she continues to open up to me, and even she is beginning to understand the depth of what we are uncovering together.

"This is all so tragic, Rosa," I say, trying to catch up on my notetaking.

"Maybe life just ain't simple, Missy. Maybe all the stupid, manipulative crap we do comes down to love gone wrong. Or maybe it's a lack of faith? Or both? Who knows? I loved someone who didn't love me back and then he betrayed me—with my sister, mind you. It makes you wonder what's wrong with you and you wonder why it is that you don't deserve love, because you see others who have love. It's just...love's a funny thing, don't you think, writer girl? I mean you want it, but then you do so much dumb stuff when you're in love, you don't recognize yourself. Loving someone makes you stupid and weak sometimes. I guess that's why they say love is blind."

Her words echo in the small room for a minute. I think about how I reacted to Perry when he mentioned my sister's beauty and how I became jealous. Essie is pretty. People have told her for years. I notice one of the guards shift his eyes to look away; he's been paying attention to the conversation, and even he knows that what Rosa said is profound. Love does make you do stupid things. Inexplicable things. Regrettable things.

For a few minutes, there's silence. I'm not sure what to say or what to ask next.

"What," Rosa says, pulling me out of the quiet trance, "you got nothin' else? I ain't ever seen you this quiet."

I do, but I'm afraid to ask, and yet I want to know. I swallow, collect my thoughts, and then I ask her. "Tell me what happened with your sister."

"I will," Rosa says, "and then you gotta to tell me about yours. Fair is fair."

I see the guard give me the signal that ten minutes remain. I know I have to make this fast. "Okay, but will you go first?"

"Sure, Missy. It won't take but a minute. She wasn't nice. My mom favored her, because she was, you know, prim and proper—more like her and less like my father—all girly and never swore. But Al liked me 'cuz I was direct, and probably because of my big chest, if you know what I mean. We were in a relationship, and he swore up and down that he loved me. Every day he told me. Then, my sister, the snake, moved in on him and stole him from me. She was manipulative and he was taken by her beauty. He shoulda stuck with the one with the brains. I hated her for what she'd done. Hated them both. And then, unfortunately, they died in a tragic accident months later."

"Killed by a train, right?"

"Yup," she says, looking down at the floor. "You could probably say 'wrong place, wrong time.'"

I don't ask her if she set it up—or had someone set it up. I want to know the details, and I don't want to know the details at the same time.

"So yeah, that's my sister in a nutshell. What about yours?"

The guard nods to me. I have eight minutes left. "Well, I found out yesterday—which is really why I didn't bring the cookies, because I was so distraught—that she is now working with my agent to write a book, which she conveniently never shared with me. She never told me about it."

"She's tryin' to follow in your footsteps, that's why. She's tryin' to be like you." I don't want to believe it. How has everything gone to pot? "So she did it behind your back." Rosa is looking me in the eyes. She waits for me to respond.

"Yes. And our relationship over the last several months... maybe even the last year...has become unrecognizable. We barely talk about anything meaningful."

"You watch out for that one, I'm telling you. Can you move out? Get a place of your own or shack up with your man?"

"I'm the one who brings home the money for us to live together in our apartment. I support her. Her part-time salary couldn't carry us, let alone just her. If I did that, I don't know what would happen to her."

"Oh, I see. She's mooching off you."

I freeze thinking this through. Is Rosa right?

"This is the thing, Missy. She's a mooch. She wants a free ride. She's taking advantage of your kindness."

The guard shouts, "Time's up," and interrupts us.

Rosa leans in to say her final words for the day: "She's selfish. She thinks only of herself. Here's what I see: you're loyal to her, but who is she loyal to? Sounds to me like she takes an awful lot from you but doesn't offer anything in return. You know what that's called, writer girl? It's called *reciprocity*, one of my favorite new words I learned. But it's true. Relationships can't be one-sided. They require give and take, not just take. And she—well it seems to me—she just keeps on takin'. What exactly has she done for you except give you *agita*?"

She looks me straight in the eye, and I can feel myself become a little ill hearing the words come out of her mouth. Rosa Manetti's got this pegged. Hearing it from her perspective helps me know that it's true.

Then she says something else before they escort her out the door: "One more thing—Can you talk to the warden and get a Catholic priest to come visit me? I need to make a confession."

As the guards each take her by the arms, she gives me one last nod, and she vanishes down the long, dimly lit hallway.

Chapter 24

Alice cannot look me in the eye. The woman who knows how to finagle book deals and coerce people to do exactly as she wishes when brokering publishing contracts is unable to meet my stare. Sitting in her posh office on Madison Avenue, I am staring at her, watching her fidget with things on her desk–the letter opener, her stapler, the tape dispenser. She reorganizes manuscript pages and opens and closes her desk drawers looking for just the right pen. I've never seen her so uncomfortable. She adjusts the glasses on her face. I'm waiting for her to explain her relationship with my sister.

"Your sister has talent," she says, posturing herself to look out her high-rise window. "I loved her story. We just want to see where that talent can take us."

"Well, I'm happy for her," I say, my hands neatly folded on my lap, calmly reminding myself to breathe in and out. "I just wish someone had shared the news with me, you know, had been honest. Is this the way you typically do business?"

She fidgets in her chair. Clearly, I have hurt her with my comment. It was meant to sting. "Essie made me promise to keep it between us. She doesn't want anyone to know, and I couldn't violate her wish as a client. She didn't want anyone to know in case..."

Her voice trails off, but I want to hear the rest of the sentence.

"In case what?"

"In case she doesn't succeed at it." There. I dragged it out of her.

I pick up my now cool cup of coffee that Lila brought each of us and take a sip. It tastes bitter.

"Oh, I see. So we are all just supposed to pretend as if she is not working toward something in case it fails. We are not supposed to know what she's up to behind closed doors, in case it flops. And I, the sister who lives with her and supports her and cares for her, am not allowed to know about her literary endeavors. Just keep Veronica in the dark. Is that the way this is supposed to go, Alice?"

Alice is a seasoned negotiator. She has the capacity to be tough as nails, all while wearing a brilliant smile on her face. However, she can't worm her way out of this one and how she has made me—her other client, the current money-making client—feel. Our relationship feels tainted. I don't want any part of it. I wish I could break my contract with her right now and start fresh with someone new, but I think I am legally bound to this book deal. I'm tied to this agent, as slimy as it all feels. Her calculated misstep has led to a changed nature of trust, one that is lacking in confidence.

"Well, I don't know what you want me to say. I see talent, and when I see talent, it's my job to foster that talent. I don't need your permission. We have signed a one-book agreement, and she has three months to get me the final manuscript. I'm sorry for the way it unraveled behind your back, but it was the wish of my client. And as you know, I value the relationship I share with my clients."

"Do you?" I say, flabbergasted by the hypocrisy.

I stand, realizing that no amount of discussion or fighting is going to change the fact that my sister and my agent have conspired to keep the truth from me. I feel a wound I haven't ever felt before. I'm not sure how to traverse this type of psychological landscape, but I know one thing: I'm tired of providing for a sister who sees me as nothing more than a financial means of survival. "I assume she will be getting an advance?" I ask Alice.

"I can't disclose the financial terms of my deals, Veronica. You know that." Alice removes her eyeglasses and places them on the desk. Her tone is condescending.

"I know a lot of things I didn't know a few days ago, Alice. Thanks for allowing me to see first-hand your agency's unscrupulous behaviors," I say.

I pick up my briefcase, and without another word spoken, I am out the door.

*

On the walk to The News, in order to take my mind off my racing heart and anger, I pay attention to the people I pass on the streets. I wonder how many people are wading in troubles of their own. I see both women and men dressed for work scurrying down avenues and dodging across streets. Summer looms, and flowers are blooming in front of businesses and along the avenues. Everything looks lovely and bright, and yet I feel weighed down by darkness.

When I enter the newsroom, calm washes over me. Having essentially grown into an adult working here, and as it's the only job I've ever had, I find familiar comfort as I step through the fog of cigarette smoke and relish the sound of the clicking of typewriters. My palms are sweating from the brisk walk. Normally, I would hail a taxi; today, however, moving my feet was therapeutic. And all the while, I have absolutely no interest in returning to our apartment later.

The tension at home has been so thick you can cut it with a knife. There is little dialogue. Essie and I rarely interact, which is probably good, but on the rare occasion that we are in the apartment at the same time, she hides in her room, and I hide in mine. Gone are the nights of playing Scrabble or watching a television program. I can't remember the last time we watched something and laughed together. Malcolm still gets her to and from work, and she seems more than happy to be out of the apartment than she does being inside the apartment. Her appointments with her activity therapist have slowed, and I wonder if the pain has subsided. I also wonder if she's been lying to me about that as well. Was the pain always as bad as she said it was? I'm curious about all of these things now, given our strained state of existence. After a while, you stop asking, especially when she fails to share anything at all.

But that doesn't mean I'm not going to ask her about her finances. It's time that she contributes to our living arrangements now that she's making a living. Why should everything fall to me? Fair is fair.

"There she is!" Robert says when he sees me, his cup of coffee in one hand, a cigarette in the other. "How's everything coming along?"

"Fine." I toss my briefcase onto the chair of my desk. "I've had a day already. Do you still have that Scotch in your office?"

Robert looks at me, bewildered. "You want a drink at this hour?"

"Yes, I do," I say.

"It's a little early for the hard stuff," Robert says.

"Who determines that? Early or not, it's the right time for the hard stuff for me." He can tell I mean business and motions for me to step into his office. He closes the door behind me, and pours me a little swig of Scotch. I swallow it in one gulp.

"Okay. What gives? What's going on?" He sits behind his big, maple desk and motions for me to sit in the guest chair across from him. Before I do, I pour more into the glass.

"It's probably not wise for me to talk about personal things at work. It's unprofessional." I take another swig.

"It can be, but I'm your oldest friend in the place, so tell me what's going on. I always have time for you." He stubs out his cigarette and focuses on me.

I can feel the tears build, but I'm tough. I won't cry. I refuse. I will not let my sister's behavior affect me this way.

"Aw, it's all just a bunch of nonsense, Robert. I feel silly talking about my private life. I'm here to work on my stories and make this newspaper some money. I shouldn't be mired down in my own problems. I've got work to do."

He's looking at me, unsure as to how to respond. Finally, he says, "Okay, so give me the shortened version, just so I can know what you're dealing with."

"My sister has gone behind my back. She just conveniently decides not to share her life with me. First, with Malcolm, and now with something else. I can no longer trust my own sister, and if you can't trust your own sister, who can you trust?"

Robert fidgets for a second, as I begin to stand and make my way toward the door. "What has she done?" he asks. "I can't help you if I don't know."

"She neglected to tell me the small details of her life and did it behind my back. I found out by happenstance that my agent just sold the book she's written. Now she'll be a published author—which is great—she just conveniently chose not to tell me about it, that's all. Secretly wrote the story by hand so I wouldn't hear her typing. Did I do that to her? No! I've allowed her to be on my journey the whole way—the journey that supports the two of us. There's something rotten about it, that's all."

Robert sighs. "I thought it was something worse," he says.

"Worse? What could be worse than your blood relation keeping things from you?"

"Well, perhaps she admires and has been inspired by you. This is not the end of the world—it's just a little misunderstanding, a bump in the road. You two will patch it up."

I look at him fiercely. "Misunderstanding? You must be kidding." I don't feel like myself. Inside me, anger swells. "Thanks for the drink," I say, placing the empty glass on the edge of his desk.

For the rest of the day, I throw myself into my work. I learned the psychology of using work as a distraction years ago when working with my first mentor. "Whenever something goes wrong, I just focus on work. It makes all the other stuff fade away for a while," he said to me. I've never forgotten what he said and how he said it, the pain of whatever he was going through at the time feeling like a heavy blanket for him, something that's tough to surmount. And so I do as he had said all those years ago. I dive into my work. It allows me to forget about the troubles with Essie. The piece I wrote with Bill about Rosa went to press yesterday, and the newsroom is buzzing with calls and rumors about what will happen to the DeCarlo family. Will there be arrests? Who's going to rat out others to save face? How will Rosa fare through it all? The public sees Rosa as a hero of sorts—the one who protected her family name and was a victim in all of this. The female Al Capone. Letters to the editor are written in support of her release from jail stating that she deserves a second chance.

Ever since I met her, I think about Rosa a lot. Her story gets to me. Somewhere deep down inside her, there's a vulnerable person. I know it. It's why I wrote the articles the way I did—because I could "see" her—with empathy. She didn't ask to take over her father's position as a mafia don, but she had no choice. Her Uncle Joey was manipulating her and set her up so many times to fail or take the fall. And if she didn't do what Joey said, she would have been chastised. She might have been killed. And I believe her when she says she never wanted the power. She told me as much.

"You might be surprised to know the real me, if you can believe it. But I don't like bein' called a pussycat. Don't paint me as a softy, though, writer girl. I hate that. Don't print anything mushy about me. I got an image to uphold, for my father's sake," she said to me a few weeks ago during one of our chats.

I made a promise to Rosa then.

And unlike other people I know, I don't break mine.

Chapter 25

Everything comes to a head at some point or another. Eventually, people get what they have coming to them. Bad eggs rot.

Rosa's words echo in my head as I read the next installment of our article in The News this morning. It's been the thrill of my life to write these articles for the newspaper. It's been a turning point in my journalistic career to dive into Rosa's life. My work as a novelist, on the other hand, is at a halt. Inspiration for fictional writing isn't grabbing me of late.

"Great piece this morning," Perry says. He carries a copy of The News folded under his arm, opens it, and finds the page where the story appears. "I just love this part: '*Rosa Manetti has eyes like fire and tells stories that both curl the blood and make you examine your own conscience.*' Great writing, Veronica. I feel as if I know her."

"Thank you. That means a lot coming from you." I plant a little kiss on his cheek. No sense trying to hide our office romance. The cat's out of the bag now.

"How's about a late supper tonight? Afternoon game, but I should be free by eight."

"Sounds good to me," I say, and with a quick wink and a grin, Perry heads over to the sports department.

I turn to read the article he's written, something I do every day. When he's not covering the games, he's been writing about the Dodgers and the ownership's unhappiness with the current condition of the ballpark. Apparently, the team's location is in jeopardy. Perry isn't sure how the Dodgers will resolve their woes, but he's optimistic something good will happen. The team's devoted fans won't want to see the Brooklyn Dodgers leave New York.

"Hey, Veronica, Alice Hawthorne's on Line 9," I hear Susana yell to me across the room.

We haven't spoken since I stormed out of her office several days ago. *Breathe*, I think, as I pick up the telephone, knowing I have to be mature about this situation and can't lose my cool in the office.

"This is Veronica."

"Hi, Veronica. It's Alice. Can we please meet for coffee? I don't like the way things ended the other day."

"I don't like being lied to, Alice."

"I didn't lie. I just couldn't discuss it."

"I don't like being lied to by my sister or my agent, especially when they're colluding."

There's a long pause as silence fills the space between the telephone lines. I just wait for her to come up with something clever to say.

"Meet me for coffee so we can talk about it like we should."

"Why can you talk about it now all of a sudden? What's changed?" I'm genuinely curious.

"Essie has given me permission."

"Oh, I see, the princess has granted you permission?" I ask, the words dripping with sarcasm. That comment hinders rather than helps the situation at hand.

"Coffee tomorrow at Mel's place on the corner. I'll see you there. Eight o'clock." She hangs up abruptly before I can decline.

Later that afternoon when I'm done for the day, I meander home. Walking slowly, I bide my time looking in store windows and taking in the sights. I'm not looking forward to being in the apartment. Luckily, I'm confident I will beat Essie home and have just enough time to change my clothes and dodge back out to catch up with Perry for dinner.

When I open the door to the apartment, however, Essie is there. She is sitting in the chair where she watches television, and she is eating a plate of food.

"Hello," she says, when she notices I'm surprised to see her.

"Hello." I can't offer more than that. I'm incapable at the moment.

Moving toward the kitchen, I pass her as I unload a small bag of food I picked up from the grocer. Fresh fruit, lettuce, string beans, and bread. I'm putting the fruit away, when she appears in the doorway of the kitchen.

"You're angry with me," she says, matter-of-factly.

"That's an understatement," I say. "Anger can go away. You've kept secrets from me, and for no good reason. Why?"

"You don't need to know everything."

"Is that so?" I'm seething.

"I wasn't up to sharing it with you," she says, folding her arms, a queer little smile turning up the corners of her lips. She is enjoying this little game she's playing. It's off-putting to see her in this light. I never dreamed it was possible that inside of my sister is a wickedness—one I've never noticed or has not yet been unleashed. I stare hard at her, trying to fight back tears. I think of how I've cared for her, and how little I've received in return. Rosa's words echo inside my head: *Here's the thing: you're loyal to her, but who is she loyal to?*

"You've left me speechless, Essie," I say, finally, exhausted by the way she treats me. "I'm not sure what to say anymore. I'm not sure why someone who's supposed to love me has kept me in the dark."

"Remember your words down the road. Remember these very words you have spoken, Veronica," Essie shouts.

She says it in a foreboding, dark way, and I can't make any

sense of it.

"What the heck does that mean?" I ask, raising my voice.

She takes her drink in her hand, turns on her heels, and moves down the hall to her bedroom, where she promptly slams the door.

My heart is beating fast. I'm angry twenty-four hours a day. I want to scream at the top of my lungs. I wonder if my mother were alive if any of this would be happening. I'm angry at my mother. I'm angry at my father for gallivanting out of our lives and leaving me to tend to things. I can sense that there is a missing piece of a puzzle that I cannot figure out–there has to be. Essie's change in demeanor leads me to no other conclusion. And no one will give me answers.

Quickly, I change into a pair of slacks and a blouse and comfortable shoes. I want to leave here and never come back. I want out of this hell I'm living in.

I grab a light sweater and make my way out of the door. I'm due to meet Perry in a half an hour. On the sidewalk, I see the newsstand and the stacks of newspapers. The headline on the evening edition reads: *Tommy DeCarlo Taken Down By Cops.*

I pick up the newspaper, pay for it, and find a bench to read what's happened. In a few minutes, I understand the gist of the story–Rosa Manetti has taken down Tommy DeCarlo and family from behind bars.

Something in me rejoices for her.

*

"You can move in with me," Perry says, taking a sip of his cocktail. He's in a great mood. The Dodgers won the game, he's completed his story, and now I've got him all to myself.

"I don't think your family would look too favorably on that. I'm not sure mine, what's left of it, would, either."

He puts his drink down and looks at me across the table.

"And we care about what they think because...?"

I smile at him. He has a point. "Because it's not really proper. I'm an old-fashioned kind of girl. Remember, I write romance stories. *Cinderella* fluff."

"Well, they're made-up stories. Ours is a real one. I like to think we have a pretty good romance brewing between us," Perry says. He's still looking at me, and he's not touching his food. He seems a little fidgety.

"I'd say so." The mere sound of his voice calms my nerves.

"I wasn't really prepared to do this at this moment, but I have been carrying this around for a while, so maybe this is the best time," Perry begins. He stands, moves away from his chair, turns my body to face him, and gets down on one knee. "I love you, Veronica DeMarco. I want to spend the rest of my life with you. You're my best friend and my love. Will you marry me?" From his pants pocket, he pulls out a box. Inside is a beautiful, antique-looking diamond ring.

I lean down and hug him, tears of joy springing from my eyes. His eyes look pretty misty, too.

"Yes. I love you, Perry. Nothing would make me happier," I say.

The people around us who have been watching start clapping, and Alberto, the owner comes over with a bottle of champagne. The trio of musicians begins to play a song, and the man on the accordion is smiling at the two of us.

I look at the ring on my finger and feel so proud and blessed to have this man by my side. With all of the other nonsense that surrounds my life and my family, he grounds me and brings stability and joy. I trust him with my life, and I know where my real home is going to be from this day forward.

With him, I have freedom.

Chapter 26

When Perry drops me off in a cab at eleven o'clock, I kiss him goodnight and tell him I can't wait to take the next step with him. I watch the cab pull away with my love inside it.

As I open the door, I see Essie sitting in the same chair she was sitting in earlier. The lights are dim, and the glow of the television reflects in her eyes.

"Where have you been?" she asks. "Out with Perry?" The ring that should be on my finger is in my purse. I took it off in the taxi, just in case she was awake when I walked through the door. My instinct was right. I can keep a secret, too. "Robert wants you to call him right now," she says. "He's called at least ten times looking for you."

Without another word to her, I walk toward the phone and dial his number. He picks up on the first ring.

"Thank goodness you called! We've got breaking news! You're the only one who can do it!"

"Do what?"

"Rosa Manetti wants to talk with you tonight," he says. "In person."

"At this hour?"

"She wants to see you. The prison has called the paper

looking for you. She needs to see you right now."

"I don't want to go there by myself. It's late. It's creepy." My heart starts to pound.

"I know. I'm coming with you. I'll be at your place in ten minutes." Robert hangs up.

Essie looks at me, having listened to my side of the conversation. "You're leaving?" she asks. I can't wait to tell her I'm leaving for good, that I'm going to marry Perry and start a new life, but there's something in the way she asks me the question that makes me believe the person I've known and loved my whole life is still in there, somewhere. What's going on with her? She begins to pout and looks much different from the person who slammed her bedroom door four hours prior. "What's the pressing story?" she insists.

Despite that I am feeling a bit sorry for her now, I remember how it went earlier, and I can't help myself. I can't hold my tongue, because I want to get back at her. I've held it in for far too long.

"I'm sorry, but I'm not at liberty to tell you what's going on. I'm sure you understand. Some things cannot be shared. It's between editor and reporter, much in the same way novel writing is between agent and writer. You understand that, I'm sure. Confidentiality and all that."

"What a rotten thing to say, Veronica! You are so horrible!" Essie screams at me. She's right in one respect. It was a horrible, childish thing to say, but I'm not a horrible person. I'm frustrated and exhausted from the game playing in our sibling relationship.

I turn to face her, anger coursing through my veins. "Look in the mirror sometime, Essie. Take a good, hard look at yourself, and when you do, maybe you'll see what the rest of us see. An angry, bitter woman, who will do anything to make those around her miserable. Especially her sister who has only cared for her all these years, supported her, and tried desperately to make her as comfortable as possible. After you've reflected on your deceitful and unkind turn of nature over these last many months, come talk to me!"

I don't even wait for the taxi to arrive. I exit the apartment, and this time I'm the one who slams the door shut behind me. On my front stoop, I reach inside my purse and put my ring back on.

I've had enough of her. She doesn't give a damn about protecting me or having a reciprocal relationship, and she certainly didn't have a problem keeping things from me.

I'm not hiding anything anymore.

The taxi pulls up with Robert inside, and I remember what I made yesterday and put in the refrigerator. I run back inside to grab it, making sure not to make eye contact with Essie. When I return to the taxi, I climb in and we make our way to the prison.

*

My heart hasn't stopped racing the entire ride in the taxi. I couldn't bring myself to say anything more to Robert about Essie and our situation, so I listened to him ramble on about work and the big stories of the day.

"Do you have a cigarette?" I ask him.

"Of course. I always have my cigarettes," he says, clearing his throat.

"May I have one, please?" Robert doesn't hesitate. He shakes one out of the pack, hands it to me, and then takes one for himself. I place it between my lips, inhaling the scent of tobacco. Leaning toward him, he lights my cigarette. I inhale, roll down the window slightly, and exhale a plume of smoke.

"I'm glad you're willing to see her tonight. It sounded urgent."

"Did you actually speak to Rosa?" I notice my hands are slightly trembling.

"No, the warden."

The prison is even creepier in the evening than it is during the daylight. It looks like the setting of a movie, the moonlight highlighting the walls, and I see it as a metaphor for hope and light for those who might eventually leave the trappings of prison behind them. The taxi pulls up at the guard gate, and we exit the cab. I take one more drag, then stomp out the cigarette. As we approach the entrance, the guards see me. Some of them know me by now—some even call me Miss DeMarco by name. The guard who first walked me into the room to speak to Rosa is here, and he says hello and walks Robert and me through the doors. The warden is there waiting for us, looking tired and irritated to have to do this at this late hour. His keyring seems to have grown exponentially.

"What's all this about?" I ask him.

"It's out of my hands now. I just do what they tell me to do," he says, pointing to the men in suits. There are two gentlemen dressed in dark suits standing outside the room. They look official, but they do not speak. One of them says to the warden. "Only she can see Manetti." Robert looks crushed. I know he was hoping to meet her in person.

"Can I bring this? Please?" I'm asking the warden, almost pleading with him. He opens up the box and looks inside.

"One piece. Cut it here. She can only have it with the guards present. It doesn't go anywhere else."

"Thank you," I say in a whisper.

It takes us a minute to cut the cake, the warden inspecting it thoroughly before clearing it. "Let's go," says the warden.

I look at Robert, and he gives me a pat on the back for encouragement. Everything about this situation is eerie, unsettling.

"I'll wait here," Robert says, ushering me along.

The warden begins to walk toward what the guards refer to as "the talk room," and in minutes, I am there. This time, the prison guards enter the room but stand by the door. The two men in suits move into the room as well. I sit in my prescribed chair and wait for Rosa. I feel anxious. When she finally materializes, she looks different. Clean and tidy. Freshly showered. Her face doesn't look as tired. She looks younger. There's a lightness to her eyes, the dark circles less prominent.

She sits in the chair across from me. The two men in suits remain on either side of us, about two feet away, both guards just inside the door.

"How 'ya doin', writer girl? You got another gift for me? I hope it's food, cuz the crap they serve you in here ain't fit for animals."

I reach over and open the lid of the small box. I wait to see her expression.

"Aw, kid. You're gonna make me cry. Did you get me a piece of Italian cream cake?"

"I made it. They would only allow me to bring one piece. Do you want a bite?"

"Do I?" I hand her the fork, and with her shackled hands, she dives in. Her eyes practically roll to the back of her head; she's reeling with delight.

"Oh my God, writer girl! You've done good. You've done real good. Maybe you're more of a *paisan* than I thought." I smile at her and she winks at me. "You're one of the good ones," she says.

"So tell me what's going on! My heart is pounding. What is happening?" I lean my body toward her, because she is whispering a little; she's not talking as loudly as normal.

"Nothing for you to worry your pretty little head over. I got them. I got the whole DeCarlo family," she says.

"I know. I read all about it in the evening paper. You're the biggest news story in New York tonight."

"Well, sometimes you gotta do what you gotta do, even if you risk death for it."

"Death? Is someone trying to kill you, Rosa?" It sounds like a naive question when it comes out of my mouth. I feel stupid for saying it, and she can see it in my face.

"Everyone's gonna want me dead, Veronica. Everyone. That's why I wanted to see you tonight. Just in case, 'ya know..."

She makes a gesture with her hand across her throat, as if to indicate being silenced for good.

"What?"

"Are you gonna actually make me have to say it? Seriously?" She smiles at me, one of those crooked, mischievous smiles of hers. I wonder what she would have been like under a different set of circumstances.

"Say what?" I ask, playing dumb, but trying to fight back tears.

"You've been good to me, kid. Those stories you wrote in the paper, they helped me, 'ya know? Helped people see me differently. Do you know I've been gettin' letters from strangers sayin' they're rootin' for me? Fan mail—go figure! Some even say they're proud of me. I'm getting letters from total strangers who don't know me, and most of them women. I have a bag of mail that they won't let me take into the cell, so I have to read them in here with two guards. But letter by letter, I'm making it through them. They are kind letters for the most part. A few pieces of hate mail, but mostly good stuff. You did that. You did that, writer girl. You made that happen."

"All I did was write the truth as you told it to me. It's my job, Rosa."

"Yeah, I know all that, but you've been kinder to me than anyone I've known in years, and I just wanted to see you and say thanks for it all. You and I, we made a friendship in this stinkin' rat hole. And unlike other people, I'm loyal to the grave. I ain't got many friends, if you know what I mean. But you..." She stops for a second and swallows hard. She doesn't need to continue. I know what she's saying, what she means.

I don't know if it's because of the emotional day I've had, but the conversation is getting to me. It feels full of doom, and I start to cry and reach for a tissue in my pocket.

"Wait! What the hell is that on your finger?" Rosa's expression makes me laugh a little.

"Perry proposed," I say, choking out the words through my tears.

"You're crying 'cuz of that, not over me, right?"

"No. I'm worried for you. I'm sick about your situation."

"Ah, kid, don't be too worried. We're all born and we all die. Now, back to that ring. When did he propose?"

"Earlier tonight."

"You're kiddin'! And I've gone and ruined your nice evening." She seems genuinely upset by the fact that she may have affected the outcome of our celebration. I set her straight right away.

"No, Rosa, you didn't ruin my night. My sister alone is responsible for that. You've actually made my night. I am happy to be here with you."

"You don't look happy."

"I am. It's just my sister–"

"Your sister, what? Stop worrying about her now. You gotta be happy you found a good guy. Things will fall into place. Stop avoiding happiness. Stop dodging love. You'll regret it. You know I'm right about this, writer girl."

I stop for a second and hear her words. They sound familiar and resonate. When Robert suggested I go to the banquet with Perry, he told me I was dodging love–dodging relationships–because I felt responsibility for Essie. Maybe I have been. My love and feelings for Essie have always led me to put her first, sacrificing everything for her. I've never been resentful that I've prioritized her comfort and wellbeing over my own. Prior to falling in love with Perry, providing for Essie and working to support us both were my top priorities.

"How'd he do it, kid? Did he get down on one knee?" Rosa still wants the details, and I laugh when she calls me kid. She's barely ten years older than I am.

I smile at her. "He did."

"Aw, romance. Just like in your story."

"You read it?" I ask her.

"You told me to! You gave me that book as a gift, so yes, I read it. Now stop changin' the subject. That ring's a beauty! You deserve it, honey. You do. And as for that sister of yours, it sounds like it's time to exit stage left and ride off into the sunset with Perry Como. I'm a romantic at heart, believe it or not, and you've been through the ringer with your sister. Sometimes, you just gotta let go."

"Perry Spada," I say, correcting the last name. I smile at her, feeling a wave of exhaustion and elation come over me.

"After all this time together, and you still don't get my sense of humor?" she says with a wink.

"Oh Rosa. I don't want to think about my sister right now. I know you're right. I've been her caretaker all these years. It isn't so easy. On her deathbed, my mother made me swear to take care of Essie."

"And you have. You kept that promise." I get the sense that if Rosa weren't in shackles, she might hug me.

I nod. It is the truth, but I'm here with Rosa, and I don't want to talk about Essie anymore. "Let's talk about you, Rosa. I came tonight because you wanted to see me."

"Well, I worry for you, writer girl. You've had a lot on your plate with that one. Don't let someone else's misery play into your happiness–or your future. I learned a long time ago that if someone can't be genuinely happy for you, they do not belong in your life. You've sacrificed for your sister, but you gotta start living your own life now. You have a lot to look forward to–"

"Three minutes," the man in the suit says.

"Hey, we usually get a five-minute warning," Rosa shouts back.

"Not tonight, Manetti. Three minutes." The man in the suit's face is expressionless.

Rosa takes a deep breath and stares at me for a few seconds. We don't want to waste the precious one hundred and eighty seconds we have remaining. "Listen, if anything happens to me, I don't want you to be sad. I'm a sittin' duck in this prison. Lots of my sort of people have died in jail, or so they say. In case things get ugly, I just wanted to tell you how grateful I am to you. You started out as a diversion to get my mind off things, but you became so much more. I'm indebted, writer girl. Remember, I am a tough bird, and you can't let anything you read haunt you. You got me?"

"I'm not sure I understand."

"You will. You will. You're a smart one. Now, promise me you're gonna just keep on livin' your life the way you know you should...the way we just talked about."

She's scaring me. I fight back tears.

"Ah, damn, writer girl. No cryin'. You're gonna make me cry. Remember, you're a tough bird, too. Promise me."

I don't entirely know what I'm promising, but I just say the words, because time is limited. "I promise."

"That's-a-girl. And thanks for getting me the priest. I got a lot off my mind. Poor man had to listen to me drone on. I actually made of list of things to confess. It was a long, messy list, honey. Two full pages. Made it a lot easier. And as for the cake, I haven't tasted anything that good in a long time."

The warden hadn't filled me in on the priest's visit, so I pretend I knew it had happened. Nonetheless, it seems to have lightened her burden, so I'm glad for it.

"Thirty-seconds," the man in the suit says emphatically. I shift in my chair, looking at Rosa. I want to remember her, this moment, and this strange relationship we've forged here among these four walls in this dingy, green meeting room. I reach across the table and touch her hands wrapped in handcuffs. We have never touched before, but I'm holding onto her, squeezing her hands because I can't seem to find any words appropriate for the moment.

I'm still clinging to Rosa Manetti when she leans in and whispers to me, "And for the record, I didn't kill my sister and my ex. I didn't do it. It truly was an accident, gettin' hit by the train. I had nothing to do with it, but I figured, why not let people think

I'm ruthless? I had an image to uphold. The rest of them people who died, it was self-defense: I had to protect my family. But you, I don't want you to think I'm that awful a human being."

"Time's up, Manetti" the suit says.

Deep down, I knew she didn't do it. I give a half-smile and am forced to let go of her when the two suits grab her, and hoist her up out of the chair, leaving the crumbs of the cake on the table.

"You're gonna be just fine," she says. "Godspeed." As the men in suits whisk her to the door, she turns her head toward me and gives me one final wink.

Those are the last words I hear spoken from Rosa Manetti's lips. After that, the prison guards escort me back to the warden's office and Robert.

*

By the time I return home at three in the morning, Essie's door is shut, and I tip-toe to my room. As I climb into bed and my head hits the pillow, the tiredness consumes me. I'm awash in memories of the night—of Perry, his proposal. My right hand touches the ring on my left finger beneath the covers. Only Rosa knows we are engaged. I did not tell Robert. I did not tell Essie. Under normal circumstances, this would be the happiest night of my life. But then I picture Rosa's face. I see flashes of her sitting across from me tonight, trying to explain that she's a target and that she may not make it. I flick the light on, grab my notebook, and write down everything I can remember she said to me, just for me, so that I'll always remember.

I'm in this apartment that feels cold and barren—barren of love and understanding, support and sisterhood. It's a lonely place to dwell. Where once I could have shared all of this with Essie, I no longer feel I am able.

Ironically, on one of the happiest nights of my life, tears wet my cheeks. I've kept so much bottled up for so many months, maybe even years. There's an unwelcome pit in my stomach. An intuitive feeling that something terrible is about to happen.

It can only be described as a sense of dread and foreboding that lurks behind the guise of light, of love.

Chapter 27

Impatiently stewing, I cross then uncross my legs. The coffee shop is bustling, but there's no sign of Alice Hawthorne. She is late. Somebody's fed money into the little jukebox. A series of Elvis songs fill the place. As much as I like his music, it's not helping to cheer me up. Alice called this meeting, not me. I'm growing more annoyed by the minute. I'm not a fan of tardiness; it's a quality I loathe in people. Making people wait for you is a sign of selfishness, that their time is more important than yours. I'm on very little sleep and am growing more agitated by the minute. I look at my watch. Another five minutes have passed.

If she does not arrive by quarter past, I promise myself to get up out of the chair and leave. There is no excuse for her unprofessional behavior. My eyes still sting from the tears I shed last night, despite the makeup used to cover up the puffiness this morning. In a straight skirt and pink short-sleeved blouse, I picked out today's outfit specifically to cheer myself up. I should be on cloud nine about my future with Perry, but I'm worried sick about Rosa. I'm also consumed with grief about the disintegration of my relationship with Essie.

I dread breaking the news to Essie that I'm leaving. It's difficult to put into words, but the act of actually doing it fills me with anxiety. Even now. Even after what has transpired. Perry and I will marry. I'm moving out. Psychologists will tell you that you grow, change, and mature as the years progress. Boy, are they right! I've learned a lot this past year. I also learned I have a breaking point. Maybe some of Rosa's toughness is rubbing off on me.

I'm not sure how my relationship with Essie can be repaired at this point. I'm not sure how to fix what's broken when she has no self-awareness to realize her role in it. Maybe my outburst last night had some effect on her. I couldn't say. I didn't see her before I left to meet Alice early this morning.

Just as I'm about to stand and take my leave, Alice comes rushing through the door. Clearly, she knows she's late. Not a hair is out of place, her stylish clothes looking like they came right out of a fashion magazine.

"I know, I know, I'm tardy," she says, her lips ruby red. She pats me on the shoulder in a condescending way. "Do sit down. We have things to discuss."

"If you think I'm looking forward to this conversation, I'm not." I can't help myself. I don't want to sit back down. She motions for the waitress to bring us coffee.

"I know you're not. But the conversation needs to be had. Please sit. So here it is. I'm sorry I kept things from you about Essie. She begged me not to tell you. That's all I can say at the moment. I'm sorry. I didn't mean to hurt you."

"Maybe you didn't intentionally, but you both did nonetheless." I'm still standing. She's infuriating. Her tone is belittling. How could I not have noticed this about her before?

Alice crosses her legs, and then crosses her arms. She leans back in her chair and studies me, then points to the chair for me to sit. "I can see you are bitter. I can see you've changed."

"Oh, is that so? And maybe I'm just seeing you for the first time in your truest light." I'm not a fighter, but I find myself in this predicament. Fighting for myself.

"Oh, Veronica. You are blowing this whole thing way out

of proportion," she says, almost mocking me.

The blood begins to boil in my body. I feel I might jump out of my skin. Who is she to comment and disregard the way I feel? It suddenly dawns on me that I want nothing to do with her. Nothing at all. How could I have been so blind? She is a judgmental, meddling, callous businesswoman. Someone who cares little for people and more about what she yields from people. I see that clearly now as she stares at me.

"Let me ask you this: How do I sever my contract with you? I no longer want you to be my agent," I continue.

"Oh, you think you can do better on your own?" She laughs it off nervously, probably thinking I don't mean what I say.

"I don't know if 'better' is the right word, but I'd rather find someone who is not a judgmental and secretive ass."

Alice is seething. I've never seen her this way. "You cannot break your contract. It's binding!"

I reach in my briefcase and pull out my latest contract, where I underlined in yellow with a highlighter what I knew I might have to regurgitate back to her.

"Let me refresh your memory, since you are clearly not up to date on your own contracts. It says here, and I quote, *'If your agent has not fulfilled the promises outlined in the contract, been unethical in any way, or has misrepresented you or your work, Author may submit a termination letter. Should a conflict of interest arise, the agreement can become null and void. Agent requires thirty days in writing to terminate the working relationships and representation.'*"

Alice is speechless. She doesn't know what to say, because I have just won the argument. I continue, "Oh, and if any of this doesn't seem right, I'll have my lawyer contact you later today or tomorrow. You'll have your thirty days notice as soon as I write the letter. Do we understand each other? I want to terminate my contract with you, Alice. I believe you crossed the ethical line and dove right into unethical, and I also believe that we do, in fact, have a conflict of interest. Good luck with Essie!"

Her mouth is agape. I can no longer look at her. I leave Alice and my coffee behind. I'm too angry and prideful to stay one more second at the table. I can't trust her, and I don't want to give it another try. It's over. I'll take my next book elsewhere.

Or maybe I'll just take a break from writing books.

Either way, on principle alone, I cannot stay with Alice.

*

By the time I arrive at The News, I've started to calm down a bit. Perry is sitting at my desk with a bag of croissants in his hand waiting for me. He's smiling from ear to ear, as I should be, if only the other aspects of my life could be as positive.

"Hello, Love," he says. It's the first time he's called me that, and I notice it.

"Hello," I say. He looks at my hand, the one with the ring on it, and brings it to his lips and kisses it. "How are you?"

"You won't believe my evening after I left you and what's happened since," I begin to say, peeking inside the brown bag he hands me. My tummy is rumbling. I need something to eat. The croissants smell divine.

"Why didn't you call me?" he asks.

"It was three in the morning. I didn't want to wake you."

"You know you can call me at any hour."

"Yes, I know." He's right. I probably should have called him, but I didn't want to be on the phone in my apartment with Essie there.

"So, tell me what's happened," he says, leaning on my desk.

"Let's see. Where do I begin? Okay, I got home, got in yet another fight with Essie—didn't tell her about our engagement. Robert had been chasing me down, and I had to return the ten messages he left with Essie at the apartment. Turns out we ended up going to the prison at eleven-thirty at night to see Rosa, who had requested to see me. Only I was able to see her, not Robert.

Two guys in suits watched the whole conversation, and she basically thanked me for being her friend and told me she thinks her days are numbered because of what she did to the DeCarlo family. Essentially, she believes people are out to get her."

"I'm so glad Robert went with you and you didn't have to go alone," Perry says, bringing his cup of coffee to his lips.

"Yes, thank goodness. The whole visit had an eerie feel to it."

"I'm so sorry," Perry says. He reaches for my hand and holds it gently. "It was terribly disturbing."

"I know how much you've started to care for her."

"I do. It's so weird, Perry. What do you think that's all about? I mean, she's done some awful things, yet I see her as Rosa, not as the person she was."

"Because you have a kind and forgiving heart, Veronica. You see the best in people, not the worst." Perry takes a deep breath and looks at me sweetly.

"I'm not so sure about that. I just fired Alice. I don't want to work with her anymore. I have to send a letter, and in thirty days, the relationship ends. She can continue on with Essie, but I honestly have no interest."

"But what about the book deal?" Perry takes a big bite of his croissant. I do the same. These are some of the best I've tasted.

"I don't care about it at the moment. Right now, my only worries are you, Rosa, and doing my job well at The News. If I'm a good enough writer, I'll find another agent."

"She won't blackball you, will she?" Perry asks. It's a question I hadn't thought of before now.

"I don't know." I sit in the chair and cross my legs.

"Let's hope she's not that awful." Perry sighs.

"Yes. Let's hope." I contemplate this for a moment.

"Well, worry no more. How about as a nice treat we go to the Yankees game this afternoon and see your buddy Mickey Mantle? I don't have to cover the Dodgers. Day off." From out of his back pocket, he presents me with two tickets to Yankee Stadium.

"I think I like your idea. Let me check a few things off my list first, then we'll go," I say to him, and I kiss him on the cheek. "I could use some baseball as a distraction."

*

"How did you get these seats?" I ask him. We're sitting directly behind the Yankees dugout. I can't believe how close we are to the field. I can hear the players talking.

"I know a few people," he says, juggling our Cracker Jacks and drinks.

It's a beautiful afternoon for a game. The sun is shining. The light hits the facade of the stadium and gives it an ethereal feel. *I'm engaged*, I think. Everything comes naturally between Perry and me; there is no pretentiousness with us. My mother would have adored him. He's everything she could have hoped for as a partner for me. She would have liked Malcolm, too, but I'm not too sure she'd be all that pleased with Essie's changed nature. Would she have been disappointed to see her two daughters carrying on this way? It would break her heart.

"You know the rumors are swirling about the Dodgers. I think this may be their last season in Brooklyn. Word on the street is it may already be a done deal. I wonder if I'll still have a job if they move."

"Are you kidding? Robert adores you. He'll find a place for you, for sure. You're one of his best writers!"

"But he's already got reporters covering other teams. I wonder if I'll get the axe when there's no team to cover."

"You're making me nervous," I say, because he is. He is making me very nervous. "You will find a place. Robert will make sure of it. I know he will." I say this because I believe it with all my heart.

All eyes are on Mantle when he comes up to bat. He walks

out of the dugout and toward the plate with swagger and confidence. People are shouting his name. "Let's go, Mickey!" they chant. "Hit it outta here, Mick!" they say. The fans are clapping for him, cheering him on. When he hits a double and makes his way to second base, Yankee Stadium erupts. He's so beloved–I adore watching him play. My father never took me to baseball games. He never much cared for the sport. I remember begging him to take me to a game when I was about twelve, yet he never took the time to take me. My mother took me once. I remember it distinctly, because a few days later, I learned she was ill.

"That guy is going to be one of the great players of the game, Veronica. I can just sense it. He already is, but I think he's going to have a magnificent baseball career," Perry says. I have to agree. Mickey Mantle is a New York treasure.

When Berra comes up to bat, he rips one into right field and Mantle comes in to score, touching home plate. He trots our way toward the dugout and catches our eye. He gives a little nod, as if he knows us, but I know it's just because that's how he is. Even so, it makes me feel special.

"He must know you're one of his super fans," Perry teases.

"I think he knows he's got a stadium full of them," I shout back over the cheers.

It's fun to be here as the Yankees beat the Red Sox. I feel a part of this city as a writer for The News, but nothing beats watching baseball with Perry–along with all the other intense fans that love the game as we do.

Chapter 28

Three days later on a Saturday morning, as I place a piece of rye bread into the toaster, the telephone rings. By the third ring, I reach for the phone. It's never good news when a call comes at this early hour.

"Hello," I say. Essie is sitting in her chair doing a crossword puzzle with the television on, sipping her coffee. I still haven't told Essie about Perry. I'm still hiding my engagement ring. I don't know why I'm waiting to tell her, I just am.

"Hi Veronica," Robert says. By the tone of his voice, I can tell something ominous is about to be shared. "I'm so sorry to have to tell you this, but Rosa Manetti's dead. Apparently, she committed suicide in her cell."

Suicide? What?

"That can't be. No. I don't believe it," I say, stunned, and falling into the kitchen chair. I feel faint. Essie appears in the doorway, looking at me.

"That's the report coming from the prison. We're going to run a story shortly. I didn't know if you wanted to help write it. I'm so sorry," he says again.

As crass as it sounds, I wonder if he's sorry she's dead or sorry that any additional feature stories about Rosa won't sell papers anymore—besides today, of course. This is big news—probably the biggest story of the month. Rosa and the DeCarlo family have been front page news on every newspaper in the city—it's even garnered national attention. Morbid curiosity will make people want to read about Rosa and her death. But that's the news business. It can be quite macabre. Sometimes I feel ashamed to be working in an industry that makes money from sensationalized stories at the expense of others. But right now, all I can think about is Rosa.

"Who called you?" I ask Robert. My hands are shaking.

"We got a call from the Chief of Police in the prison's district. I have Jones on the story, but I would appreciate the tact you would bring to the story. This isn't a regular obituary. It's got to be published for the evening edition, and that's pushing it." I see Essie fold her arms as she watches me have the conversation.

"Let me dress, and I'll be right in," I say, swallowing hard, fighting off the nausea. None of this makes sense. Rosa was worried they'd *kill* her. How could it have been suicide?

I hang up and sit there for a moment in silence. I lean over, trying to catch my breath. Essie's still in the doorway. Then, she speaks.

"Who's dead?"

"Rosa Manetti," I say, looking up at her, a tear running down my face.

"I guess that's the end of your Rosa Manetti stories," she says.

Bile rises in my throat. What a cruel and insensitive thing to say to me. I think of Rosa and the way she felt about her own sister. I'm not too far from feeling that way about my own. Essie turns and walks back to her chair. I'm disgusted by her words.

I want to tear into her, tell her what an awful person she is, but I can't. I don't have the energy.

Rosa Manetti's dead. And by her own hand. Just like her mother.

I begin to piece it together. That's why she wanted to see me—to say goodbye. Once she got the DeCarlo family, maybe she felt she had nothing else to live for, that she'd always have to watch her back. *They want me dead*, she had said. She squealed on them, and now it's over. They're behind bars and Rosa is no longer with us.

The toast is burnt. I have no interest in eating at all. I dump it all into the garbage can. Quickly, I brush my teeth, dress in slacks and a blouse, toss my hair in a bun, and grab my briefcase from the foyer.

Essie doesn't even acknowledge me as I walk out the door.

And I have nothing to say to her.

*

Ed Jones, Robert, and I are huddled over the copy we are editing together. It's a massive story, and as we've been the ones to publish Rosa's exclusive story, we want to get this one right. We've been on the phone all day, verifying sources, especially from the prison. We're editing and editing, examining every little word, trying to get this story the way it needs to be. It has to be just right.

"We have to write the truth about Rosa telling me they'd be after her—the DeCarlo family. She said those words to me the last time I saw her. That has to be in there." Robert knows it belongs in the story, but he's trying to find the right way to say it without having the newspaper threatened by the mob. "Why are you deliberating? It's good the way it is," I tell him.

"I don't know. Is it too blunt?" He's rubbing his chin as he examines the copy.

"Too blunt? It needs to be shared, Robert. For Rosa's sake. We don't want our readers in the dark about this. It's how it went down. Those were the words she said to me. I owe it to her to tell the facts." I cross my arms and stand back, looking at the two men.

Robert looks at me crossways. He runs his fingers through his mostly grey hair.

"Blunt it is," he says, looking from Ed to me. The News has

been the paper of record regarding Rosa Manetti. Robert takes a long drag of his cigarette, giving the article one last look, and then he blesses the story. "Let's get this published now," he says.

That's it. After working on the story for nearly four hours, we have it the way we want it.

"Good working with you on it," Ed says to me. He's a middle-aged man with warm eyes and a brilliant smile.

"Thanks, Ed. Good working with you, too."

He leans back in the chair, studying me for a second. "You'd make a good investigative reporter, wouldn't she, Rob?" Ed says, more as a fact than a question.

"She would, but she likes features and fiction." Robert stubs out his cigarette in the ashtray, folds his arms. I laugh when others call him Rob. He's much more of a Robert to me.

"Well, that's a wrap," he says. "What are your plans, Veronica?"

"I guess I'll head home now. Perry's covering the game, and it doesn't matter where Essie is. We never speak."

"I'm off to see the Missus," Ed says, standing and stretching, interrupting our conversation. "Promised her a night at the pictures to see *The Pajama Game*. There's no going back on that promise now." He grabs his hat and says goodbye.

"I think you and I need to go out for an early dinner," Robert says. "I don't want you to be alone. I know you became fond of Rosa Manetti."

Suddenly, I'm sad again. The reality of her death is sinking in. Writing the story took my mind off her actual passing, because I had to do right by her. It was my duty as a human being first, then as a reporter.

"Ok. That sounds good to me. Where shall we go?" I ask.

"My favorite place," he says. Within minutes we are in a cab heading to the west side and his favorite place—as it is Sinatra's—Patsy's. We hop out of the cab, check in, and are whisked to a table.

"I called ahead," Robert whispers to me.

I've never been to Patsy's, but I've certainly read about all the celebrities who've helped put this place on the New York City map, none more so than Frank Sinatra. Understated but warm and welcoming, Patsy's is humming with patrons. It smells divine. I realize that I haven't eaten all day. Only coffee has fueled me.

Robert and I are seated against the wall with photographs in frames above our heads. "That's Sinatra's table over there," Robert says to me as we get comfortable.

When the waiter comes over, Robert orders us each a glass of wine, as we peruse the menu. It feels strange to be here with him in this manner. We haven't done this in a while. I've been to his home with his family on many occasions, but dinners out are not a regular thing for us. I've let the idea of grilling him about my mother go for the time being. I have too many other things to focus on at the moment. We study the menus, then pick our dishes—Robert selects the linguini, and I choose the ravioli. He orders an appetizer for us to share. The wine is delivered, and Robert raises his glass to make a toast.

"I know it may seem a little inappropriate to be toasting when you've lost Rosa, but here's to Rosa and what she brought to you, to our paper, and to the city by taking the bums down," he says. We clink glasses. But he's not done. "One more toast—to you, Veronica. I'm very proud of you and all your hard work. You have become an excellent reporter and an integral part of the newspaper." We clink glasses again. I thank him for the kind words.

Patsy's is a lively place, filled with happy people. People are laughing, drinking, and enjoying each other's company. Robert and I sit for a moment, taking it all in.

"You like this place, I can tell," he says.

"I do." I take a sip of the wine and smile at him.

"I can't believe I'm about to do this, but I want to talk to you about something."

"What is it?" I ask. He's got me worried for a moment. This sounds serious.

"More of an ask, actually. I need to ask you why you're not wearing your engagement ring."

"How did you know about that?" I'm shocked. Genuinely. I've done a good job keeping it quiet for now.

"Perry told me. He's worried about you. Frankly, he's very worried about you and Essie."

"I know. I'm worried about Essie and me, too. Everything's changed." I look at Robert, and he's looking at me—really looking at me. He's not distracted by work, by what story is breaking, or who to send off to cover an accident or murder.

"So, you gave me a little insight last time we talked. What's going on?"

Robert has opened the door to conversation, and I take it. For the next half hour, I give him a peek into my horrible home life, my hopeful life with Perry, and the disastrous situation with Alice Hawthorne. He listens as he's never listened before. I detail what Essie said to me this morning when I learned of Rosa's death. When I finish spewing the abbreviated version of my life over the last several months, I'm almost out of breath. I've taken only two bites of the appetizer.

"I'm glad you've told me all of this," he says. "You are right. I had no idea what you were going through with her. I'm sorry to hear she's treating you so poorly."

The waiter brings our dinners to the table.

"Yes. Me, too." I cut a piece of the ravioli and take a bite. Either I'm starving, or this dish is near perfection.

"Where exactly is your ring?"

"In my purse. I've become accustomed to taking it on and off."

"Let me see it," he says.

I reach into my purse, pull out the ring, slide it on my finger. It is beautiful. Robert grabs my hand and looks at it. "It suits you perfectly. Perry did a good job."

"I love it. And I love him." It feels good to say it to someone.

"I know. It's obvious when you two are together."

"It is?"

"Everyone at The News thinks you're a match made in heaven, if there is such a thing." He says the second part with a wink.

I smile at him. It's good to hear this after the horrible day we've been through.

"Rosa liked Perry." I take a sip of the wine.

"Did she meet him?" Robert asks genuinely.

"No, I just told her all about him. I think she loved knowing he makes me happy."

"But didn't she kill her sister and her own former lover?"

I don't want to betray Rosa's confidence, even in death. She didn't care that people thought she did it. I knew she didn't, even before she told me she didn't do it. Nevertheless, I play along. "That's the story," I say.

Robert raises an eyebrow, as if to indicate he knows I know more than I'm letting on, but he doesn't press me.

"Well, you can't keep the engagement from Essie. She's going to find out about it sooner or later. I think you have to level with her. Tell her the truth. If this Malcolm fella really loves her, perhaps he'll step in and unburden you from feeling guilty. She can't be your responsibility for the rest of your life."

He's right. I know he's right. And I'm being a silly, scared mouse about all of this.

"Did Perry ask you to speak with me?"

"Maybe he did," Robert says, taking a bite, "and maybe he didn't."

Chapter 29

There is no funeral for Rosa Manetti. No service. The newspapers sold out, because the story was so sensational. It's still amazing to me. One minute a person is here, and the next minute, she's gone. Watching my own mother take her last breath is not something you soon forget. When my mother passed, I thanked God that she was finally at peace. The pain consumed her in the end. Rosa may now be at peace, but for different reasons.

Essie had stoically mourned our mother. I was drenched in tears, and she was the tough, brave one, muddling through. I never saw her cry about our mother. Never once, come to think of it. That's an odd thing to remember about one's only sister, but it stands out in my mind.

It's early on a Wednesday morning, and I find myself in a cab directing it to the prison. I don't know why I feel the need to be there, I just do. I'm not sure where else to mourn Rosa.

The taxi pulls up in front, and I tell the guard that I'm here. He calls the warden to clear me. I get out and one of the guards takes me inside the thick, double doors. He's one of the newer guards, but he knows who I am.

"Hello, Miss," he says.

The warden's assistant greets me and takes me to the warden down the hall to see him.

"Sorry about Manetti," the warden says to me.

"Thank you. I'm not sure why I'm here, I just felt I had to be here for some reason. Maybe say a little prayer and have a proper goodbye." My voice is shaking when I say this.

"We have a chapel. You can only have a few minutes because I can't keep the guards away from their jobs for too long."

"I understand," I say, giving him a half-smile.

He directs two guards to escort me to the chapel and gives me ten minutes tops. I can sense he wants me to make it quick, but he's also been decent to me over these many months. I'm appreciative for the few minutes, especially as I've arrived without warning.

The guards escort me to the chapel, and I step inside. It's nothing like our beautiful church, but there are a few pews, and I kneel. The cross hangs above, and I close my eyes and pray. I pray for Rosa's soul—that she has made it to heaven. I close my eyes and pray for everyone who was hurt. I pray for the DeCarlo family. I can't help myself. They are all people, as tangled up in crime and messed up as they may be.

After several minutes, I make the sign of the cross, and turn to see the guards, who are trying to give me my privacy. I dab my eyes with my handkerchief.

Rosa's gone, and I've said my goodbyes. The guards walk me back to the warden's office, where I say my final farewell to him as well.

"Well, your newspaper has certainly helped us out," the warden says.

"Really?"

"Yes. We've received numerous donations from folks who have given money to help keep the prison up. One told me your stories led him to donate. He wants me to use the money to grow the library and plant a garden." He chuckles.

"Despite that she killed herself in here?" I ask him, honestly.

"Despite that. The stories you print seem to touch folks in certain ways. There are some rotten people in this world-I've seen many of them in here. And Manetti, she was a piece of work. But she wasn't the worst of the worst," he says.

Strangely, I find comfort in that.

*

"You went where?" Robert asks as I enter his office. It's more of a scolding, in fact. It's raining so hard outside that his office is particularly dark, and the lights are dim. It's only eleven o'clock in the morning by the time I arrive at The News.

"To the prison. I don't know why. I just wanted to be there. You know, to say goodbye."

"Well, that's that. No more going there. You've had enough prisons for one year."

"But you were the one who sent me there in the first place!" I say, incredulously. He did send me, and he knows it. He's contradicting himself.

"I know I did, but now we've made the mob mad by writing what we've written. I don't want you gallivanting around unnecessarily."

"But the DeCarlo family is behind bars."

"Yes, but we don't know about the fringe." He's leaning in as he says it.

"Okay, okay. No need to overreact. I won't go anymore. It's not like it's my favorite place, or anything."

Perry sees us chatting and pops his head in. "Morning all," he says.

"Morning," Robert says in return, stretching out in his chair and placing his feet on the desk. "Do you know where our girl has been this morning?" He's pointing to me as he says it.

"The prison?" Perry knows me.

"How did you know?"

"She told me she might go," Perry says, shuffling his feet. "How was it?"

"Well, the warden didn't expect me, but it was fine. I felt I needed to be there."

"She's got a big heart, my girl," Perry says, putting his arm around me. "She's got a heart of gold."

"And that's why you love her," Robert says, smiling.

"And that's why I love her."

I feel bashful, but I won't lie. My heart did go pitter-patter when he said it.

"Okay, okay, outta here, you two love birds," Robert says, shooing us out the door. "I've got work to do—and so do you!"

We can't help but laugh. His reaction to our display of affection is funny.

"Can I talk to you for a minute before you go back to your desk?" Perry asks, as we make our way toward my desk.

"Of course."

We walk over the corner of the room. Perry looks at me intently. "I'm pretty certain the Dodgers are going to move out of Brooklyn."

He'd mentioned it at the ballgame, and I had heard all the rumblings and read his stories, but it seems he knows something more than he's letting on. "'Dem Bums are gonna leave town, Veronica. I'm not sure what that means for me, and I've just asked you to marry me."

I look at him unsure what this means.

"Oh, do you want to take back the proposal?"

"No, no, you silly goose. Of course not. I just hope I have a job." There's worry visible on Perry's face. I place both my hands in his and look him in the eyes. "You will have a job, Perry. You're so talented. Of course, you'll have a job. Robert will just move things around is all."

"I just had to share to get your thoughts. Put in a good word for me, will you?"

"I don't need to," I say. "He already thinks the world of you."

Chapter 30

Christopher Masterson is a top lawyer in the city. Robert kindly arranged for me to meet him. He's slick and savvy. He's tall and a bit intimidating in his expensive suit and greased-back dark hair. His desk is meticulously organized with piles of papers strategically framing his blotter. Sitting across from him, I notice how chiseled his face is, the edges of his hair beginning to show signs of graying. In the thirty minutes I've been with him, he hasn't smiled once.

He reviews my contract line-by-line and makes notes about my circumstances and feelings of mistrust. He believes divorcing myself from Alice is an open and shut case. His fees are high, but I'm willing to pay them in order to have an efficient lawyer who will get the job done cleanly and swiftly.

I must break these ties with Alice. At the end of the assessment, Christopher Masterson calls my book publisher and speaks to him directly, letting him know that "the contract between Veronica DeMarco and Alice Hawthorne has been compromised and is null and void," and that his law firm will be representing me for the time being. He and the publisher speak about the particulars of new representation. By the end of the call, I'm assured that I can still publish my books under new guidance.

"Of course! Saves us money," the publisher had told Mr. Masterson. Now I have peace of mind.

Mr. Masterson then calls Alice Hawthorn's office while I am there and requests that the pages of my current manuscript be returned to me directly and swiftly, as under the nullification of the contract, my work is my property.

At the conclusion of our meeting, Mr. Masterson explains that he will draw up the final dissolution papers, and when I have completed the second book, at that point, I can do whatever I would like–hire a new agent or work directly for a publisher. The decision is mine. Agent or no agent, I vow that the next person I work with will be someone I can trust–someone I will fully vet beforehand.

"I appreciate everything you've done for me," I say. We both reach out to shake hands.

"I am happy to help. Robert's been a friend and client of mine for years. I am genuinely pleased to have been of service." Just then I see a wee little smile creep across his face.

*

Four days later, when I receive a brown package that is delivered to my apartment and is addressed to Ms. DeMarco, I open it. I assume the manuscript is mine, because Mr. Masterson called to tell me that Alice's people would be sending my pages back to me. Thankfully, the divorce from Alice is almost complete.

The tragedy of opening the package is that I do not find my work–my pages–inside the package. Instead, I see a note addressed to Essie that reads: *Here is your final manuscript for review, Essie. Let's meet soon, Alice.* The mistake of opening it is mine, but how could I have known it wasn't for me? Addressed only to "Ms. DeMarco," I genuinely thought it contained my returned manuscript. When I lift the note that's on top of the pages and see the title of my sister's work, I almost fall over. *A Family in Ruin: The*

Tale of Two Sisters - by Esther DeMarco.

My mouth drops. She's using her formal name. And the title is jarring.

Essie comes through the door from work and sees me holding the package.

"Is that for me?" she asks, her tone full of indignation and contempt.

"It is. I thought it was my returned manuscript, so I opened it. But it's meant for you." I hold it out for her to take.

She walks toward me and snatches it out of my hands. "You should never open my mail!"

"As I said, I thought the package was for me. My lawyer told me that my manuscript was on its way over, and I saw it was addressed to Ms. DeMarco—no first name. I assumed it was for me."

"Well, it's mine!" Her face has turned an unusual shade of red.

Mr. Masterson had relayed to me that Alice Hawthorne has a new secretary he's been dealing with and that Lila had resigned. Maybe that explains the lack communication and the omission of a first name on the package.

Essie attempts to huff past me, but I won't let her go by. Using my body, I block the hallway and the path to her room.

"Well, I did see the title of your work of art. Is it going to take me having to purchase your book to find out why on earth you have been so wicked to me over the last year? What exactly have I done to you to make you treat me with such disdain? I have been nothing but kind to you! And all the while, you've been secretly writing about our relationship in a book?"

"It's fiction, stupid," she barks back.

"Sure it is." I'm trying to remain civil. She never wanted me to read it. Wrote it in the silence of her room. Handwritten page after handwritten page. The truth is, I'm using every ounce of restraint not to strike her.

"You are to stay far, far away from my writing career," she

snarls, pointing her finger in my face. She looks unfamiliar. I hardly recognize her.

"Gladly," I say. "And while we're at it, I'll stay far, far away from you, too. I'm done being treated in this manner, Essie. I'm leaving. I didn't tell you yet, but now seems as good a time as ever. Perry and I are engaged. We're going to be married. I'll pay the rent until the lease runs out in January, but after that, you are on your own. I'm done paying your way just to be mistreated by you. I'm not sure what's happened to you, but you've become such an unkind and angry person. Has Malcolm had the pleasure of engaging with your new demeanor?" I can't help but to be smug. She's earned it.

She moves toward me and puts her forefinger in my face. "You will NOT speak to Malcolm!" I hit a hot button.

"Oh, don't worry. I won't. I don't need to. He'll find out all on his own," I say, as I move away from her. In a complete rage, she picks up our mother's favorite vase from the end table and throws it at my head. Luckily, I duck in time and it crashes into the fireplace. I freeze, both afraid and in utter shock. She is shaking with fury. She's gone completely mad.

Neither of us had heard the sound of the front door opening during our fight, and then we turn and see him. Malcolm is standing in the foyer holding Essie's umbrella that she must have left in the cab. He's looking at the two of us in disbelief. His face is pale. He stares at Essie, speechless. Perhaps he got a glimpse into what I've been dealing with for months.

"She's all yours, Malcolm," I say, as I make my way toward him and the door.

I turn to Essie. "I'll arrange to have my things moved out. Don't touch any of it." Then, to Malcolm, I say, "Please don't let her touch any of my things."

Before I walk out the door, I share one final thought with Essie: "I have spent thousands and thousands of dollars catering to you all these years. It pains me to see you in this light. I honestly have nothing left to say to you." I take the umbrella from Malcolm's hand, stepping past him, and opening the door to the rainy, August air. "I will have Perry fetch my manuscript when it arrives," I say to Malcolm.

The rain is coming down fast and furiously. I pray it will wash away our sins.

*

I put the coin in the payphone on the street and cross my fingers that Perry will pick up the phone. I can't remember if he has a game to cover tonight, my mind is so garbled. I don't know where to go. The phone rings and rings and rings. No answer. I put another coin in the slot and dial The News. I ask for him. I wait. He's at the game, they tell me, covering the Dodgers.

It takes me a minute to realize what I've done. I've just walked out on my sister, the only relative that I feel close to, at least for a time. I could call my father, but what would that do? He's going to find out about this at some point, if he doesn't know already. Essie will call him immediately, like she always does. He tends to side with her on all matters and did the same when we were younger.

I begin to walk toward The News, my sanctuary, the place that makes me feel normal. I love the place because I can always be myself here. No one judges you. There's no time for bickering and childish behavior. We work. We respect each other. I realize I'm in need of comfort. I miss my mother. I miss Rosa. I miss the old Alice, the old Essie—four women who were in my life and now are not.

I can feel the tears coming, but I'm batting them back as I walk.

When I arrive at The News, I realize it's after five o'clock. Of course, editors and reporters are still working, but I wonder if I've missed Robert. He knows so much about my family, and as he continually reminds us, says it is his pleasure to help us as needed. He worries about us, I know. Maybe I should have asked him to interfere on our behalf.

He's in his office, smoking a cigarette, still here. Still working.

My hands are shaking. I've never had to ask anyone for help; I've always been self-sufficient. Working vigorously since the age of 18, I've had to make it on my own. Daddy was a bit of a help in the beginning, but I've carried Essie and me for years.

I've never been so angry.

I've never felt so alone.

Robert sees me through his glass office window, smiles, and waves. He motions me to come over to him, and I do, taking a deep breath, feeling ready to tell someone the story.

"You're soaked. What's happened, kiddo?" he asks. "What brings you back here?"

"Do you really want to know?"

"Yes, I really want to know. Sit down." Robert pulls out a chair for me. He looks concerned.

"Essie and I had a knock-down, drag-out fight, and I left, telling her I'm moving out," I start to say. Robert leans in as I relay what happened, what was said, and how Malcolm heard the end of the argument and witnessed Essie's temper tantrum.

He listens intently as I fill him in on the details, especially when I tell him that she threw a vase at my head. That I'm lucky I have good reflexes. He seems horrified by this and is genuinely worried for me.

"She threw a vase at your head?" I nod. "I don't like the sound of this. I don't like the idea of that manuscript and the fiction she's spinning, and possibly to your detriment!"

"I know. She has hurt me on every possible level."

We both take a minute to pause and take it all in. Robert offers me a glass of Scotch from his cabinet, and I take it. He pours himself one, too. "Can I have a cigarette?" I ask.

He doesn't argue with me, pulls one out of the pack, and lights my cigarette. I'm clearly having a breakdown—drinking scotch, smoking a cigarette, and realizing all too quickly that I'm homeless. I have to ask him now.

"Where will I stay tonight? I don't have a home."

"With Perry. He's going to be your husband—he is here to support you. That's what marriage is about. Sharing the good times and the bad. He will want to know what's happened. I would want to know what's happened if it were Connie."

"Or my mother," I say. I can see the comment stings, but I don't care. I had to say it.

His glance pierces me. Clearly, he doesn't like when I bring up her name. We both remain quiet as we listen to the sound of typewriters—several reporters outside his office are typing their stories.

Robert gets up from his chair, walks toward the door, and closes it. He turns to face me.

"I suppose this is the day I'm going to break my promise, the one I made to your mother—and to your father. The one I've wanted to break time and time again but had to honor as your mother made me swear to her on her deathbed that I would never tell anyone. But I know Essie knows."

I can hear the conflict in his choice of words, in what he is saying. "What does Essie know?" I ask.

Robert takes another big swig of his Scotch and sits down in his chair, facing me. He leans over his legs and places his forearms on his thighs.

"Essie is adopted. Your father is not her biological father. And you are not his daughter."

"I am adopted, too?"

"No," he says, pausing and taking a breath. "I'm your father." He looks up to the ceiling and then says, "God forgive me."

"You are my father." I say it matter-of-factly. I'm surprised, but not surprised. The inscription in the book definitely made me wonder how far my mother and Robert's relationship had gone.

"Yes."

Now, I'm panicking. "And was my mother my mother?"

"Yes."

"So, you did love my mother?" The questions are flying out of my mouth.

"More than anything in this world, besides you, of course."

"But how could you do this? To me? To Essie? Who are Essie's parents?"

"I don't know who her biological parents are. Your mother and father, when they first married, could not have children. They struggled for a while, so they adopted Essie. Your parents had marital troubles after that—real troubles—and almost split up when Essie was small. During that time, your mother and I, well—let's just say, I loved her since we were kids." There it is. Finally, the confession.

"And she loved you. The book. Her 'Darcy.'" I'm stating these facts as if I'm filling in the blanks, but I still can't help but feel foolish. Who I am is a big lie.

"She did, but she had some infatuation with your father and felt a sense of duty—for Essie's sake. He treated her badly, and yet she kept going back. I couldn't understand it. Why do some women like to be treated badly? And then you came along, and they stayed together. I would have taken care of all of you. I told her to leave him if she was unhappy. I would have married her, raised you both."

"Does he know I'm not his biological daughter?"

"He does."

"Then why did they both pretend?"

"Because of the money."

"What money?" Why does everything always come down to money? It ruins lives.

"The money your mother had from her parents. Your

grandparents were very wealthy. That's why your dad's never really worked all that hard. He lived off the money that was your mother's, that she inherited. Then, when she died, it all went to him. He didn't want to give it up, so he made the choice to live with the things he knew weren't true. It really was all for the money."

Listening to Robert explain the details makes it seem as if it's happening to someone else, as if I'm watching someone else's life unfold, not my own. I feel akin to Mr. Dobson–Lawrence Dobson–the man I interviewed about finding a twin brother and the truth about his famous parents. Mine aren't famous, but I feel the same way he did. Everything is spinning. Everyone has lied. Lawrence Dobson was angry about the deception. So am I.

"That explains why he wanted Essie and me to go out on our own and helped us only a little. So, the rest of the money is his?" My head hurts.

"He gave you some of the inheritance to get you two started in Greenwich Village. But, yes. That's how he affords the house and lifestyle in New England."

"And you think Essie knows this?"

"I know she knows. I just never dreamed she'd tell the family story in a book."

"How do you know she knows?" I realize I'm firing questions at him, but I need answers. I'm owed answers.

"She found something that belonged to your mother and pieced it all together. I'm not sure what it was, but it was something. She tried to blackmail me. She told me that if I ever told you about the history, the situation, she would make sure everyone knew what happened. She said she would air our dirty laundry that she was adopted–that I am your father. She wanted to ruin my career. And she didn't care how it affected Connie. I do love Connie, and I don't want her to get hurt in all of this."

"When was this?" I'm shocked by the depth of Essie's manipulation.

"Six months ago."

"So Connie doesn't know?"

"No."

"Will you tell her?"

"I will now. I should have told her years ago. But a promise is a promise."

"Let's hope she's understanding after all this time." Poor Connie. I hope she has the fortitude to hear the news. It happened long before Robert came into her life, but still.

"You've known what a horrible person Essie is for this long and you let me continue to live with her? Endure her nastiness and loathing? I can't believe it! I can't believe what my life has become in a matter of hours." Exasperated, I begin to feel like I can't breathe. "You're my dad. And you never told me." I'm shaking my head and raising my voice.

Then, I begin to sob. I'm struggling for air. Robert closes the blinds to his windows so the few people who are in the newsroom can't see what's happening. I'm inconsolable.

My mother. My supposed dad. Robert–my biological father. Essie. All of them knee deep in secrets.

Trying to catch my breath, I begin to hyperventilate. Robert gives me a paper bag.

"Breathe into this. In and out, in and out–" he says. I'm trying with all my might not to pass out. I'm breathing the best that I can. I've been kept in the dark, on purpose, by everyone.

As I begin to come out of it, Robert has me sit in the chair with my head between my knees. He dials the phone. I hear him speaking. It's Perry. He's coming to get me.

My gut instinct is to run and hide. I want to get far away from all of these imposters–these people I thought were my family. Rosa's face pops into my head. More than ever before, I can understand how she felt about her own sister. Twisted and toxic family dynamics.

Robert keeps trying to talk to me, tries to apologize. I won't look at him. I can't look at him. I don't want to hear anything he says.

A little while later, Perry appears in the doorway out of breath.

"What's going on?" he says, looking from me to Robert, confused and concerned.

There's a long pause. Neither of us answers. I rise from the chair, a little unbalanced, take a few steps toward Perry, loop my arm through his, and say, "I will tell you all about it, Perry, but right now, all I want is to get the hell out of here."

Perry puts his arm around me. He can feel me shaking and gives me a squeeze, leading me out of the office.

I refuse to look back.

Chapter 31

Two days later, and I'm on Perry's couch in the apartment, still wearing my pajamas. I haven't left his house. I've stayed in the same clothes and slept in a couple of Perry's shirts. He offered to go to my apartment and collect my things. I only wanted him to get one thing: my manuscript. He did go and retrieve it. But as he's the kindest sort, he also packed a suitcase full of my clothes and unmentionables in a bag before he left. How brave of him not to be intimidated by Essie.

Robert has called Perry's apartment seven times wanting to talk to me since I learned the truth. At every attempt, I have refused to speak with him. When I think about it from an outsider's perspective, I can understand the clandestine nature of Robert and my mother's relationship. However, I'm not sure as to what I owe the pleasure of Essie's horrible treatment of me. I never did anything to her. I didn't create the circumstances. I like to think that in all the years we've spent together minus the last, I've been a help to her. A true sister, a friend. We were raised as sisters, but in her twisted mind, blood is thicker than water, and in reality, we don't share the same blood. Maybe she resents me for not being blood relations, our mother, and our circumstances. Maybe she knows more than I know. I don't care anymore. My brain actually hurts from thinking about all of it.

Perry is leaning on the counter staring at me, legs crossed, sipping his coffee. I can tell he wants to have that conversation with me—again. He's so supportive and gentle. He wants to talk this through, wants to be a pillar of strength for me. I appreciate it, I do. But when you hit rock bottom, it's tough to climb back up. I'm having trouble focusing on anything. On everything.

"I think we need to get you dressed, take a cab to your place, get the rest of your things, and get to work. You still have a job. You haven't been fired. And I have a job. I haven't been fired," he says, as gingerly as possible.

"How can I? My boss is my father."

"Yes, but no one knows that. We are the only ones who know."

"Yet," I say. "Until Essie's book comes out, which will probably air all our dirty laundry—things that she's known but never shared with me. When I think of how I've been the one propping her up, helping her, supporting her! I feel so incredibly used."

"And you have every right to feel that way. But guess what? You don't have to live with her anymore. You and I are going to start a new life. We are going to marry—heck, I'd go down to the courthouse and marry you right now! I love you. I want to be with you, and I want your life to be better than it has been these past months."

"Perry, ever since you've known me, I've been dealing with my sister's antics."

"I know. You must be exhausted. And that's why we're going to navigate these circumstances together." He smiles at me, that wonderful, warm Perry smile that makes the world seem right. In all of this mess, he's been the one who's kept me grounded and sane. "So, what do you say? Let me go with you to your apartment and help you pack a suitcase of the things you need. I know what I've already packed for you isn't enough."

It's the right thing to do, I know. I'm dreading it, but it

must be done. Essie has no idea that I know the truth, and I'm not going to let her know I know. I'm going to walk into MY apartment, the one I pay for, and gather my things. I'm going to leave. I'm going to tell her that when the lease is up, I'm taking my name off it. She can take over the payment if she can afford it. I won't resign it.

The hurt still swishes inside my stomach. There's nothing she can do or say to make me feel better.

*

I tell Perry I will go to the apartment ahead of him to get started. Essie shouldn't be home–it's a workday for her. Besides, Perry has some calls to make; he'll take a separate cab to our apartment.

The taxi driver pulls up in front of our apartment. I feel as if I've been gone for months. It's only been seventy-two hours. Yet, the place feels completely changed and unfamiliar now. Perhaps that's why they say sometimes you can't go back. It's too hard. Everything is altered.

I put the key in the door, turn the handle. I'm miffed to see the apartment untidy and completely out of sorts. Remnants of the shattered vase are still on the floor. Dirty dishes are on the coffee table. I look at the fireplace and see Mickey Mantle's ball is still there. I walk over, grab it, and slip it into my pocket. No one is going to keep this special keepsake from me–or throw it at my head.

Just then, I hear a door open and Essie appears in the hallway. She is disheveled, her hair a mess, her eyes stained with tears. She looks older, sadder, and distraught. I tell myself not to feel sorry for her, mentally reminding myself of all she has done.

"Why are you here?" she asks, limping toward me.

"To get my things. Why are you here and not at work?"

"I don't feel well."

She is stating the obvious. She looks awful. The old me

would make her homemade chicken soup and brew her hot tea. The old me would cater to her every need. The new me is disgusted just looking at her. I still can't get over all the things she's kept from me, that she blackmailed Robert, and the way she deceived me with Alice. There's nothing left here. It's all been ruined.

"Sorry to hear," I manage to say, and I walk past her and to my room, closing the door behind me. It seems gloomier than usual, the dark green floral wallpaper adding to the melancholy. I open the blinds to let the morning light in. I'm not going to engage with her. I didn't expect to find her in this state—whatever state this is—I'm not sure. But I have come to accomplish a task—to get myself organized. To get out.

I pull a suitcase from underneath the bed, place it on top, and open it. I sift through drawers and pack things I might need, realizing I can't take it all with me right now. Perry said he would carry my typewriter for me when he gets here, which I appreciate. His place is small; it's going to be crowded with the two of us there every day. We agreed to look for a new place that will hold both of us sufficiently, maybe even a location closer to The News.

Not expecting an apology from Essie, part of me wonders if she's even capable of understanding just what she's done—the magnitude of it all. I've thought about this a lot over the last couple of days. Even if we did learn the truth about our upbringing, our parents, and her adoption, we could have remained a family. We could have figured it out together. But she's severed all of that now. She's a million miles away from me, and I'm not sure she has any interest in repairing anything. I remember an old friend of mine from high school saying something profound about friendships one day in study hall. She said, "Why are we afraid to break up with friends? We break up with boyfriends when they do not suit us. The same should be true with friends, right?" The same could be applied to supposed sisters, as well.

The photo on my dresser is one of the three of us—my mother, Essie, and me. I pick it up gingerly and look at it. I glance at myself in the mirror. How could I never have seen it before?

As I've aged, I look more and more like my mother. Dark hair, dark eyes, olive skin. Essie looks nothing like either of us. My mother would always say Essie looks like our father's side of the family, especially our Aunt Marina, a woman from Northern Italy, whom none of us had ever met. I wonder now if an Aunt Marina even existed, or was she just a made up character to fill in the blanks for our dysfunctional family. At this point, I find myself second-guessing everything that ever came out of my mother's mouth. Out of Robert's mouth. Out of my father's mouth.

I put the photo back on the dresser and continue packing. I hear the television, but she obviously won't even try to speak to me after our knock-down, drag-out fight. She threw a vase at my head. She broke our mother's favorite vase, not that I care a lick about it at this moment.

Leaning all my body weight onto the suitcase, I barely get it to close. I walk toward the door and take a look around my room.

At the last second, I walk toward the dresser and grab the photo, stuffing it inside my purse.

Perry should be here any minute. I hope he arrives quickly; I don't want to have a conversation with Essie again. I check my watch and hope he's nearly here.

The suitcase is heavy. I carry it into the living area and place it next to the front door in the foyer. I see Essie look at me out of the corner of her eye. In that moment—a moment where I should hate her, despise her for the ways in which she has mistreated me for nearly a year—I'm unable to hate her. I pity her. I'm sad for her. She sees me looking at her, and like a child, she turns her back to me.

It isn't the first time.

Perry raps on the door, and I open it for him. "This way," I say, nodding toward the bedroom. Essie's back remains to us, and she won't speak to him, won't look our way. We walk down the hall and away from her.

I flick the light on in my room and point to the typewriter on my small desk. He picks it up as if it weighs nothing. "Don't say anything to her. She's so rotten," I utter in a whisper.

"Okay," he says. "Whatever you want."

He exits my bedroom, and I close the door behind me. Then we walk past her and out the front door without another word being said.

Chapter 32

The next morning, I'm back at my desk at The News. Robert and I have not spoken. In fact, I'm not sure what I'm supposed to be working on now that Rosa's gone. I'd been given a lead about a story—a new restaurant in The Village owned by a wealthy woman who wants to recreate recipes from her family's Greek heritage—but for some reason, I'm just not that excited by it. I realize I miss hearing Rosa's stories—and relaying those stories to readers.

Eddie Crawford, the features editor, stops by my desk, his suspenders a little lopsided, his curly hair slightly messy. It's part of his character, I'm convinced. He always looks a bit disheveled.

"Hey, Veronica, you working on that restaurant piece?"

"Well, I've barely started, to be honest."

"Good. I'll give that story to Gabe and I'm gonna give you your choice of features, but it's gotta be done by Friday. Choice number one: That beatnik writer Jack Kerouac is on a book tour, promoting his new work called *On the Road*, which is getting good reviews, or choice number two: It looks like Ted Williams is gonna be the MVP of the season, but Mickey Mantle is the most valuable player, especially here in New York. As the season is almost over, we'd like to run a feature on Mantle. Since you did wonders with Manetti, wanna cover Mickey?"

"Is this a trick question?" I ask. "Are you serious, Eddie?"

"As serious as a heart attack. We can set up a conversation with either of them, I'm sure. We'll pull strings and get it done."

He must have seen my face light up. I've heard about Kerouac, but Mantle? There's no contest.

"I'll take Mickey."

"Thought you would," he says.

*

"Wow! That's incredible, Veronica!" Perry says to me, as we pack up to leave The News that night. "I'm kind of envious, to be honest."

"Well, you get to chat with players and write about them every day."

"Not Mickey Mantle, though."

"Eddie got it set up for tomorrow. I'm going to interview him at Yankee Stadium. They said I'll have thirty minutes with him. I can't believe it. Should I bring along my signed baseball you gave me?" I'm still in disbelief. It's a wonderful distraction from all that is going on in my private life.

"Not sure I'd do that. Remember, you have to act as a reporter, not a rabid fan." He's smiling as he says it, egging me on a little.

"Right. I have to remember that. I'll probably get tongue-tied. Will you help me with questions for him?"

"Of course. Anything for you, darling." He kisses me on the forehead. "But no swooning over Mickey, you hear me?"

"I hear you," I say, laughing. "I only swoon over you, as you are well aware. He's a great ballplayer, but you've got all the charm, mister."

I reach for his hand and gently lean into him as we exit the building. When I look to my right, I see him.

"Malcolm?"

"Hello, Veronica. Hello, Perry. I'm sorry to come to your place of work, but—"

"How long have you been waiting here?" I ask.

"Only about thirty minutes. I was going to come in, but I wanted to get my thoughts in order."

"Of course," I say. He looks upset and worried. I gesture for him to come and sit at one of the small round tables The News has set up on the sidewalk in front of the building. I occasionally take my lunch out here.

We sit, and Malcolm begins to fidget. Perry and I both notice it, and glance at each other. This prompts Perry to ask Malcolm if he'd like to have a private conversation with me, alone. Malcolm answers, saying that he would prefer it, that it's hard enough to say what he's about to say already. Always a gentleman, Perry says he completely understands, rises from his chair, and gives my hand a squeeze, saying he will wait for me at his desk while I speak with Malcolm. My heart begins to beat a little faster, feeling the weight of Malcolm's own anxiety about the forthcoming conversation.

When Perry disappears into the building, I start the conversation.

"So, feel free to share what you want to share, Malcolm?" He takes a breath, then begins.

"It's your sister. I'm not sure what's going on with her."

"That makes two of us," I say, leaning back and folding my arms across my chest. Malcolm had witnessed the ugly scene that night, unbeknownst to either Essie or me, and saw Essie throw the vase at my head. I can't even begin to imagine the conversation that happened between them after I left.

"She won't tell me what's happened. She won't communicate, and so I'm asking you."

I picture what she looked like yesterday and remember all too well how out of sorts she was. I feel backed into a corner; on one hand I want to tell Malcolm how awful she's been to me, but I also think he loves her. I have to be careful with my words. This

I know.

"She and I had a very big disagreement, as you saw. Just as she is keeping things from you, she has kept things from me for quite a while. Things that I am just now finding out about."

"Can you share what those things are?" he asks, innocently enough. Because the newspaper business has made me leery and savvy simultaneously, I'm reluctant to share. This is the impact of being a member of the press. You're on high alert and don't want information ever to be held against you. You guard your mouth and are careful when you speak. Also, as much as she has hurt me and gone behind my back, I refuse to do the same. I have no interest in interfering in any way in their relationship. Essie needs to answer these questions, not me.

"I wish I could, Malcolm. As you know, I think you are a wonderful person, and you've always been kind to me and my sister and Perry, but I'm afraid she has to tell you. The things I found out were from another source, and I'm not at liberty to share. I'm so sorry."

"I understand and respect that," he says. "I just can't seem to get to the heart of it."

"I understand that, as well. Hearts have been broken. Mine's been shattered into a thousand pieces, and I'm not sure how or if that will ever change."

"I was going to propose, you know, but I'm not so sure now," he says, reaching into his pocket. "I have a ring."

He places the box from Tiffany's in front of me and opens it. I see an exquisite diamond in a beautiful setting, twice the size of mine, not that I care. She would have loved comparing the extravagance of her ring to the quaintness of my own. I wonder if she will ever see it. What a shame if not. She would have been a very happy and fortunate woman. Malcolm comes from money and could provide well for her. She would have been set for life.

"It's just stunning. Truly." I mean it. The ring is a work of art; it's incredibly regal looking. Something a princess would wear.

I hand it back over to him.

"But how can one enter into a marriage when one of the parties won't speak or explain anything to the other party? I was hoping to glean something from you in my desperate state to understand. But I'm not sure I can be with a woman who keeps secrets and cannot share her world with me. I'm totally in the dark here, unable to get clarification or understand her."

"I feel the same way," I say.

His face is full of frustration, and I ache for him. He looks miserable. But in the long run, would he be more miserable with her? Who is to say?

"Let me see if I can fill in a few of the blanks. I can tell you the thing that is true and happened the other night, the thing that prompted me to move out. She and my agent went behind my back. Essie has written a book, one that she never told me about. I'm guessing it's based on our family history. I saw the title, though she claims it's fiction. But Essie and Alice conspired against me, keeping me from knowing the truth about their collaboration, about Essie being a new author. To think I live with Essie night and day; yet, I came to find out she wrote the pages by hand so I would not hear the clicking of typewriter keys. There had to be a reason for that. There is more, Malcolm, but that is all I can share right now. I wish I could shed more light, but I can't. Others are involved, and it's not my place to share such stories. Does that help at all?"

"She went behind your back and is publishing a book?"

"Yes, despite that I've always been up front with her and have shared all my writing topics and projects with her, she didn't feel the need to do the same. And my agent didn't feel the need to share anything with me, which is why I had to leave her agency. It's still so hurtful."

"I would have done the same," he says. "Who can blame you?"

"She also was horrible to me when Rosa Manetti died. I know she was a criminal and all that, but she and I formed a unique bond when I was interviewing and visiting her in prison as I wrote the articles for the newspaper. Essie was rude to me when I learned of her passing and said, 'Well, I guess that's the end of your Rosa Manetti stories.' She said it right after I got the call when I was in a state of despair. I couldn't believe it. I'll stop there."

Malcolm takes the small ring box from the table and puts it back in his pocket. "Since she won't apologize for her behavior, I'll apologize for her. What she said to you is unconscionable. I'm sorry she said it."

"Me, too," I say. "And please don't apologize on her behalf. That's her responsibility."

We sit listening to the New York streets as we reflect on our situations. The weight of Essie's aloofness and coldness always gets the better of me. Now, as this sweet man tries to make amends for her, I once again feel sad for the loss of our relationship. I haven't bad mouthed her, I tell myself. I have only relayed the truth as to what has transpired.

Malcolm moves toward me and pats my hand. "This is an unfortunate situation, indeed," he says. "I don't want to upset you any further, Veronica. Thank you for sharing what you have shared. The rest is up to Essie. I appreciate your time."

He gets up, shaking his head in disbelief, and turns to walk away. I wonder if I will ever see him again.

Chapter 33

I'm sitting in a room in the bowels of Yankee Stadium, underneath the stands. Even from here, you can smell the field, the dirt, the sweat. I'm in awe of all the history inside this place. Mickey Mantle is due to arrive, and the representative who works for the Yankees brought me here to this holding room to conduct the interview. The newspaper didn't send a photographer for two reasons: first, because Eddie said he'll use the good stock photos the newspaper has on file of Mantle, and second, because Eddie wanted me to have the full time with Mantle for the interview without the distraction of having photographs taken. I turn to the page in my notebook with all the questions Perry and I constructed, hoping Mickey will give me a solid interview. There's nothing worse than someone who isn't talkative. The room is stark, the ghosts of Yankee Stadium at bay.

I peruse the questions one by one, silently reviewing them in my head. There are so many things I'd like to ask him. I can feel my heart pounding inside my chest. I take a deep breath and remind myself that I am more than capable of writing this piece. I'm thankful Eddie offered it to me. I wonder if Robert put him up to it.

When the door opens, Mickey Mantle is ushered inside.

His handler reiterates that we have thirty minutes for the interview. Mickey sits down in the chair across from me. He's in slacks and a blazer, not in his uniform. He smells of cologne and looks like he's ready for a day at the office rather than a day on the field.

I'm slightly nervous, but surprisingly not any more so than I was when interviewing Rosa Manetti. She was formidable. I'm expecting the same demeanor of the Mickey I bumped into at the banquet: kind with boyish charm. I'm relieved when I find out that he does not disappoint. He is all of that and more.

During the interview, I try to focus on every word he says and to not get distracted by the fact that I'm interviewing one of the Yankee greats. Surprisingly, he knew I was the reporter who covered the Manetti stories. Said he'd read every word of every article. He's amenable, funny, and charming, and before the interview ends, I make sure to tell him about my treasured Mantle baseball that Perry gave me that brought us together. He enjoyed hearing that story.

When the Yankees representative comes to take him away, I thank him profusely. He thanks me in return and asks me to make him look as good as I made Rosa Manetti look in the *Rosa's Revenge* series. I laugh, and he vanishes down the long, dark hallway underneath Yankee Stadium. I sit there in silent contemplation long after he is gone, making notes about the things he said, and secretly hoping I will not only make him proud with the article, but also Perry, too.

*

On the way back to The News, I can't help but to smile in the taxi, despite the last couple of weeks I've had personally. The grueling business of being a reporter definitely has some perks, especially when you get to cover stories about people like Mickey Mantle, Rosa Manetti, and even sweet Mr. Dobson. The truth of the matter is that you learn a little something from everyone you interview. Too often, we shy away from the life lessons we can glean from others. That's the hard truth about my business: as writers, we take away so much more than we give. Our job is to share that knowledge with others in the most ethical and clear way as possible.

It's not going to be too difficult to write a story about Mickey Mantle. He's having an incredible season. His optimism is high. His team is strong. And his outlook is inspiring. The article, which will be chock full of memorable quotes from Mantle, will take me no time to write, and I already know my angle: *Oklahoma charmer inspires fans with his dazzling baseball talent.* He'll look good in the press without having to try too hard. They already love him so much here in New York.

Looking back, I suppose I did the same thing with Rosa's stories. Her brutal honestly during our conversations moved me to write features that made Rosa seem less scary, because she became less scary to me. Readers saw her as a real person and as someone who got forced to do things that she didn't want to do in the first place. There's no denying she was tough, and she did things she later regretted, but her circumstances led her down that troubled path. Her father was no help, and her mother even less helpful. I have a quick flashback and remember walking into that holding room at the prison for the first time and being intimidated by her. Her cold stare and her unkempt hair caught me off guard. Then, by the end of the series, and even when I was done writing the articles, we were eating cake together. I miss those conversations.

I thank the taxi driver, pay him, and walk into the newsroom to get to work on the story. There are so many ideas running through my head as to how I want to start the piece. I want to tackle writing it now, while everything's fresh in my mind. There's an inordinate amount of pressure to get this story right—there will be a lot of eyes on it.

Eddie waves to me from across the room as I arrive back at my desk and comes running over.

"How'd it go?" he asks. His eyes are wide with curiosity.

"It was fantastic. Thanks, Eddie, for giving me this one. I loved interviewing Mantle. It was really special. Did you know that a Mickey Mantle baseball is what brought Perry and me together?" There has to be some bright spot to all the darkness that's invaded my life recently.

"I may have heard a whisper of it," he says.

"It's all true," I say.

Eddie smiles and gives me a wink. "When do you think you'll have it done, kid?"

"Whenever you need it," I tell him.

*

"So, how'd you do?" Perry asks, seeking answers as quickly as possible. It's suppertime, and he looks cute with an apron tied around his waist.

He pours me a glass of wine. The kitchen smells of rosemary and thyme.

"I think I did well. I like the guy." I toss my briefcase onto the chair and kiss Perry on the cheek.

"Who doesn't? He's an American icon, even if you don't like the Yankees," Perry says. He's right. I realize how blessed I am at the moment for the assignment, for the opportunity to share a story about Mickey Mantle, and to be up close and personal with him.

"Was he a cool cat?" Perry asks.

"Cool and oozing with Oklahoma charm." I smile, teasing Perry a little.

"You didn't fall in love with him, though?" Perry asks, chiding me.

"I think one extraordinary love in my life is enough for me," I respond, lifting the lid to take a peek at what's inside the pot. "And I appreciate all the help preparing for my interview with

Mickey. I sounded like a baseball aficionado. He told me to count my blessings."

"Am I such a blessing?" He's smiling from ear to ear.

"You are."

"And you are my blessing. I also love that you love the game as I do–it makes me love you even more," he says.

It's a sweet thing to say. When I think about the circumstances that brought us together–our affinity for the Yankees and Mickey Mantle, the signed Mantle ball, and working at The News–we are pretty fortunate. While the rest of my personal and family life crumbles, Perry is my constant.

He strengthens my faith in people.

Chapter 34

In an excerpt from an article written by Perry Spada in The News today, September 25, 1957, Brooklyn Dodgers owner Walter O'Malley insists that the team is not moving to Los Angeles.

"Speculation grows regarding the Brooklyn Dodgers potential move to Los Angeles. Despite the vote of approval to allow the team to leave New York back in May, owner Walter O'Malley has continually insisted that the franchise will not relocate. Amid the rumors and growing resentments, only 6,702 fans showed up at last night's game. Fans shouted 'Dem Bums' to the team's players. Ownership is being deemed traitorous by its bitter fans, and the team's final game may have been played at Ebbets Field. The manager, players, coaches, and staff wait to see if there will be an announcement made about the team's future."

I place the newspaper down on my desk at work. What does this mean for Perry? What does this means for Perry and me? If the Dodgers move, will he be reassigned here at The News? Will Robert take care of him? Will he still have a position? As his sole job is to cover the Brooklyn Dodgers, what will he cover if the team heads west?

We've talked about this on and off for months, but now it seems to be a reality. I ring Perry's desk.

"Sports desk," Daniel says, answering the call.

"Hi Daniel. Is Perry there?" I ask.

"Nope. He had a meeting off site. Can I help with anything?"

"No. Thanks, though," I say.

I glance over at Robert's smoke-filled office. He's deep in conversation with the entertainment editor, probably discussing the success of Joanne Woodward's new movie about mental illness. It's been the talk of the film scene. Robert and I have not spoken since I learned the truth about him and my family. I keep showing up to do my job and keep getting paid, despite the unnerving silence between us.

My desk is a mess with scribbled notes and copies of articles about Mickey Mantle. The completed piece is due by five o'clock today. Writing about Mantle keeps me from thinking about all the other complications in my life.

Three hours later, as I'm putting the finishing touches on my story, Perry comes waltzing over to my desk. He's whistling. He appears jovial, and he plunks himself down in the chair next to my beat-up wooden desk.

"I've just been offered a job," he says, whispering it to me over the hum of the newsroom.

"What?"

"I've just been offered a job." He is so proud of himself. If he were a peacock, his feathers would be spread wide open.

"Well, do tell," I say, intrigued by his beaming smile.

"I've just been offered a position to cover the Dodgers for the Los Angeles News. An announcement is coming in a few days from the league that will make the move from Brooklyn to Los Angeles official. The paper wants me to cover the team, since I've been the beat writer for years. How does a fresh start in California sound?"

"This is real? Not a joke?" I ask again. I'm taken aback. California might as well be another planet. It feels far and away from everything I know.

"Yes, that's right, darling. A fresh start for the two of us in California." He's grinning from ear to ear.

"And you want to take the job?" It's shocking to me that he would leave his family behind.

"Don't you want me to?" he asks, confused to hear my response.

"Well, I don't know. We'd have to talk about it. I mean, I have a job here. A life I've built."

He squints his eyes and tilts his head, confused by my comment. "This wasn't the response I imagined."

"I'm sorry," I say. "What did you imagine?"

"I thought you'd be happy to leave all this behind—Essie, Robert, memories of your mother, even Rosa Manetti. I thought you'd say, 'Good for us. It's just the break we need to begin a life together!'"

I don't know why I don't say any of these things, but the words aren't coming from my mouth. I've never lived anywhere else, and I always imagined being here, continuing with my career, continuing writing, finding a new literary agent, and living in New York City with Perry. I didn't expect I'd have to consider a relocation to the West Coast. Even if he did lose his job here at The News for whatever reason, I thought he'd find another one here.

"Wouldn't you miss your family?" It's an honest question anyone would ask.

"Of course, I would. But we can visit." He is being serious. He is considering this offer.

Nevertheless, I'm unable to muster up excitement. "Not all that often. California is all the way across the country!"

"You're in shock, I know. But it will be fine. Would it be hard to leave New York City, a place both of us know and love? Sure. But just think what's ahead for us."

"Well, for you, maybe—and I'm happy for you. But I don't have a job in California. My jobs are here."

"I'm pretty certain with your talent and savviness, you'll

get one out there."

I look down at my lap. Everything I've ever known is eroding little by little. And the idea of relocating is coming at a time when I don't have a handle on anything. Everything feels as if it's spiraling out of control. I just want to feel grounded by something.

He stands and looks down at me as I remain in my chair. "What is this really about?"

I look up at him. "I don't know, security, I suppose."

"I'm your security," he says.

"And I'm yours," I say in response. Our tone with each other has changed.

"I know. That's why I'm asking you to come to California!"

"You're asking me to uproot my life."

"Maybe I am, but your life is in a bit of chaos at the moment. Again, this would be a chance to start fresh. I understand it may be hard at first–"

"Do you?" I don't think he understands. Even though my life is in shambles, New York City is my one constant. I realize at this moment I may not be strong enough to cut that cord, too. Once a Jersey girl, I have become a true New Yorker.

"Yes," he says. He stands and places his hands on his hips, then runs his hand through his hair.

"Honestly, I don't think you're understanding that through everything, this newsroom has always given me a sense of stability. I always know who I am here. I have a sense of myself and a sense of purpose."

"A sense of yourself? I thought one of the points of life is to share yourself and your life with someone who loves you unconditionally, and vice versa. Isn't that what gives life meaning?""

"Of course. I love you, but–"

"Never say 'but' after you tell someone you love them," he says. He folds his arms across his chest.

He's right. I know he's right about that. What's happening? I can't seem to get a grip on this. He looks at me waiting for a response.

I have none to give.

My silence irritates him, and in utter frustration, he throws his hands up in the air and walks away from me.

Our first fight.

In my stupor, I don't go after him.

*

When I was a little girl, whenever something difficult happened to us, such as the passing of my grandmother or little children bullying my sister at school, my mom would bundle us up and take us for ice cream. There was a homemade ice cream parlor a few blocks from our house, and we would take the walk, knowing we were going to cheer ourselves up with one of the many flavors Mo's Ice Cream Shoppe had available that day. We even had a frequent visitor card. Essie and I would debate which was better—chocolate or vanilla—and Mama would tell us that her favorite ice cream flavor was strawberry. Essie and I would scrunch up our faces at the thought of 'disgusting' strawberry ice cream. When Mama passed, I remember walking to Mo's by myself and ordering a cone filled with strawberry ice cream in her honor and realizing it wasn't so bad. Maybe because it was Mama's favorite, or perhaps because I chose it in her memory, but ever since then, strawberry ice cream has become my favorite.

After the disagreement with Perry, I leave the newspaper and meander through the streets. Perry and I have had our first fight. In the year that we've been together, we've never had the smallest disagreement, and certainly not a fight. I know I've hurt his feelings, but it doesn't change the fact that I'm not sure about moving to the other side of the country. But maybe he's right. Maybe it would be a good thing for us. A fresh start, something new and different. I'm sure I could find a job. What would Robert say about my leaving the paper? It feels odd to think about these things, especially after learning Robert is my biological father. Come to think of it, I haven't talked to Daddy in weeks. It dawns on me how little we speak at all.

Turning the corner, I see it. It's not Mo's, but it's always been my favorite ice cream place in the city. It almost feels too chilly to eat ice cream, but I want it. I reconcile in my mind that it will make me feel closer to my mother. I walk inside Dolly's Creamery and step up to the counter.

"What can I get you, honey?" the woman asks. Her voice is softer than the hard way she looks, her eyes lined with black eyeliner.

"I'd like a strawberry cone, please," I say.

I pay for the ice cream and sit at a table in the front window. Looking out at the vibrant streets of New York City, a tear drops into my cone. Sadness consumes me. I used to love the way my mother would order a cone right along with us. "Pick your favorite flavor," she would say, as she selected her own. I miss her terribly despite the secrets she kept. The shock has turned to anger and now there's just a numbness that remains. She must have had her reasons, but those reasons seem insignificant to me now. Pile on the fact that I'm not really talking to either of my "fathers," I've disconnected from my own sister, I cannot trust my literary agent, and now my fiancé, the one person I could count on, is so angry at me for my lack of support for his career opportunity, he's walked away from me, as well.

I feel a sense of despair I've never felt before. At this moment, I'm utterly alone, and it's crushing. Honestly, I don't know what to do or where to turn. I exit the shop and start to walk anywhere, everywhere.

Chapter 35

When dusk sets on the city, I'm still aimlessly roaming the city blocks and avenues. The one benefit to this type of wandering is that you can still feel the heartbeat of the streets, and they make you feel less alone. Unable to think clearly, I feel an unusual heaviness in my chest. Sorrow has a way of affecting your whole being.

The sidewalks are covered in fall foliage, as autumn has announced its presence. Leaves rustle and dance along the pavement. I end up mesmerized by one particular leaf's swirling pattern, as it twirls and dances, getting caught up in the city breeze, especially as the gusts pick up between buildings. Bewildered by it, and as I have nothing else to do at present, I follow its lead.

After a couple of blocks, when it finally falls prey to a large bush, I pause and wonder why it has stopped here—and so suddenly.

When I look up, I see a beautiful, marble statue of a man who looks like a saint, exquisitely carved, wearing robes and pointing to his heart. The engraved sign reads: "Come to me, all you that labor and are burdened, and I will give you rest." I look up and realize I'm standing at the steps of St. Michael's Roman Catholic Church. I have gone through the motions with Essie, attending mass and events here and there at our own parish, but something is calling me to enter this church right now. I look closely at the statue, and then turn for the steps. When I reach the top, I touch the door handle and open it, stepping inside. The church is regal, with an impressive gilded altar, wooden benches, stained glass windows, and a marble statue of St. Michael the Archangel. I walk toward the altar and genuflect, then sit in the second pew.

Reaching for the kneeler, I pull it out and fall to my knees. I make the sign of the cross and pray. Tears stream down my cheeks. I have so much to tell God. I haven't prayed enough throughout this mess and am ashamed. And yet, I feel he is with me in this moment, listening. I lose track of time. When I finish praying, I continue to sit in church, basking in the peacefulness of the quiet. I ask God for forgiveness and mercy. *Where should I go, Lord, and what I should do? How do I move forward from this situation?* Needing a tissue, I retrieve one from my purse. It's been a day of tears and uncertainty.

I sit there waiting patiently for an answer, a sign, or to hear God's word. Out of the corner of the church, I see a man peer at me, and I wonder if I have overstayed my welcome. Perhaps it is time for the church to lock its doors. And yet, I remain anchored in the pew.

The man approaches, and I see his collar. A priest. He walks toward me, smiles, and then softly says, "Are you okay, young lady?"

He doesn't appear to be that much older than I am. As I'm in church, I cannot fib and say I'm okay. The truth must be told.

"I am not, in fact," I say. He sees me in distress.

"May I?" he asks, pointing at the seat next to me.

"Yes," I say, scooting over so that he can sit.

"Is there anything I can do to help ease your burdens?" His voice is a mere whisper, gentle and kind, his eyes caring.

"I don't think you have enough time to hear my story, Father," I say.

"I beg to differ—" He's waiting for me to share my name.

"Veronica," I say.

"I beg to differ, Veronica. I have all the time in the world."

*

An hour later, we are still sitting in the pew. A few people have entered, prayed, and left the church during that time, but the two of us remain huddled in soft conversation. I have told him everything—all of it—including the part about the leaf that I believe led me here.

He is the best listener. You realize quickly how most people enjoy giving their advice to you and make it all about themselves when you have a problem. That's not the case with Father Gatta. He listened the whole way through, rarely interrupting, allowing me to be sad and to grieve. He held my hand when it became too much.

"You have been through a lot," he says, gently. "And I believe you were brought here for a reason. Blessings come in all forms. Sometimes, we just have to be open to recognizing them." I nod, understanding that he believes the leaf's guidance was divine providence. "I'm not a psychologist, Veronica, and I am leery to offer advice that may not be beneficial to you, but just as you want to be forgiven for certain things—and you are—you truly won't feel free until you can forgive those who have hurt you. Trust me on this. I have been hurt as well, and the advice includes forgiving those who are living as well as those who have passed on. But it has to come from here." He points to his heart. "I think that's where you have to begin."

"I don't know how to move forward," I say.

"I think your heart will know, and from listening to you, I think you have a loving and forgiving heart. Plus, you have a good Guide," he says, looking up. "Remember what Saint Peter said: *Love covers a multitude of sins*. Forgiving someone requires you to be vulnerable and to let go of your pride. It isn't always an easy thing to do, but it can be done. And you also have to be able to forgive yourself."

I feel a wave of peace come over me. In the hour I've spent

with Father Gatta, he's helped me see things clearly.

"Thank you, Father Gatta," I say, embracing the epiphany and the clarity he has offered. "You are right. I know exactly what I need to do. You have helped immensely."

He smiles. "I don't think it was me," he says, gesturing toward the crucifix. "I think we had some help."

*

It's eight o'clock when I leave the church, and I hail a taxi.

I feel freer.

Sometimes all we need is a little perspective and guidance—someone to lend an ear, and perhaps intervention from above.

The taxi drops me at the apartment I share with Essie. I tell the driver to wait a moment, that I'll be right back.

I have my key, but since I haven't been living there, I decide to be courteous and knock. I knock several times, and then I see the handle move, and she opens the door.

Essie stands before me, a disheveled mess. It's as if she's aged a year in a month.

"What do you want?" she says to me, as I stand outside.

"I forgive you," I say.

"What?"

"I forgive you, Essie. And I'm sorry for whatever part you think I played in all of the deception and secrets. I'll never fully understand why you did what you did, or why you never talked to me about it or shared it with me, but I forgive you. And I know the truth, Essie. I know about all of it: your adoption, Robert and Mama, Daddy and the money, and you and me. Their secrets should have nothing to do with our relationship. I still love you, blood ties or no blood ties. You will always be my sister no matter the circumstances that we were put in. That's it. That's all I came to say."

I can tell she is trying to think of something to say back,

but she cannot find the words. She's dumbfounded. She cannot find it within her. Then, "Well, if that's all..." she says.

"Well, that's not all, exactly. I will always be here for you, praying for you, hoping that you will find your way. Thank you for listening."

She stands there looking at me as if I'm crazy, arms folded, but she won't deter me from doing what is right. I'm unburdening myself, and I'm doing what's right. She's been living with feelings of hurt just as I have been, which is why a year's worth of wounds, uncertainty, and betrayal are being laid at the doorstep.

What she does with it is entirely up to her.

*

"Take me to The News, please," I tell the taxi driver, as I hop back into the cab. We are off. One done, two to go. This cab ride is costing a small fortune, but I don't care.

Driving through the city, I feel a rush of adrenaline coursing through my veins. The city is alive, and so am I. It's about time all the secrets are confronted. All the lies.

I pay the taxi driver, thank him for his time and for waiting for me, and I scurry inside The News. The wind blows and lifts my skirt as I run toward the main doors to the newspaper. I find myself giggling. Maybe I've gone insane, I'm not too sure.

Barreling through the newsroom, I find my way to my desk and drop my purse in my chair. Robert's in his office on the telephone. He sees me approaching and quickly ends his call.

When I reach the doorway, he stands. "Veronica," he says.

"Robert."

"What brings you here at this hour? Are you working on a story?"

"No. But I'm working on my relationships—and I'd like to work on my relationship with you. I'd appreciate it if you would just let me say what I've come to say."

"Okay," he says, sitting back down in his chair and closing the door behind him. He's stunned and tentative.

"Everything is messed up. I hate the lies and having been lied to. I don't know why my mother did what she did and why she never felt she could tell us the truth. I understand you made a promise to her and you didn't want to break it. I get all of this stuff about your clandestine relationship, Robert. I don't like any of it. But I do like you. You've never been anything but kind to me. And clearly Mama cared for you. I'm glad to know I come from you and Mama. I forgive you, I forgive Mama, shoot, I even forgive Daddy for whatever part he played in all of it. I just wanted to tell you that. I needed time to process all that I've learned and what I've been subjected to by Essie. I'm not sure what the future holds for any of us, including my relationship with my sister, but I have to forgive it all. I have to, Robert, or it will be the death of me. And I do forgive it all. It's the only way to move forward."

When I finish that last sentence, I'm out of breath.

He sits in his chair looking at me, astounded.

"You just looked and sounded so much like your mother when you said all of that," he says, and then he puts his face into his hands and gently weeps. Selfishly, I've never thought about how much weight he may have carried all these years—thinking he was fulfilling a promise made on her deathbed and keeping a secret from his own daughter. Clearly, he loved her and wanted to honor her. Seeing his vulnerability, I recognize a valuable lesson of the heart: love continues to live on long after someone is gone.

"I'm sorry," I say. "Have I made it worse?"

He gets up, comes over to me and embraces me in a big hug—the kind I've always imagined a father giving a daughter. It's gargantuan, and it feels genuine and right. I allow myself to settle in his arms.

"No, my sweet daughter. You have made it all far, far better." And he kisses the top of my head.

*

Robert and I share a bourbon. He relays that he told Connie, and while it was a shock to her, she could understand why he didn't want to break a promise, especially one made on a deathbed. Having children of her own prior to marrying Robert, she said it was understandable, and that she would have done the same if the roles were reversed. He's lucky to have an understanding wife.

After sitting and talking with him for a bit, I'm momentarily feeling the weight of all the deception and angst falling away. It's nearly ten-thirty in the evening when I realize I must go home to Perry to make my final amends.

"I'd best get a cab to take me to Perry's," I say to Robert.

"Will you survive the next few days without him?" he asks me.

"What do you mean?" I ask. I didn't mention the fight we had. Did Perry?

"We sent him to California this afternoon to cover the Dodgers' move. Big stuff happening. He caught an afternoon flight."

I look at Robert as if he has two heads. I had no idea. Feeling deflated, I stand.

"When will he be back?" I ask.

"Next week," he says. "You didn't know?"

"No," I mutter, "we didn't get a chance to speak this afternoon."

"Well, he'll be back before you know it."

"I appreciate that," I say, and reach to give him a hug. He walks me outside and helps me get a taxi.

"I'm glad we got this time together, Veronica. I'm glad you said what you said. I'm sorry for all of it as well. Truly, I am."

"Thank you. I hope at some point you can tell me more. I want to know more about my mother...and you."

I give him one last hug before I climb into the taxi and wave goodbye through the window.

When I arrive at Perry's apartment, I reach inside my purse and pull out the key to the apartment. As I step inside the dark hallway, I flick the light on.

Standing there, the ticking of the clock sounds louder than usual.

Next to the small telephone table is a scribbled note in Perry's handwriting: *Have to go to California to cover the ballclub moving to the West Coast. Called the newspaper this afternoon, but you weren't there. I'll be back next week. We can talk more about our situation then. Love, P.*

I read the note three times over.

Settling into the quiet of the apartment, I suddenly feel the enormous absence of Perry.

The silence is deafening.

Chapter 36

Having fallen asleep with the radio on, I wake in the morning to find myself on Perry's sofa. The weekend feels like a blur.

Rubbing my eyes, I look around at the empty apartment. *This is what it will feel like without him*, I think to myself.

Part of me wants to hide here under the covers until he returns, but I have a job, and the job requires me to perform. There's no hiding from writing stories for the newspaper. Monday beckons and deadlines await.

By the time I dress, swallow a piece of toast and drink a glass of orange juice, it's ten o'clock. I telephone Susanna at The News in advance to let her know I'll be later than usual.

Too tired to make the walk and not in the mood for the subway ride, I hail a taxi. The driver attempts to make small talk on the short ride to the office. He's telling me about his grandson's baseball game, and then he starts to talk about the traitorous Brooklyn Dodgers. The only thing I want more than a cup of coffee is to get out of this cab.

Crossing the newsroom floor, the smell of paper and coffee and ink reinvigorates me.

"Hey, Veronica. How are you?" Susanna asks me.

"I'm okay. Thanks for covering for me this morning," I say.

"Oh, you needn't thank me. That's what I'm here for."

Susanna is always so pleasant, so even keeled. She's a pleasure to be around. I watch her walk back to her desk, which is just caddy-corner to mine. Within seconds, she reappears with two messages in her hand.

"These are from earlier. This fella just wanted to say 'thanks,' and this gentleman really wants you to call him back as soon as possible–it seems urgent," she says.

"Thanks, Susanna," I say, as she returns to her desk.

The first message is from Mickey Mantle's handler. "Mickey wanted me to call and say 'thanks' for the amazing article you wrote. We appreciate the good press." The story hit the paper yesterday. What a classy thing to do. We've received a positive reaction to the article, and I'm relieved that Mickey liked it.

The second message holds no clues as to what it's about. There is a name and a phone number, but I don't recognize either one. I make sure to dial the number carefully. The number of times I've misdialed ranks as my biggest flaw as a journalist. Sometimes it takes two turns of the dial to get it right.

The phone rings. It rings again. On the third ring, a woman picks up.

"Mr. Davis' office, may I help you?"

"Hello. This is Veronica DeMarco from The News returning Mr. Davis' call."

"Oh, yes, Miss. DeMarco. Please hold the line. He really wants to speak with you."

I'm in the dark on this one. I have no idea who this man is or why he's calling. I don't recognize the name at all.

"Ah, yes, Miss. DeMarco! So wonderful to hear from you," a smooth and soothing voice says through the phone line. There's an air of eloquence in the way he speaks.

"Thank you, Mr. Davis, but I'm not sure what this is about."

"Well, what it's about is something very exciting, Ms. DeMarco. A mutual acquaintance of ours, Christopher Masterson, informed me that you are looking for a literary agent to represent your book publishing career. I've looked into your work, and I'm open to new writers. Would you be interested in meeting to learn more about how I may serve your needs?"

Mr. Masterson put this man up to this? What a sweet thing to do. In the throes of everything else going wrong, it's comforting to know there are people out there willing to help you.

"I would love to meet with you, Mr. Davis. Just tell me when and where."

"Next week, and only if you stop calling me Mr. Davis. Brian's the name, and I can't wait to meet you in person."

We set a time the following week for me to come by his office on Madison Avenue. This feels promising.

I look back down at my desk where I've scribbled a few notes from the conversation with Mr. Davis...Brian. I dial Mr. Masterson and tell him what's transpired, thanking him profusely. He chuckles with delight as he hear the excitement in my voice. Imploring him to continue to serve as my lawyer and oversee the contracts, he seems quite pleased by all of it.

*

When the day ends and I have nowhere to go and no place to be, I walk toward the Empire State Building. I haven't been to the top of it in ages. On this crisp and clear autumn day, all of New York City should be visible from way up high. The sky's the limit.

Making it just in time, I join about twenty others as the last group to ride to the top.

When the elevator lets our small group off, we head in different directions, some with cameras, and others just wanting to take in the magnificent view.

I had the opportunity to go to the screening of *An Affair to Remember* back in July when the film was released. Cary Grant can make any picture romantic, and sometimes when I write, I imagine him as the leading man. That film tugged at my heartstrings like few others have, and I've wanted to revisit the Empire State Building ever since, the setting of the film whereupon everything hinges.

I look toward the East River, and it's as if I've been transported back in time. I recognize myself as a child up here with Mama and Daddy. I'm six. No...wait. It isn't Daddy, and Essie isn't with us. There's a photograph somewhere in one of my mother's boxes that I came across recently—a picture of me holding a Teddy bear at the top of the Empire State Building. Everything becomes clearer. It's the three of us. I see Mama and Robert, but they aren't in the photograph. They're joyful, laughing, as they take the picture of me. He looks at my mom and she smiles back. They have me pose, the cityscape behind me.

How is it that I remember the moment now? It's a vivid memory, as if a film clip has been installed into my brain. Being here, above the city, I feel the presence of my mother, of the love she had for me. I wonder about her short life and about the sacrifices she made. I think about her marriage to Daddy and whether or not there was real love between them. I wonder how deeply she felt for Robert and the happiness she may have given up. I think of the decisions she made as to how to raise her girls. I surmise that none of it was easy.

The clouds feel close and heaven even closer as the building reaches for the sky, attempting to touch the clouds. I wonder if Mama can see me from her spot in heaven. Goosebumps tingle my arms. I look up at the darkening sky.

I forgive you, too, Mama, I whisper softly.

I think I understand it now.

Love doesn't fit tidily into a box. There are no limits on love, and it can be very, very messy.

But it is love, nonetheless.

Chapter 37

On Monday, Perry phones from California. We have a brief conversation about the chaos in Los Angeles and he shares that everything is unfolding as is written in the newspapers: the Brooklyn Dodgers are making the move to Los Angeles. It's official. Despite this sad and disappointing news for New York and its devout fans, Perry seems upbeat and his normal, cheerful self on the telephone. We don't address the potential job opportunity in Los Angeles, or what the team's move means for his job at the newspaper.

On Wednesday, after interviewing a family in Hoboken all day for a story I'm writing, I return to The News late in the afternoon. There are people milling outside the newspaper offices wanting answers about the Dodgers. It's quite chaotic, because New Yorkers are not taking the team's departure well.

Stepping out of the taxi, I clip my press pass onto my jacket, and finagle my way through the crowd. Police are patrolling the streets outside the building. Perry will be sorry to have missed seeing this in person.

I shimmy through the door and notice there are more reporters than usual in the lobby. Outside the front doors, you can hear the hearts of Dodgers fans breaking all across the city, at least that's what I overheard one reporter say to another. The news is devastating to baseball fans here. They feel betrayed and bamboozled.

I feel a tap on my shoulder. "Excuse me. Are you Veronica DeMarco?" a slim man asks me.

"Yes, I am."

"I'm Aaron Stark. I used to write for The News years ago. Working over at a local television station now. Loved your piece on Mickey Mantle."

"Thank you," I say. "He was an easy interview."

"Sure seemed like it. He shared a lot."

"He did."

"And the Rosa Manetti stories were interesting, too. You're quite a reporter."

"Thank you. That means a lot to me."

I look away from Aaron for a moment and see Perry come through the door, a suitcase in his hand. Our eyes meet, and I see the corners of his mouth turn into a smile.

Abruptly ending the conversation, I say sweetly, "Lovely to meet you, Mr. Stark. I hope we cross paths in the future."

Perry hustles over to me, carrying his luggage, a grin on his face. The noise from conversations fill the air, but all I can hear is Perry.

"Fancy seeing you here," Perry says, when he approaches me. "I take it you're here to apologize for your horrific behavior?" Knowing he has a sense of humor about our situation puts me at ease.

"It was horrific, wasn't it?" I ask him.

"Not any more horrific than mine. It was awfully presumptive of me to think you'd be thrilled to pack up and leave, when, in fact, you do have a wonderful career at The News. You're one of the best reporters the paper has. You were right, my love. We should have talked it over fully. I got caught up in the excitement and wanted you to feel the same."

"Perry Spada. This is why I love you. This is why I couldn't wait to see you. Being in that apartment alone made me realize I'd be a fool not to go to California with you. You are my life, and I'd choose being with you over all of it—over New York, career, even what family I have left here."

"Really?" Perry's eyes are wide.

"Yes. I've thought it over and we can start our lives together in California if the job means that much to you. Honestly, I don't care where we are, as long as we're together."

He sets his suitcase down and ushers me outside the building and away from the chaos. We walk toward the nearest bench on the sidewalk under a tree. But before we sit, he takes my face in his hands and kisses me. I can feel his love, his longing, and his support in that one, sensuous kiss.

We sit down next to each other and hold hands, the autumn sun beginning to set over the buildings.

"So, truthfully, you don't care where we are as long as we're together?" Perry asks me.

"Yes. I was so worried you'd still be angry with me about our fight."

"Well," he says, "you can make it up to me."

"How?"

"By loving me," he says. He brings my hand up to his lips and kisses it. In return, I touch his face and look into his kind eyes.

"That's an easy one." I can't help but smile at him.

"Is it?" he asks.

"Promise me we are going to be alright," I say.

"My darling, I promise you. You have my word—my life."

"That means everything to me, Perry."

"Good, because we're not going to California. As luck would have it, I'm staying at The News. Robert wants me to cover the Yankees. Daniel's taking the sports editor position in Chicago to be closer to his family."

"What? Is this true?" I am speechless, and Perry sees my mouth wide open and touches it.

"You heard me. Mickey Mantle, here I come! Maybe now I can actually interview the guy!" He is laughing, and I am laughing right along with him.

"What about the job in Los Angeles?" I can't believe what he's saying.

"Well, I hadn't accepted it. And Robert talked to me about the position before I left. I did listen to the job offer, and if I'm being honest, I did consider it. And maybe for a moment, it sounded really appealing. I mean, how about the weather in California? It's spectacular! I saw it as a fresh start for the two of us, but the truth is, I'm an East Coast guy and you're an East Coast girl. I'm flattered to be offered the job as the Yankees beat writer. Besides, you were right. I'd miss my family. I also don't want to separate you from Robert under the present circumstances," he says.

"You are full of surprises, Mr. Spada," I tease.

"I called and talked to my parents about it. I don't want to force you to leave anything you're not ready to leave. And who knows? Maybe things with Essie will work out in time."

I had mentally prepared myself to pack up and move to California over the last couple of days. I'd been over and over it in my mind. But staying in New York definitely makes my heart the happiest.

"In that case, I also have some news to share with you. I received a call from an agent who wants to represent me and my work. Christopher Masterson put him in touch with me. I was so surprised."

"Who is it?"

"A man named Brian Davis."

I see Perry's face light up. "That's wonderful. I'm so proud of you," Perry says, trying to contain his own enthusiasm.

Perry lifts his arm, wanting me to get closer to him, and we sit there together for a while, just being together, realizing this is how it's meant to be.

I think of how I felt only a few days ago, of being in that

church, of being overwhelmed by despair, of talking with Father Gatta, Essie, and Robert. I've never felt as alone as I did that day, yet I believe I was being looked after. I also think of Rosa, and how she was alone...and lonely. In makes me wonder about my mother's own feelings, especially with regard to her choices in life. Did she ever experience loneliness? Regrets? I don't want to experience those feelings. I want love in my life—I need love and family in my life. And one day, perhaps, to have and love a child of our own.

What I cannot discount is that I believe it is God who shines the brightest light, and puts people into our lives for a reason. I have nothing to fear, no complaints to be made. I was loved, and am loved. So is Essie, whether she understands that or not. And then there's Perry, a man I adore and cherish. I also want Robert—my father—in my life. I want to know him as a daughter and not just as a mentor and friend. He loved Mama, and I come from that love.

The reality, I've discovered, is that when the dust settles, we know who we can count on. We know who loves us unconditionally, we know who uses us, and we know who will always be there for us. We can choose to hold on to anger or a grudge, believe we are owed an apology, or refuse to forgive. But what purpose does that serve? It's true: we can be hurt by the ones we love, whether it's intentional or unintentional, but forgiveness is mandatory to free us.

Hate runs deep, but love runs deeper.

Someday, I hope Essie will let go of all she's been clinging to, and she will find, like I did, that holding on to anger, frustration, and things you can't control will destroy you.

There is great wisdom in knowing that where there is love—even the fragments of it—there is also hope.

Chapter 38

"Mr. Davis will see you now," his secretary says. She is perfectly manicured and wearing the latest tweed fashion, not a hair on her head out of place.

I follow her as she leads me into Mr. Davis' office. He's eloquent and nattily attired. He reminds me of the actor who played Fred Gailey in *Miracle on 34th Street*.

"I'm so pleased to meet you in person," Mr. Davis says, reaching out his hand to me.

"Thank you. And I'm thrilled to meet you, Mr. Davis."

"Brian," he says. "I'm not into all that formality."

"Brian," I repeat. "And please call me Veronica."

"It's a deal. Won't you sit down?" Brian motions for me to sit in the chair opposite his desk.

"There's so much I want to talk to you about." His warm expression complements his words.

"It's all very exciting, Mr. Davis—Brian," I say. "Thank you for this incredible opportunity."

"We love connecting with good talent." He rubs his hands together, raising his eyebrows. "So, tell me what you're working on, Veronica?"

"I published my first book last year, and I have a completed novel with no representation just yet. But I'm also working on a nonfiction book," I say, casually sliding it in.

"You are multi-talented, Veronica, to write fiction and nonfiction books. I've read your work at The News. Quite impressive."

"Thank you, because the nonfiction idea relates to that."

"Is it about Rosa Manetti?" Brian asks.

"How did you know?" I ask him.

"Because great minds think alike. I was hoping you'd be willing to write about Rosa and her life. I think people would eat it up."

"I agree!" I say.

"Oh, Veronica...I have a good feeling we'll accomplish some great things together. I can feel it," Brian says. "Those stories are riveting. If we play our cards right, maybe we can even get the story made into a motion picture. Have you ever written a screenplay? My good friend works for a studio out in Los Angeles, and I just feel it in my bones. This could be a great opportunity."

I smile at Brian. Rosa would have loved seeing her story on the big screen, I know she would have. It would be an honor to tell her story. What a way to continue her legacy. And I am just the person to write it.

*

Perry and I have plans to visit Father Gatta together, so I meet him back at The News. I want Perry to meet him in person, as I want to be married in that church. I called ahead of time to schedule time for us to chat.

"I know your family would love to see us married in their church, but the bride should have some say, don't you think?" I tease Perry. He doesn't care where we marry, as long as we marry soon. We set a date before Christmas on a Saturday afternoon and reserve a room at one of Perry's favorite Italian restaurants for a dinner reception. It will be simple. That's what both of us want.

The newsroom is bustling, as is the sports department: it's Perry's first official day as the Yankees sportswriter. He's ecstatic and is already making plans to go to spring training in Florida. Robert said I could join him for a few days, so it's something to look forward to during New York's coldest months.

"Hello, lovely," he says. "Are you ready to head to the church for all the planning? I've got the marriage license right here."

"Yes," I say. "Ready to go."

I pick up my small briefcase with my ideas and notes in it. Perry smiles at me, and I feel like the luckiest girl in the world. I wish my mother were here to help me plan the wedding, but Perry's mother and sisters are filling in just fine. We will have a simple service with immediate family and a few friends and a reception at the restaurant afterwards. Of course, Perry's side will be far larger than mine. The invitation for Essie is addressed, but is unsent as of yet.

Perry puts his arm around me, and just as we begin to leave, Malcolm comes striding through the main doors of The News.

"Malcolm?" He startles me. I haven't seen him since our last conversation. "Is everything okay?"

"Well, it's been a bit dicey, but there's someone who would like to speak with you. She's waiting outside. She won't come in the building."

"It's so chilly out," I say.

"I know, but she insisted. Would you mind stepping outside to see her? She's just outside the main doors."

Perry and I exchange glances. "Okay," I say to Malcolm. "Take me to her."

The three of us exit the main doors. Essie is standing there, waiting. She looks better than the last time I saw her, but still a bit unlike herself.

"Hello," I say, walking toward her. Malcolm and Perry keep their distance, staying behind so that she and I can speak privately.

"Malcolm said he'd never talk to me again if I didn't try to connect with you," she says, the words deliberate, almost in a whisper.

"Okay, so you're not here of your own accord," I state as a fact. Why must she be so frustrating all of the time?

"Let me try that again," Essie begins. "Malcolm and I talked about it, and the right thing is to speak with you."

"Okay," I say, staring at her. "What would you like to say?"

"I'm not sure who I've become, but I don't like her. I was angry at you for having a real mother."

"You did, too; she was your mother."

"Not biologically, but in every other sense, yes." I see her lip quiver, and she continues: "I have a lot to work through in order to cope with the anger and frustration inside me, but for all of our sakes, I'm hoping we can mend some of the fences, if not all of them," she says. It's not an apology, but she is trying.

"And the book you are about to publish? What of that?"

"I've taken it off the table, revamping it. Robert doesn't have to worry. I won't share any of our family secrets publicly," she says.

"That's a relief." She knows I want more, but I'm pretty sure it's all she can give.

"Well, I just—I just appreciated when you stopped by that night," she manages to say. "And you seem really happy with Perry."

"I am. And I hope everything works out for you and Malcolm, too."

"Well, we'll see. For now, he's just happy to see me try to make amends." The attempt is definitely appreciated, though not overwhelming, but she's still got a wall up. She was deceived, too. She learned that neither our mother—nor our father—are her biological parents. There are wounds there. I understand that. She feels distant; we are distant from each other. But I'm pleased to see even this small attempt to put things right.

"Yes," I say. "Well, I'm glad to see you. Truly." I think of what it means to be kind, and I do my best to understand, to offer her kindness. To fully forgive her.

Essie nods. I catch her eye, and in that moment, I still see her. I recognize her, the girl of old, my big sister, my partner in crime, my roommate and my friend, the one I've grown up with and lived with longer than anyone. She's still there somewhere. Something tugs at my heartstrings in that moment, especially seeing Essie so vulnerable and barely able to look me in the eye. She feels ashamed, unloved, and lost, I can tell, even if she's not saying it. I take a step closer, reach for her, wrap my arms around her, and hug her.

Nothing else needs to be said.

And then, just as I'm about to pull away, I feel her arms tighten around me.

Chapter 39

It's funny, but there is some truth to marital bliss, because I haven't been able to wipe the silly smile off my face since saying "I do" to Perry two weeks ago. We've started looking at moving into a little bigger place, although we're content at Perry's apartment for now.

Malcolm and Essie did come to the wedding. I was happy she made the effort to be there. The mending of our relationship will take time. Daddy actually materialized and walked me down the aisle, but it was Robert who beamed from the second pew. I could see him out of the corner of my eye from the altar.

One welcome change is that I'm enjoying a little bit of this domestic life. I'll always write and be a writer, but it's a Saturday afternoon, and I love that the kitchen is a mess with my cooking. I'm being a little sneaky. Perry's mother gave me her homemade red gravy recipe that's been in Perry's family for decades. While he's out Christmas shopping, I'm cooking and spending time with the other Perry—Perry Como—who fills the room with Christmas music as it blares from the speakers of our stereo. The tree is lit, and tonight we'll have a romantic dinner that we'll eat by candlelight later as we appreciate the season. A little surprise for my husband.

Through the window, I see someone drop something into my mailbox. I'd forgotten to get the mail last night when I got home from work. Perry and I had both stayed late at The News, putting finishing touches on each of our articles. This time of year, I'm always eager to retrieve the mail, because I love getting Christmas cards. To my delight, as a newly married couple, we've received quite a few thus far. In my apron, I open the door to the cold air, and pull the mail from inside the mailbox.

I sit down at the table and excitedly open the first card: it's from Perry's mother and father, with a handwritten note telling us how lovely the wedding was and that they're so pleased that I'm a part of their family.

The next one is from Susanna and her husband; there's a happy, Christmas reindeer on it and words of good cheer.

The third one is a letter and has no return address, nor does it have any postage mark on it. It is specifically addressed to me. I rip it open with the letter opener, wondering who it's from, when I see the salutation:

Dear WG,

I'm sure this is going to come as a shock to you. For some strange reason, I trust you more than I've trusted anyone in my life. After you read this, you must burn it. That's your job. If you only knew the lengths I had to go through to get this letter to you.

As you are realizing, I'm not dead. I had to make a deal with the devils (the people in charge) to get me out of that horrific place, if you know what I mean. When I ratted out those bums, they let me have a lawyer to help me access my money and work out the terms, as long as I promised to "disappear" for the rest of my life with the government's help. Death to the living, I call it. I agreed to it. There really was nothing keeping me in New York City anymore.

My lawyer also helped me leave a little something for you. You'll be hearing from him shortly, and he'll tell you that you were noted in my will, so that you'll believe I'm dead and gone. It was part of the deal

I made, but I couldn't lie to you. You were always after the truth, so I figured you are owed the truth. You deserve it, unlike a lotta people I know. So I'm leaving you a few bucks. I also figured one of us should live out our days with the man we love. Think of it as a little wedding present from me.

I can't tell you where I am, but I'm sure you remember my affinity for beautiful sunsets. Fortunately, I see a lot of them. And I have met a guy. He knows me as my new name, Angela. He's nice enough and is a good companion.

After you read this, burn the letter, WG. And I'm hoping you're writing a book about a well-meaning woman who got saddled with the wrong things and made a mess of her life. She has repented, though, and continues to do so. So much more wisdom is in my brain. I think it's reading all those books. If you do tell my story in a book one day, promise to make me a glamorous and sexy character. You know, keep the big breasts and curves, but cinch the waist and describe my face more like Ava Gardner's. Full lips and sexy eyes. I'd like that.

Also, I finished reading the Bible, so now I'm informed and can be preachy, so here it goes: I've come to the conclusion that people can change. If you can fix it with your sister, do it. I wish I had. The irony of growing older is that you see things more clearly as you age, which isn't so helpful when you're young and stupid and the people you wish you could make amends with are dead and gone. Anyway, if you can't work it out, it's okay. Just do your best so you can live without guilt. Wallowing in it for years afterwards isn't good for the soul. Trust me on this.

I know your newspaper stories and the reaction to them helped me get this deal and keep me alive. And I'll never forget the cake you made me. I was at my lowest and you were able to lift me up. I'll always be thankful for what you did. And I loved reading all the mail I got in jail. Made my days. Truly. It's incredible that strangers can give you hope.

I'd say I love ya, but I think you already know I do. To be frank, your sister doesn't know how lucky she is. If I had been blessed with another sister or a daughter in my life, I'd have wanted her to be just like you.

Merry Christmas. Enjoy the rest of your life with Perry Como.
Your good friend,
–R

Line by line, I recite the letter over and over for nearly an hour, memorizing every word and hearing the sound of Rosa's voice in my head.

I sit motionless, gripping the letter, the only physical artifact I have of Rosa's, not wanting to let it go. Then, when I can say every word of it flawlessly, I walk over to the fireplace, toss the letter into the flames, and watch it burn.

–The End–

A note from the author

Dear Reader,

I hope you enjoyed this story. With my background in both baseball and journalism, I enjoyed constructing this story. It was inspired by a real story my father-in-law told me about a friend of his and two twin brothers who were separated at birth and adopted by different families. The story was a pretty wild one. Although I didn't tell that exact story as was told to me, aspects of that story inspired the telling of this one.

It was also an opportunity to set a novel in the 1950s. I enjoyed tying together the backstory of the Brooklyn Dodgers leaving for Los Angeles, a mafia woman (who was loosely based on a real-life mafia woman), and family drama, along with a love story between two reporters. And while this book has a lot of angst in it, if you've read any of my previous works, you know that I have philosophy of leaving readers with hope at the end of the stories. Because, truthfully, what's the point of life if we don't have some hope?

As for Mickey Mantle and the Yankees...my apologies, Orioles fans, but he was my late grandmother's favorite player. Her name also happened to be Eleanor DeMarco. As well, my husband had an Aunt Marina (who made fabulous pizza), and I had a priest when I was little named Father Gatta.

Do you believe Veronica and Essie eventually found their way back to each other? I'd like to believe they did. I'd like to imagine that in some fashion, they both married, had children, and grew their families with each other in it, along with Robert and his family, and even their Dad. I want to believe that Malcolm and Perry became great friends and that Veronica and Essie truly put the past behind them and loved one another fully. The hope for this future lies in their ability to forgive and move on. I believe happier times are ahead for all of them.

And if this future is possible for them, that means there is possibility and hope for all of us.

Thanks for reading,
Stephanie

thank you to...

My immediate family for their constant support...Anthony, Matthew, Eleanor, Mom, Dad, Jo & Mark

All the willing pre-readers: Anthony Verni & Leni Parrillo (thank you for the many reads and advice), Mark Verni, Elizabeth Johnson, Jim Abbiati, Jere Anthony, Dana Armstrong, Sayword Eller, Megan Musgrove, and Colleen Young

Key brainstormers and consultants: Leni Parrillo, Doug Parrillo, Elizabeth Johnson, Jenny Bumgarner, Lynn Davis, Dawn Lowman, Reana Listman

My circle of friends who encourage me (you know who you are).

The Maryland community: You all keep me going!

All my friends at Park Books and Mystery Loves Company who are wonderful at lifting up and encouraging ALL writers.

Book clubs that have been instrumental in helping spread the word about my work. I appreciate you all so much!

To those who take a moment to write a review. Every single one is helpful and matters. I'm so appreciative!

To those who share my books on social media, recommend one of my books to a friend, and/or support me with comments, conversations, and words of encouragement: I can't even begin to tell you how much it means to me.

And most importantly, to God, for giving me the ability, gift, and perseverance to tell a story.

book club questions

1. There isn't a lot of specific backstory about Essie and Veronica's relationship prior to the year that the story begins, except that the two shared a loving sisterhood. From what you glean from Veronica's storytelling, what do you imagine their relationship must have been like until Essie found out the truth that she and Veronica were not blood sisters?

2. How did Veronica feel about Essie as the story evolved?

3. Why do you think Essie resented Veronica? Was it justifiable that Essie took her own hurt out on Veronica? Why or why not?

4. Talk through the evolution of Rosa and Veronica's stories. How are the two characters similar and dissimilar?

5. Talk about Perry. What does the relationship with Perry bring to the story? How does this relationship help Veronica during her struggles?

6. Robert is both a mentor and father figure to Veronica. What happens when Veronica finds out the truth about her mother and Robert? What does Veronica think about her mother's decisions?

7. Veronica is able to forgive a lot. She finds strength from her faith and from talking to Father Gatta. Have you ever talked through a terrible situation with someone you value? A stranger? How did that help you get through your struggles?

8. Essie says some pretty cruel things to Veronica throughout the story. She also throws a cherished vase at Veronica's head. Talk through the perspectives of each woman during these scenes and how they were handling the dissolution of their relationship.

9. Malcolm is a secondary character, yet we learn a lot about him from his interactions with the other characters. How would you describe him? Why do you think he stuck with Essie during her lowest moments?

10. Mr. Dobson's story in the beginning of the novel is a foreshadowing of what's to come in Veronica's own family's story. What did Veronica glean by writing Mr. Dobson's story, and how might it have helped her handle her own family's secrets?

11. Even though Rosa is in jail and she has done some horrible things, she ends up being the story's wise sage and a heroine of sorts. How did Rosa's experiences in life help Veronica? How did Veronica help Rosa?

12. Veronica's relationship with Alice becomes tainted and another disappointment in her life. While it isn't stated in the outcome of the novel, do you believe Veronica forgave Alice for keeping things from her with regard to Essie?

13. What did Mickey Mantle bring to the story? Why were his insights important to the story?

14. Faith, God, and forgiveness is sprinkled throughout the story. How did the characters grow, change, or need faith in their lives?

BOOK CLUBS

I LOVE ATTENDING BOOK CLUB MEETINGS!

IF YOUR GROUP IS INTERESTED IN READING ANY OF MY BOOKS AND WOULD LIKE ME TO ATTEND YOUR BOOK CLUB EITHER IN-PERSON OR VIRTUALLY, EMAIL ME: STEPHANIE.VERNI@GMAIL.COM

STEPHANIEVERNI.COM

Other Books by Stephanie Verni

BENEATH THE MIMOSA TREE

Annabelle Marco and Michael Contelli are both only children of Italian-Americans. Next door neighbors since they were both five years old, they both receive their parents' constant attention and are regularly subjected to their meddlesome behavior. In high school and then in college, as their relationship moves from friendship to love, Annabelle finds herself battling her parents, his parents, and even Michael. She feels smothered by them all and seeks independence through an unplanned and unexpected decision that she comes to regret and that ultimately alters the course of her life, Michael's life, and the lives of both of their parents.

BASEBALL GIRL

Francesca Milli's father passes away when she's a freshman in college and nineteen years old; she is devastated and copes with his death by securing a job working for the Bay City Blackbirds, a big-league team, as she attempts to carry on their traditions and mutual love for the game of baseball. The residual effect of loving and losing her dad has made her cautious, until two men enter her life: a ballplayer and a sportswriter. With the encouragement of her mother and two friends, she begins to work through her grief. A dedicated employee, she successfully navigates her career, and becomes a director in the front office. However, Francesca realizes that she can't partition herself off from the world, and in time, understands that sometimes loving someone does involve taking a risk.

INN SIGNIFICANT

Two years after receiving the horrifying news of her husband Gil's death, Milly Foster continues to struggle to find her way out of a state of depression. As a last-ditch effort and means of intervention, Milly's parents convince her to run their successful Inn during their absence as they help a friend establish a new bed and breakfast in Ireland. Milly reluctantly agrees; when she arrives at the picturesque, waterfront Inn Significant, her colleague, John, discovers a journal written by her late grandmother that contains a secret her grandmother kept from the family. Reading her grandmother's words and being able to identify with her Nana's own feelings of loss, sparks the beginning of Milly's climb out of the darkness and back to the land of the living.

FROM HUMBUG TO HUMBLE: THE TRANSFORMATION OF EBENEZER SCROOGE

How, exactly, did Ebenezer Scrooge stay true to his word and change in order to become a better person? What good deeds did he actually do to leave behind his life as an old miser and curmudgeon? What became of Tiny Tim? In this follow-up novella based on the great Charles Dickens' A Christmas Carol, long-time Dickens fan and writer Stephanie Verni imagines Scrooge's path to redemption that includes philanthropy, family, friendships, and love. Dickens fans will be treated to insights as to how Scrooge changed his ways in this heartwarming tale full of Christmas spirit as we revisit old Scrooge, Bob Cratchit, Scrooge's nephew, Fred, Isabelle, Tiny Tim, and more in this charming Christmas tale.

THE POSTCARD AND OTHER SHORT STORIES & POETRY

In this collection, which includes 22 short stories, you will read about tales of love, heartbreak, middle-aged meltdowns, gossips and unkind women, abusive relationships, a last-ditch message in a bottle, witches and brooms, baseball, and living with a grandmother, among others. Written over a span of twenty years, The Postcard and Other Short Stories & Poetry will warm your heart and leave you feeling as if you've made a few new friends among the pages.

ANNA IN TUSCANY

Travel writer Arianna (Anna) Ricci relocates from the United States to Italy for a year on assignment to cover the regions of Italy. She is also on a quest to write a story of love about La Festa Degli Innamorati—otherwise known as Valentine's Day—for her magazine's website. Living in her cousin's apartment in Siena in Tuscany, Anna meets her neighbor, Matteo, an older gentleman who lost his wife several years prior, and they form a friendship and begin to play cards every Wednesday evening, along with Matteo's son, Nicolo. Before long, Anna, who has suffered through two previous heartbreaks, uncovers a love story that spans decades, and learns a few things about love as she finds her own way in Italy.

THE LETTERS IN THE BOOKS

Can a handwritten letter found inside a book change the course of your life? Empath Meg Ellis believes it can. One snowy evening in early December on the night of Midnight Madness, a kick-off to the holiday season in Annapolis, Maryland, four downtrodden people walk into Meg's bookstore at different times throughout the evening and become recipients of her inspirational letters. Over the course of a year, Meg's clandestine, handwritten letters help positively change the trajectory of these vulnerable characters' lives. Before long, Eva Levoni, Reid Jones, Lily Webster, and Dimitri Vassos become connected; prior to that night, they were not. Friendships form, romances bud, and their bonds become strong. Additionally, Meg's backstory reveals why she takes the time to write the letters of encouragement–a handwritten letter she received years prior after losing someone she loved. Meg, too, finds herself on a journey of her own.

***

To stay in touch with Stephanie and hear about her work, visit her website at stephanieverni.com, or email her at stephanie.verni@gmail.com to sign up for the mailing list.

Made in the USA
Middletown, DE
13 November 2024

64531827R00155